CLOSE TO KILLING

"This is Fire River country. It's ours. You know what they say about fire. . . . Step too close and a fellow can get himself burned down mighty easily."

"Let me know where *too close* is," Shaw said, taking a deliberate step forward. He stared at Gunnison, his hand hanging at the edge of his poncho. His big Colt stood out of sight beneath the poncho, but only an inch from his fingertips.

Behind Shaw, Lori Edelman saw things were about to get out of control. "Bo Hewes, how dare you ride in here and let these bullies threaten my guest when I'm trying to bury my husband!"

Hewes relented. He clenched his jaw tight again and gave a sharp jerk of his head, signaling Gunnison and the others to back off. "This is a funeral. You men step down and help. Take turns with the shoveling," he said gruffly. To Lori he said, "All right, let's get Jonathan laid to rest." He turned to Shaw. "This day belongs to my brother. You brought him here; you've been properly thanked for it. Don't push your luck with me."

"Luck was made to be pushed," Shaw said flatly.

CROSSING FIRE RIVER

Ralph Cotton

A SIGNET BOOK

SIGNET
Published by New American Library, a division of
Penguin Group (USA) Inc., 375 Hudson Street,
New York, New York 10014, USA
Penguin Group (Canada), 90 Eglinton Avenue East, Suite 700, Toronto,
Ontario M4P 2Y3, Canada (a division of Pearson Penguin Canada Inc.)
Penguin Books Ltd., 80 Strand, London WC2R 0RL, England
Penguin Ireland, 25 St. Stephen's Green, Dublin 2,
Ireland (a division of Penguin Books Ltd.)
Penguin Group (Australia), 250 Camberwell Road, Camberwell, Victoria 3124,
Australia (a division of Pearson Australia Group Pty. Ltd.)
Penguin Books India Pvt. Ltd., 11 Community Centre, Panchsheel Park,
New Delhi - 110 017, India
Penguin Group (NZ), 67 Apollo Drive, Rosedale, North Shore 0632,
New Zealand (a division of Pearson New Zealand Ltd.)
Penguin Books (South Africa) (Pty.) Ltd., 24 Sturdee Avenue,
Rosebank, Johannesburg 2196, South Africa

Penguin Books Ltd., Registered Offices:
80 Strand, London WC2R 0RL, England

First published by Signet, an imprint of New American Library,
a division of Penguin Group (USA) Inc.

First Printing, August 2009
10 9 8 7 6 5 4 3 2 1

For Mary Lynn . . . of course

PART 1

Chapter 1

Cresta Alta, the hill country, Old Mexico

His name was Lawrence Shaw and he was rightly known as the fastest gun alive. . . .

When his bullet hit the first bandit squarely in the chest, the impact of the shot slung both the man and his tired horse sidelong to the ground. The bandit landed facedown, dead upon arrival, but his terrified horse thrashed and whinnied and managed to struggle back onto its hooves.

"No, *Senor, por favor!*" the second bandit shouted immediately as Shaw's big smoking Colt swung toward him. Yet even as the bandit tried to bring the proceedings to a halt, he managed to cock the French revolver in his right hand. In reflex, Shaw fired. His second shot lifted the man from his saddle and flung him backward to the ground. The bandit lay stretched out, gasping for breath. His horse, the better looking of the two rangy desert barbs, spun with a loud whinny and raced away across the sand.

Shaw sighed as he slid down from atop his mule and watched the stream of sand dust billow up behind the fleeing horse. The blanket that had served as the bandit's saddle flew from the horse's back and drifted to the ground.

"Looks like it's you and me," he said to the first horse, a speckled gelding, as it shook itself off and snorted and stood on spread hooves, staring blankly at him. Beside him the ragged mule raised its muzzle and sniffed the air toward a line of blue hills to the right.

Shaw punched the two hot, empty cartridges into the gloved palm of his hand and dropped them into his pocket. He replaced them with two fresh rounds from the gun belt draped over his shoulder beneath his dusty poncho. With his Colt hanging in his right hand he walked forward to where the second bandit lay panting, managing to clutch his bleeding chest.

"You did not . . . have to shoot me . . . ," the bandit said, struggling to sit up but not making it.

"Yeah, but I wanted to," Shaw said matter-of-factly. He let his words hang for a moment, then said with a nod toward the stream of rising dust, "It looks like the best cayuse got away."

The bandit managed a weak nod—he understood. But then a look of confusion set in as it seemed to suddenly dawn on him that it was he and his *compañero* who had come to do the robbing. "You . . . were awaiting us . . . to steal our horses?" he asked.

"Wasn't waiting," Shaw replied, "but I saw you coming." He reached out a boot and kicked the big French revolver farther away from the man's reach. "I figured you were up to no good." He added grimly, "I'm tired of riding this *federale* pack mule."

"Damn . . . I feel foolish," the man said, his voice failing. His eyes went to his friend's body on the ground a few yards away. The man had been a young American outlaw known as Claw Shanks. "It was Claw's . . . idea."

"It makes no difference now," said Shaw. He'd heard of Claw Shanks, enough to realize that his death was no big loss to either side of the border. Then he looked all around and asked quietly, "Have you been to Valle Del Maíz lately?"

"*Si* . . . of course," the man groaned, "only . . . a month ago."

Shaw could see that the Mexican was fading fast. Fresh blood began to trickle down from the corner of the bandit's mouth, and a circle of darker blood widened on the ground beneath his back. "Did you see an old witch there with a covey of trained sparrows?"

"A *bruja* . . . ?" The dying bandit stared at him through dim, waxy eyes. "With *trained* sparrows . . . ?"

"*Si, me oyó*," said Shaw. *You heard me.*

"You . . . kill me, then you ask me this?" the bandit rasped, his voice weakening.

Shaw only stared at him.

"You . . . must be loco, Senor . . .," the man managed with his dying breath.

That was no answer. . . .

Shaw stepped over and looked down at the dead man. He'd really wanted to know about the *bruja* and her sparrows, whether she and her birds had been real or imagined. He had been drunk on mescal, tequila and peyote wine for well over a month when he'd pulled himself atop the lank ragged mule and rode bareback out across the desert floor. The night before he'd left the dusty adobe village of Valle Del Maíz, he had sat watching an old *bruja* wrapped in a ragged, flowing black cloth as she tossed a covey of paper-thin sparrows upward from her knobby fingertips in a circling glow of firelight.

Sparrows . . . ? He still questioned himself in reflection, seeing the small birds assembled in a wavering line, suspended in midair, awaiting their command. He'd never seen anything like it, yet there they were, eight or ten of them, perhaps even a dozen. They had spun and fluttered and hovered above her weathered fingertips, dancing on air like playful children.

"Sparrows . . . ," he repeated to himself, and he shook his head at the absurdness of it. He looked back down at the two bodies.

How drunk had he been?

He considered the question for a moment beneath the narrow shade of a battered top hat he'd scavenged somewhere over the past week. All right, he'd been about as blind drunk as a man could be and still be counted among the upright and breathing. He pictured those small birds chirping and dipping, catching something in the purple night air—crumbs, no doubt sprinkled freely from those weathered mystical fingertips.

No, he decided as the birds appeared clearly in his mind, being drunk had nothing to do with it. He couldn't dismiss it as some drunken hallucination. The old *bruja* and her sparrows had been real, as real as anything he'd ever seen here in this land of black shadow and blinding sunlight. He saw the birds dip and spin and flutter on their tiny wings, sparks from the fire skittering up into the black night around them.

As real as two dead men in the sand, he told himself, having to force the birds from his mind. For the sake of his sanity, he had to put the incident away, real or not. He gave the dead bandits another passing glance, then gazed out across the endless desert floor. Enough of witches and dancing birds, he told himself. He had lost a month in the grip of heavy drinking. Now he had to finish regaining his rattled wits and get back to business—the grim business of killing.

His friends Crayton Dawson and Jedson Caldwell were somewhere out there ahead of him. He should have caught up to them a month ago, but the need for drink had come upon him like some terrible, sudden fever, and he'd fallen before he could hang on and stop himself. *Dancing sparrows . . . Jesus.* He sighed. Would it be like this for the rest of his life?

He gathered the reins to the tired horse standing spread-legged above its dead rider. He checked the animal over and found nothing wrong with it that some water and a little rest wouldn't cure. He ran a gloved hand along its wet flanks and loosened its saddle cinch.

"We'll pick up your friend along the way," he said to the black-and-white speckled barb. Lifting a goatskin canteen from its saddle horn, he picked up the dead man's hat and poured a puddle into its upturned crown. Kneeling, he held the hat by its brim while the animal drank.

When he had given the thirsty animal two hatfuls of water, he pitched the wet hat aside. He picked up a bandoleer of ammunition from beside the dead man and checked the bullets before draping it over his shoulder. From the man's deep shirt pockets he pulled out a leather bag and shook seven shiny new gold coins out onto his palm. "Gold from the Sonora depository robbery." He shook his head knowingly and added, "Shame on you, Claw Shanks."

Dawson will want to see this. . . . He pulled a rawhide string, closed the top of the bag and shoved it down behind his gun belt. Seeing a bulge in the man's other shirt pocket, he reached down and pulled out a battered metal whiskey flask. He sighed. He shook the flask gently, judging its contents as half-full.

A few days ago he would have given his horse for a deep drink of whiskey—if he'd had a horse, that is, he reminded himself. By then he'd already sold his horse for whiskey—or had he lost the animal somewhere . . . ? He didn't know. *Here goes* . . . Unscrewing the cap from atop the metal flask he took a long, deep smell. He waited for a moment, not knowing what to expect. Then he screwed the cap back on with a feeling of satisfaction. He could not have done that a week earlier. The *urge* had left him. Well, it hadn't left him, but it wasn't raging inside him the way it had been. He started to pitch the flask aside. But then he stopped. *Don't get carried away*, he told himself. He shoved the flask inside the worn saddlebags behind the speckled barb's saddle. Whiskey wasn't the problem. *He* was the problem, he reminded himself, turning, leading the speckled barb over to the mule.

When the urge was not upon him, he could swim in a sea of whiskey with no desire to drink a drop of it. Or he could have a drink, two drinks, three or four, and push the bottle aside. But when that drinking urge hit him hard the way it had over a month ago, and those painful memories came flooding in at the same time, he was powerless. He didn't know which one brought on the other, but once the drinking urge and the bad memories got together, he became a man helpless atop a wild, raging beast. All he could do was hang on and ride it out.

Did that make him a drunkard? Well, yes, he expected it did at that. . . . He swung atop the mule and led the horse, letting it rest for a while without a rider on its tired back. He'd have to give the drinking matter some more thought, but not right now. Soon though, he told himself. He looked off at a dark boiling sky far east of him, and rode on.

A thousand yards from where he'd left the bodies lying on the ground, Shaw found the spooked horse that had run itself out. When he reached the animal he didn't stop. He simply stretched out from his saddle and gathered its dangling reins. The little bay fell in alongside the other horse in tow and walked along easily, drawn toward the smell of rain on the eastern horizon.

When the three riders reined down at the sight of the two men lying dead in the sun, a young gunman named Bobby Freedus pointed at Claw Shanks. "That's ole Claw, deader than hell, sure enough," he said. "Damn, there's Paco too!" he added, pointing toward the Mexican.

"Yeah," said Merle Oats, the older of the three dusty, trail-bitten bounty hunters, "careful your loud mouth don't cause us to join them." His eyes searched the barren sand with suspicion.

The third man, a half French, half Sioux called Iron Head, said under his breath, "I said those shots meant trouble."

"Yeah?" Oats spit and replied gruffly, "When was gunshots out here ever a good sign?"

Iron Head didn't answer.

"Free Boy, shake them bodies out," Oats said to Bobby Freedus. "See if whoever killed them overlooked them German coins."

"Hell, it ain't likely," said Freedus. Instead of stepping down from his saddle, Freedus crossed his wrists on his saddle horn.

Oats stared at him coldly. "Humor me."

Freedus let out a breath. He didn't like being told what to do, but he stepped down anyway and walked forward, leading his horse. "I never liked being near these two when they were breathing in and out. Dead ain't going to be no better."

"Help him," Oats said to Iron Head in a short tone of voice.

The half-breed glanced at him crossly, but stepped down and did as he was told, catching up to Freedus.

In a lowered voice, Freedus asked Iron Head, "Is he getting on your nerves as much as he is mine?"

"More," the half-breed replied.

"Think I ought to kill him for us?" asked Freedus with a dark grin.

"I don't think you can," Iron Head said flatly.

"Any-*damn*-body can kill any-*damn*-body," Freedus said with a swaggering confidence, nodding toward the two bodies. "There lays cold proof of it. All it takes is guts to get the job done."

"I know," Iron Head said, leaving his meaning open to Freedus' interpretation.

Freedus gave him a stern look from beneath his lowered brow. "Don't smart-mouth me, *injun*. I got the guts for the job."

"Then do it, or shut up about it," said Iron Head.

Freedus stalled for a second, wishing he'd never mentioned the matter. "Aw, forget it, injun," he said finally as they stopped and stood over the bodies. "I was just making conversation."

"Yeah, that's what I thought," said Iron Head in a sarcastic tone.

From his saddle Merle Oats watched closely, making sure he saw their every move as the two rifled through the pockets of the dead bandits. *Lousy sonsabitches . . .* He didn't trust either man as far as he could spit. Seeing the half-breed lift something from the dead Mexican's pocket, he called out quickly, "Hey, what's that? What have you got there? Bring it on over here!"

Iron Head gave Freedus a disgusted glance and growled under his breath, "What a suspicious turd." Then he straightened up from over the Mexican and held up a gold coin. "It's one of the stolen German coins, sure enough," he called out to Oats. "But there's no more on him."

"On neither one of them," Freedus added, straightening up beside Iron Head.

Sonsabitches . . . He'd have to see for himself, Oats

thought. He urged his horse forward with his boot heels, then stepped down and jerked the coin from Iron Head's upheld fingertips. "Yeah, that's one all right," he said gruffly. "Where the hell's the rest of them?" His voice took on an accusing tone.

"How would I know?" said Iron Head. "We got here at the same time, remember?"

"Yeah, I remember," said Oats. "We follow these sonsabitches for a week, and then some other bastard steps in and takes our prize. Life ain't fair, and that's the whole of it."

Iron Head looked down where the two bandits' tracks had intersected with a single set of hoofprints. "We go after the one who took the gold. At least there is only one now."

"That's easy enough," said Freedus.

"You're not real smart, are you, Free Boy?" Oats said with a bitter expression. "Whoever the *one* is, he just killed *two* of Jake Goshen's gunmen. Does that tell you anything about him?"

Bobby Freedus considered it, then replied, "That he's a Texan, maybe?"

"Jesus," said Oats; he shook his head.

Iron Head did the same. But he added, "Whoever he is, he must've got the drop on these two. But we know he's out there. We'll be ready for him."

"I sure as hell hope so," said Oats, sounding none too sure. "Meanwhile, cleave these twos' heads off. We still got some bounty coming from the government."

"About forty dollars," said Iron Head. "At least that's something."

"But it ain't the damn gold, is it?" Oats snapped

back quickly. "It's hardly worth the stink and the flies from carrying them around."

"We'll get to the gold," Freedus offered, not about to try to explain to Oats that the Texas remark had only been a joke. Nobody was in a joking mood; that was clear enough. He stooped down and pulled a bowie knife from his boot well. "So long as we're carrying a head or two around it shows the *federales* we're bounty hunters."

Iron Head gave a flat grin. "It shows that our hearts are in our work."

Oats let out a breath and calmed down. Freedus was right. If they were ever going to track down Jake Goshen and his gang and get their hands on the stolen German coins, they needed good cover. Bounty hunting for the Mexican government was perfect, for now anyway. "Get to cutting," he said to Freedus in a friendlier tone. He nodded off toward the black storm clouds in the distance. "We're going to catch up to him. We don't need rain washing his tracks out."

Chapter 2

———

Shaw had not been lucky enough to outride the storm, or outflank it, as he'd hoped to do. In fact, he'd ridden right into it. But that didn't bother him. Weather played no favorites, he reminded himself wryly as he ripped a corner off a dirty shirt he'd found inside the speckled barb's saddlebags. Beyond the narrow rock overhang lightning twisted and curled, followed by pounding thunder.

He wrapped the cloth around a piece of downed tree limb and lit it with a wooden match. Holding the flickering torch before him, he half walked, half crawled into the low open crevice. The sound of a snake's rattle moved away, deeper under the hillside as he ventured forward.

"As long as you're leaving anyway...," he murmured toward the snake under his breath, his big Colt out and cocked in his right hand.

Only by a stroke of luck had he happened upon a small cave as he'd put the speckled barb up a mud-slick trail, the other horse and the mule trudging along

behind. When water rushing down the trail reached
halfway up the horses' forelegs, he coaxed the animals
upward onto a rock ledge where an overhang pro-
vided some shelter from wind and water. It was there
he'd spotted the black entrance to the cave and saw
the weathered leather shoe lying in the dirt just inside
the crevice opening. Curiosity had gotten the better of
him.

Torch in hand, he managed to stand in a crouch as
the cavern widened, revealing its dusty six-by-fourteen-
foot floor. Across from him he saw the last three inches
of the rattler's tail slide away under a rock wall. He
looked around carefully in the flickering torchlight,
then lowered the Colt back into its holster.

Seeing a wide drag mark across the dust and a set of
fading boot prints leading back toward the entrance, he
stepped forward, holding the torch in front of him. As
the black shadow gave way to the dim light, he spotted
the half-skeletal and half-mummified remains of a man
lying beneath a thin cover of dust. He stopped and
stared, his expression stoic, as he was not the least bit
surprised by his discovery.

This was not the first dead man he'd found in this
desert wasteland, and he doubted it would be the last.
Death was too commonplace to cause concern, he
thought, looking all around the dusty corpse until his
eyes came upon a black leather bag. *A doctor's medical
bag . . . ?*

Kneeling over the dusty bag, he reached out a
gloved finger and pulled the top open, noting a bare
spot where a name had been removed. "All right,
whoever you are," he murmured sidelong to both the

corpse and the medicine bag, "let's hear your sad story. . . ."

Outside the small cave the storm pounded along the rock lands and roared across the endless desert floor. Shaw held the torch closer to the open bag, tipping it with one hand until its contents spilled freely into the dirt. Among an assortment of gauze and medical instruments he saw a small blue bottle of laudanum and a larger half-pint bottle of what his trained eye identified as rye whiskey. Opening the cork and sniffing the contents confirmed it.

He recorked the bottle and laid it aside, along with the laudanum. First the flask of whiskey he'd taken off the dead bandit, now this. He shook his head. "Where was everybody when I needed them?"

He walked in a crouch back to the entrance, then stooped down and looked out at the horses and the mule, seeing the three huddled closely against the rock wall. They were wet but no longer being battered by the blast of wind-whipped rain. It would have to do, Shaw told himself, turning back to the corpse, the leather bag, and the fading boot prints leading back to the entrance.

In moments he'd scraped together enough twigs and dried scraps of wood and brush from the dirt floor to start a small fire. While the blaze flickered off the jagged rock walls, he searched the corpse's pockets, noting the thick black stains surrounding two bullet holes in the dry, decomposed chest cavity.

He finished searching the pockets—trouser, suit coat and shirt—and found nothing. He sat back on his heels and gazed all around again, looking for anything he might have missed. *No money . . .* Again he was not surprised. But a man dressed in a suit and string tie—a doctor no doubt—carrying no identification? He glanced again at the leather bag, then at the boot prints.

"Somebody went to a lot of trouble dragging you in here," he murmured to the skeletal face covered by only the remnants of thin parchment skin. He thought about the two dead bandits he'd simply left lying where they'd fallen, the same way they would have left him had things gone their way. The law of the desert, he reminded himself, reaching out and flipping the leather bag shut with finality.

Who went to this kind of trouble for a man they'd killed and robbed? Better still, he asked himself, looking at the bottles of whiskey and laudanum lying in the dirt, who killed a man and left good liquor and dope behind? Nobody he knew of, not even himself, and he was no bandit. He stared blankly at the corpse for a long silent moment, then said with a sigh, "All right, Doc, it looks like you'll be coming with me. . . ."

By the time the storm had passed and the land had begun drying, the sun had moved over into the low evening sky and lay simmering in a pool of fiery red. Shaw watered the animals in the storm's runoff and divided a small portion of dried oats he'd found lying loose in the speckled barb's saddlebags. The barb had brought his attention to the loose grain by poking its nose back toward the bags and stomping its front hoof in frustration.

"Okay, I hear you," Shaw said.

While the animals ate, he'd wrapped the thin, brit-

tle body in a threadbare blanket that lay rolled up behind the barb's saddle. Dragging the wrapped corpse
from the cave, he laid it over the mule's knobby back
and tied it down loosely with strips of cloth he ripped
from the blanket's edge. Looking east toward the border, he envisioned the rocky desert trail leading toward a small supply town he'd passed through over
two years earlier.

"Banton . . . ?" he said aloud, recalling the small
dusty border town. He glanced toward the blanketed
corpse as if playing a guessing game with the bundle
of dry hide and bones. After a moment he let out
a breath, considering the long, harsh trail stretched
out before him. "Yeah, Banton," he said to the corpse.
"That's where you're from."

When the speckled barb had finished eating, Shaw
stepped over, slipped its bit back into its mouth, picked
up its reins and said, "That's all the handouts you'll get
for a while." He swung up into the saddle, tapped his
boot heels to the barb's sides and rode away, leading
the mule and the bay behind him.

Shaw rode until the sun had sank below a stretch of
sand hills and broken rock west of him. He stayed up
above the wet flatlands and skirted the rock hillsides,
giving the land its proper drying time. By noon tomorrow he knew the blazing desert sun would have done
its job. The streaks of muddy water that he now saw
stretched across the rolling sand flats below him would
be gone, boiled back up into the endless Mexican sky.

In the last blue light of evening, a large desert vulture batted down from the sand hills and broken rock
to his left and soared off into the darkness above his

head. The sound of the large fleeing bird called for his attention. He knew of no animal other than man who could scare a vulture from its roost. Yet instead of looking up along the edge of the hillside he gazed straight ahead.

Easy . . . If there were someone up there, they weren't about to skylight themselves to him. He was in no position to let someone know he was onto them. Keeping his head down, he effortlessly quickened the barb's pace a little, veering slightly upward into a stand of chimney rock and saguaro cactus. Once inside the shelter of rocks he'd have all the time he needed to find out who was dogging him, and why.

When Shaw and his animals had vanished into the looming darkness, higher up on the hillside, another winged scavenger lifted from its perch on a rock and batted out across the night sky. In the darkness a tall Mexican known as Juan Facil Lupo—Easy John—stepped forward in a black riding duster and a wide black sombrero and turned quietly to the three other men spread out along the rocks behind him.

"I recognized the two outlaws' horses, but I do not recognize the man riding Claw's speckled barb," said Lupo, in good border English. He searched the faces in the darkness until he found the one he sought, a wiry Scots-Irish gunman named Maynard Lilly. "What do you make of it, Senor Lilly?" he asked, intentionally avoiding the opinion of his scout, the man who had misled them into the hillside of roosting vultures.

"I say it's Claw's horse certain enough," Maynard Lilly replied. "If that is not Claw Shanks riding it, I say we need to know just who it is."

"*Si*, you are right," said Lupo. "Perhaps the body on the mule is that of Claw Shanks himself." He considered something for a moment, then added, "But if that is Claw's body, where is Paco Zuetta?"

After a moment of silence, a young Texan named Booth Anson, who wore the fringed buckskins of a trail scout, said, "Why do we even give a damn? If Paco and Claw are dead, our jobs are finished here. I say leave this man alone. You can head on back to Mexico City, send me and Wallick and Lilly home to Texas."

"Oh . . . ?" Lupo turned to the cocky young scout. "Perhaps you'd like to stir up some more vultures and send them his way, make sure he knows the four of us are trailing him?"

Anson felt the sting of Lupo's words. "He didn't see us," he replied.

"What makes you so certain?" said Lupo, showing the scout more patience than he was accustomed to showing anyone. His fingertips tapped idly on the butt of his holstered Colt as he spoke.

Anson noted the tapping fingers. Instead of answering Lupo's question, he responded in his own defense, "How was I supposed to know these hills are full of vultures roosting anyway?"

The third man, an Arkansan named Wilbur Wallick stepped forward and said in an even tone, "It's not so much that you should have known they're roosting here, as it is that you should have had better sense than to stir them up." He looked at the Scotsman. "Is that what we're saying, Lilly?"

Instead of answering, Lilly tipped up his dusty

derby hat and stared coldly at Anson, who stood close by. "I say if you were any kind of scout at all, you would not have stirred up this hillside full of gut pluckers and got us seen up here."

"I said, he *didn't see us*," Anson repeated insistently, glad it was Lilly he now defended himself to instead of Lupo.

"Aye, but do you *know* he didn't see us?" the Scotsman asked, pushing for the same answer Anson had ignored a moment earlier.

"I know *because* I was watching him," Anson shot back angrily at Lilly. He wasn't about to take any guff from the older gunman. "I know *because* he didn't even look up. I know *because* it's my job to know. That's how I know."

Lilly gave a dark chuckle. "Yes, of course you *know*, you bloody young *frisk*, ya." He looked away in the darkness and spit and grumbled under his breath.

"What did he call me?" Anson asked no one in particular.

"Don't act like a child," Lupo said stiffly, still keeping his temper under control. "Get the horses. Let's get behind this man and see why he has Claw's and Paco's horses. I want to get to him before those bounty hunters do." He gestured a nod back across the desert floor and added gruffly, "Now get moving, pronto!"

"All right, but first I want to know what he called me," Anson insisted, staring hard at Lilly even as Lupo turned and walked away toward the horses.

"He called you a *frisk*," said Wallick. "Now come on, let's go."

"What does that mean?" Anson asked the Scotsman, standing in a way that blocked him from walking toward his horse.

The Scotsman gave a short, tolerant smile. "It means whatever you bloody well *choose* for it to mean." He wagged a finger in warning. "Careful your choice doesn't lead you to an ugly spot."

"An ugly spot?" Anson's hand drew nearer to the butt of his holstered Colt.

Wallick tugged at Anson's arm. "Let it go, it means nothing."

"Unhand me." Anson rounded Wallick's grip from his forearm. But he took a breath and let his blood simmer a bit. "Whatever I *choose* for it to mean, eh?" he said to Lilly.

"Correct you are, laddie," said Lilly. He stepped past Anson as the young scout gave way for him.

"So what if I take it to mean that I'm one strapping fine fellow? Is that what it means, then?"

"I could not have explained it better," Lilly said, feigning cordiality over his shoulder. Yet as he walked he closed his hand around the bone handle of the big bowie knife he carried holstered just under his left arm.

Wallick grabbed the young scout's forearm again. "Let it go," he insisted, lowering his voice this time and speaking almost in a whisper.

"I don't answer to that son of a bitch," Anson grumbled.

"No, but you do answer to Lupo," said Wallick. "We all three do. You best keep that in mind, else you'll end us all up back in prison with that iron collar around our necks."

"I know who I work for, Wallick," the young scout said harshly, keeping his voice lowered. "As far as I'm concerned, let the bounty hunters have this saddle tramp. We came looking for Claw Shanks, nobody else. If he's dead, the deal's done."

"We don't know that Claw's dead," Wallick replied under his breath as the two men reached their horses behind Lupo and the Scotsman. "If he's not, we best find him and take him back to the general alive, the way Lupo said we would."

Anson offered no further words on the matter. He swung up atop his horse and gazed in the direction of the border. "Do you know how long it's been since I seen my own country?" he said to Wallick, not expecting an answer nor waiting for one. "Too damned long." He gigged his horse forward.

"Proceed quietly," Lupo ordered in a hushed tone. But the young scout murmured a curse word under his breath as he rode off ahead of the others.

Beside Lupo, the Scotsman said, "I have never known a man so irritating as our *dear* Mr. Anson. I couldn't blame you were you to lift your long-barreled Colt and empty it into his back."

"It was you who told me he is a good scout," said Lupo. He kept his voice and manner even and under control, as was his custom.

"I told you he knew his way around on both sides of the border, not that he was a good scout," said the Scotsman. He arched a brow and added, "A good scout should understand that he can get himself killed quickly out here and never be missed, eh?"

Lupo didn't answer, nor did he look toward the

Scotsman. "I must get this job done, Senor Lilly. Serving my general and my country is the first and most important thing to me. I must let nothing else bother me or deter me from my task." He gigged his horse ahead of Lilly and Wallick a few feet to keep from having to converse with them. The Scotsman looked at Wallick and shook his head with a knowing grin.

"They call him Easy John, huh?" Lilly said under his breath to Wallick when Lupo had ridden far enough ahead.

"Yep, Easy John is what they call him," said Wallick. "Easy John, they say."

"I'm beginning to see why," Lilly said with a shrug and a sigh, heeling his horse forward.

Chapter 3

Anson had no trouble finding the lone campfire glowing in a clearing on a rocky hillside, even though he could tell the man who built the blaze had taken precautions to not be easily spotted from the trail. "He should have killed that fire before he turned in," the young scout whispered to Lupo and the Scotsman who stood crouched down beside him.

"That mighta helped him some," said Anson. He stared at the small circle of dim firelight as he spoke. "Some pretty good tracking if I do say so myself," he added a bit haughtily. After his earlier mistake regarding the roosting vultures, he needed to reestablish himself as trail savvy.

Lupo didn't answer. He wasn't about to comment on Anson's prowess as a scout, nor was he going to mention that almost anybody he'd ever known could have found a campfire in the middle of the night, especially trailing a man who had no idea he was being followed.

"Let's not fall for the oldest trick in the book," Lupo

said quietly. He looked at the horses and mule standing at the outer glow of firelight, the blanket-wrapped corpse lying on the ground near their hooves. He noted the low flames and the ragged poncho spread over the man sleeping close to the flickering fire. He slept with a saddle as a pillow, his battered top hat covering his face.

"Trick? It's not a trick," Anson said defensively. "I just caught him off guard. He's ours now. I'll walk in alone and wake him up if you want me to." He jiggled the rifle in his hands.

"No," said Lupo. "We're all moving in closer. You and Wallick lead the way. When we get close enough Lilly and I will lag back and shadow you, in case this does turn out to be a trick."

"That's playing it safe enough, I reckon," Anson said, his tone dripping with sarcasm.

"I'm honored that you agree with me," Lupo replied in the same sour tone. He stared hard at him in the grainy moonlight. "Now, will you do as I say, or do I tell the general you refused to follow an order?"

An order . . . ? Anson fought back the urge to remind Lupo that he was not a soldier and that Lupo was not his superior officer, only his employer, the way he saw it. But he managed to hold his tongue for the time being. "You heard him, Wallick," Anson said, gripping his rifle at port arms. "Follow me. . . . Try not to trip and fall over your own feet."

Wallick just stared at him sullenly.

The two moved forward slowly, quietly, keeping an eye on both the figure sleeping near the fire and the body wrapped in the blanket lying near the horses. A few feet behind them Lupo and Lilly crept along, watching both sides of the campsite, ready for anything. When Lupo decided he and Lilly had gone close enough, he held a hand out to his side and halted Lilly while Anson and Wallick crept closer and stopped at the outer circle of firelight.

"Watch the body lying near the horses," Lupo whispered sidelong to the Scotsman. "If this is a trick, it will come from there. . . . He thinks we won't expect anything from a dead man."

Lilly didn't reply.

Lupo looked toward him in the darkness but could no longer see the wiry Scotsman's silhouette. "Lilly? Do you hear me?" Lupo whispered, searching the dark purple moonlight.

Still no reply.

At the edge of the dim circle of firelight, Anson and Wallick heard a thud followed by a deep grunt, as if one of the two men had tripped and fallen. Anson looked back over his shoulder. "Now who's making all the noise?" he murmured under his breath. He turned back quickly and studied the man sleeping beneath the spread poncho until he was certain the disturbance hadn't awakened him.

Behind him, he listened to the faint sound of footsteps advancing toward him and Wallick. "Here they come," he whispered to Wallick as he took a cautious step forward. "Let's get this done while there's still some time left to get in a good night's sleep."

"You're too late for that," a voice said gruffly behind him.

"What the—?" Anson and Wallick spun around and

saw Lupo standing only five feet behind them, his palms raised, his eyes wide in fear. But it wasn't Lupo's voice they had heard.

"Drop the guns," Shaw said, standing behind Lupo, a forearm around the Mexican's neck, his Colt cocked against the side of Lupo's bare head.

Wallick's gun hit the ground at his feet. But Anson stalled, looking the situation over warily.

"You heard him, Anson," Lupo shouted in a frightened voice, "drop the gun!"

"Not so fast," Anson said. "First I want to know what the deal is here."

"What the deal is?" said Lupo in disbelief. "He cracked Lilly's skull, and he is holding a cocked gun to my head! For God's sake, you fool, what's the matter with you?"

"Nothing's the matter with me," Anson said defiantly, keeping his eyes on Shaw's shadowed face in the darkness. "Just because he's got the drop on you don't mean that I ought to throw down my gun and—"

Before he could finish his words, Shaw's gun swung away from Lupo's head and fired. The shot hit Anson solidly in his left shoulder and spun him backward to the ground like a scarecrow. The roar of the shot resounded in the Mexican's ear. Shaw shoved him away, then stepped forward and reached down to pick up Anson's rifle from the ground where it had fallen. Wallick and Lupo crouched near the ground, Wallick with his hands chest high, Lupo cupping one hand to his right ear.

"I—I cannot hear anything," he said, his voice still shaken by the sudden impact of the gunshot.

"Shake it off," Shaw said with no show of concern. He stepped away from the wounded Anson, picked up Wallick's gun and shoved it down in his belt beside a Colt and bowie knife he'd taken from the knocked-out Scotsman. "It's better than what you deserve, slipping around bushwhacking folks in the dark."

"We were not out to harm you, Senor," said Lupo, managing to hear Shaw through a thick ringing in his head. "We just wanted to know what you're doing riding Claw Shanks' barb. We saw the body on the mule. We thought it might be Shanks."

"Are you friends of Shanks?" Shaw asked Lupo as he reached down, lifted Anson's Remington from its holster and shoved it down behind his gun belt.

"No, we're not friends of his," said Lupo. "We were tracking him and Paco Zuetta. I'm an investigating agent for the government of Mexico. We are investigating the robbery of the National Bank in Mexico City."

"I see," said Shaw, not sure if he believed a word of it. He eyed Lupo in the grainy moonlight. "Shanks is dead, so is his pal, Paco. But it was neither one of them you saw tied over the mule."

"Then whose body is it?" Lupo asked.

"I don't know," said Shaw. "I found it in a cave among the rocks. He's been dead a long time."

"I see." Lupo pondered the matter. "Did you kill Shanks and Paco?" he asked with a tone of authority, seeing this man was going to be hard to deal with, having the upper hand on them. As he asked he looked Shaw up and down, noting all the guns in his position.

Not liking the Mexican's tone of voice, Shaw didn't

answer. He motioned for Wallick to help Anson to his feet. Then he turned his gun sight back toward Lupo.

"If you did kill them, I'm sure it must have been in self-defense," said Lupo, softening his tone at the sight of the big Colt pointed at him. "I know the kind of men they were. I only need to know what happened in order to report to my superiors." He kept his hand cupped to his ear. "If you will, *por favor.*"

"Don't belly up for this sonsabitch!" Anson growled, clutching his upper shoulder in pain. He glared at Shaw in the pale purple moonlight. "We ought to haul him to Mexico City for a trial and a long stretch in the—"

"Keep your mouth shut," Lupo shouted, his head pounding above the ringing in his ears. He said to Shaw, "Pay no attention to him, Senor. I had him released from jail and brought him along as a scout. But I'm afraid he is turning out to be an idiot." He turned a harsh stare to the wounded scout.

Shaw looked the Mexican up and down. "Who are you, Mister?" In the pale moonlight he noted Lupo's good clothes, good English and good manners in spite of the smell of sand and horse sweat.

"I am Juan Lupo." Out of habit he gave a slight head bow. "I serve the emperor of Mexico under Generalissimo Manuel Ortega."

Juan Facil Lupo . . . *Easy John*, Shaw remembered, recognizing the name right away, but making no mention of it. "You're searching for the gold stolen from the Mexican National Bank," Shaw said.

"Oh . . . ?" Lupo gave him a suspicious look. "What do you know of the stolen German coins?" he asked.

"Nothing. But that's all I've heard everybody talking about since the day the gold was stolen," Shaw replied. He thought about the shiny new coins he'd taken from Claw Shanks' body. He wasn't about to mention them. "You figure Shanks and his pal had something to do with that big robbery?" he asked Lupo.

"Never mind what I think," said Lupo. "I am the *only* one who should be asking the questions, not you."

"But I'm the *only* one holding a gun," Shaw said flatly. "The one you were about to bushwhack."

"If we were bushwhacking you, Mister, you'd be lying dead back along the trail hours ago," Anson growled through his pain.

Lupo shot Anson a cross look. "As I said before, we were not going to bring you harm, Senor," he replied to Shaw, "only question you about Claw Shanks and Paco Zuetta."

Shaw looked away for a second as if dismissing the matter. Then he said to Wallick, who stood beside Anson supporting him, "You best stop the bleeding."

"Don't tell us what we need or don't need," Anson said in an angry, scorching voice.

Shaw gestured a nod back over his shoulder and said to Juan Lupo, "Your other man is knocked out back there where I left him. I shooed your horses away. With any luck, you should have them rounded up come morning." He backed away a few steps. "Start walking. Stay away from my camp until I clear out of here," he warned. "I'll leave the shooting gear along the trail a couple of miles ahead." He touched two fingers to his forehead and backed away into the darkness.

"What if we're come upon by Apache?" Anson called out, his voice sounding strained by the throbbing pain in his wounded shoulder.

"Keep your mouth shut, Anson," said Lupo. He turned and stomped away, walking back toward the spot where Lilly lay stretched out on the ground. When Wallick and Anson had caught up to him, he stood over Lilly, who lay moaning on the dirt.

"I never seen a man slip up and get the drop on four men at once," Wallick said. He stooped down over Lilly, pulling him upward as the Scotsman groaned and murmured in confusion.

"You have seen it now," said Lupo, disgusted, but keeping it from showing. He helped him raise Lilly to his feet. "Let's get after the horses, before they wander out onto the desert floor."

"Once we gather our cayuses, I say we quit this chase," said Anson, holding his bloody shoulder. "Claw is dead, so is Paco. I'm wounded, Lilly is knocked senseless. This whole thing has gone to pieces, if you ask me."

"It was you and your roosting vultures that put us here," Lupo said in a tight and lowered voice. He had just caught a mental flash of himself spinning around, grabbing Anson by the throat and choking him to death with his bare hands. But he fought hard to keep from turning the dark vision into a reality.

"I'm not blaming anybody," Anson said, "although if I had been—"

"One more word, and I'll drag you back to the general in chains," Lupo said, with no anger in his voice, only resolve. He picked up Lilly's hat, slapped it against his thigh and shoved it down onto the Scotsman's addled head. He looked back at Wallick and Anson. "Both of you, spread out, find the horses," he said. "We still have a job to do, wounds or no wounds."

Lilly staggered in place, but began to realize what had happened to him. "I—I didn't know what hit me." His hand went to his empty holster. "My gun is gone."

"Of course it's gone. He took it," said Lupo, struggling to hold on to his patience.

"But don't worry," said Wallick, "he's going to leave our shooting gear along the trail."

Lupo just stared at the dull-witted gunman for a moment. Then he looked back toward Shaw's camp as he saw the glow of firelight go out, leaving a rising gray spiral of smoke in the night. Clutching his fists tightly, Lupo said almost to himself, "So you saw us coming and you set your trap. And like fools we fell into it."

"Outsmarted by some ragged-ass saddle tramp," said Anson in a sarcastic and accusing tone, as if he had nothing to do with being caught by surprise.

"Oh? A saddle tramp?" said Lupo. "Is that what you say he is?"

"Yeah, that's what I say he is. I can't say for sure," Anson said, pressing Lupo ever closer to a breaking point, "since you didn't even manage to ask his name."

Lupo said, "Maybe I didn't have to ask his name. Perhaps I already know who he is."

"If you do, maybe you ought to let me in on it," Anson said, gripping his wounded shoulder. "I'd like to know the name of the man I'm fixing to kill as soon as I come upon him again."

But instead of answering, Lupo only smiled slightly to himself. He decided he'd rather let Anson find out for himself who had put a bullet into his shoulder. He gazed back toward the spot where the campfire had been only moments ago, seeing even the smoke dissipate into the night. He knew that by now the lone gunman had vanished into the rock hillside as if he'd never even been there.

"Let's get after those horses," Lupo said, looking all around and seeing neither sign nor silhouette of the animals against the purple night.

Chapter 4

━━━

At dawn, after searching the rock lands the rest of the night, the four men found two sets of horses' hoofprints in the blue-gray light and followed them down onto the desert floor. The two sets of prints joined another set in a patch of soft sand and, a few hundred yards farther on, Anson pointed out a fourth set of prints trailing down out of the rocks from a different direction.

"All right," Anson said, "I've found them for you. Now I've got to get off my feet for a while." He staggered toward a large rock alongside the trail.

"Nobody stops. . . . We keep moving," Lupo said. "Once the sun is standing over us, it'll boil our brains out. If we don't find those horses soon, we've got to stick and get off these flats back into the rocks." He walked toward Anson, waving the tired scout back into pursuit of the horses.

"Damn it," Anson cursed. But he was savvy enough to know that Lupo was right. Gripping the dark blood-stained bandanna tied around his upper shoulder, he swayed back onto the hoofprints and struggled on. Lilly, sore and cross from the pounding inside his knotted head, followed silently alongside Wallick, until the four managed to once again space themselves out single file in the rising morning sun.

An hour later, as the morning sun began scorching their backs through their shirts and coats, they stopped and stared ahead through the wavering heat at a gathering of black spots in the distance. "Apache, you reckon?" Wallick asked.

"What's the difference who they are?" said Anson. "Whoever they are, they've got us dead-to-rights in this damned furnace."

The four stood squinting in glaring sunlight. "It's not Apache," said Lupo. "They wouldn't be out in the open this way."

"Why wouldn't they?" Anson lamented. "They probably watched us from afar. They know we're afoot, got no guns, no way to protect ourselves or outrun them."

Lupo didn't bother to answer. He trudged forward, leaving the other three to decide whether or not to follow him.

In the distance, at the far edge of the sand flats, Merle Oats stared through a powerful brass-trimmed naval telescope at the four exhausted hikers. "Well, well, look who we got coming here," he said with a dark chuckle. "If it ain't ole Easy John Lupo himself."

Beside him Bobby Freedus sat with his wrists crossed on his saddle horn. He shook his head, squinting toward the four, unable to make them out with his naked eye. "What are we going to do, give their horses back?"

Merle Oats held the big telescope with both hands for a moment longer. Then he lowered it and laid it across his lap for a moment before shoving it down into its leather sheath. "Yeah, I expect we will," he said, "else this desert is going to bake them into the ground."

"That's no skin off our backs," said Freedus. "Lupo being dead wouldn't hurt my feelings at all."

"Maybe," said Oates, "unless he's found information about the gold that we need to know." He looked back at Iron Head, who sat holding the reins to the four lost horses. The two dead outlaws' heads hung in bloodstained feed sacks from the half-breed's saddle horn. "Lupo can keep us from toting these stinking sonsabitches all the way back to Mexico City."

"I don't mind us toting them," Freedus replied.

"That's because I'm doing all the toting," Iron Head said sourly.

Oates continued grinning, as if not hearing the other two. "Beside," he said almost to himself, "I would kind of like to see his face when we come leading their horses up to them. He'll be beholden to us whether he likes it or not." He gave another dark chuckle.

Bobby Freedus managed a crooked grin, starting to like the idea himself. "Come on up here, Iron Head," he said over his shoulder. "I'll lead a couple of those horses myself, if it'll keep you from feeling put-upon."

Twenty minutes had passed by the time Lupo and the other three recognized the riders coming toward them at an easy gallop. As the men drew close enough for him to spot his and the others' horses being led by Freedus and Iron Head, he murmured a curse under his breath.

"*Hola*, gentlemen, and a good morning to yas all," Oates called out as the three reined their horses down twenty yards away and put them at a walk. "Nothing like a good long morning stroll to steady up a fellow's constitution, eh, Easy John?"

Easy John . . . Lupo gritted his teeth, but he only stared at him grimly, dirt covering his black duster, his hat, his face and boots.

Oates chuckled under his breath as he lifted a canteen strap from his saddle horn and pitched the half-full container to Lupo. "What brings you fellows out onto the desert floor at this hour? I hope you're not overextending yourselves in this heat."

"Those horses," Lupo said flatly, uncapping the canteen and throwing back a drink. "We've been searching for them all night."

"These horses?" Oates said in mock surprise. He motioned Freedus and Iron Head forward. "Whatever might have happened to cause you men to lose your horses?" His speech was taunting and goading. "We heard gunshots in the night. Don't tell me you were set upon by horse thieves."

"They're unarmed too," said Freedus with a grin of satisfaction.

"My, my, but they sure are," said Oates, shaking his head. "You four are some brave *hombres*, traveling this wild desert frontier without firearms."

"Stop mocking us, Oates," Lupo warned. "I'm not in the mood. We followed a man riding Shanks' speckled barb, leading Paco Zuetta's horse behind him." He capped the canteen and pitched it back to Anson, who caught it with his good hand, uncapped it and drank. Wallick and Lilly closed in around him, eager for their turn at a mouthful of tepid water.

"You don't say," said Oates, with a wizened expression.

"He caught us off guard last night," said Lupo. "He spooked our horses and took all of our firearms."

"That's a damned shame," said Oates. "We came upon the same fellow's trail. Lucky for him he was long gone, else we would have chopped him down, us not being *off guard*, as you say." He gave a smug grin, adding, "It'd been a hell of a sight better for you boys."

Beside him, Bobby Freedus muffled a laugh. But his laughter stopped short as Lupo stepped forward and jerked the reins of his and Wallick's horses from his hand. Backing away and handing Wallick his horse's reins, Lupo turned his harsh stare from Freedus back to Oates. He gave a nod toward two bloodstained feed sacks hanging from Iron Head's saddle horn. "I see you've managed to gather some bounty for yourselves."

"We have, indeed," said Oates, changing from his teasing tone to a more civil reply. "This is Paco and Claw, trimmed back some for traveling, of course."

"Of course," Lupo said flatly, watching flies circle and buzz above the two dark bloody feed sacks.

"I expect if you was of a mind to you could sign as

witness to us having brung them in," Oates said. "It would keep us from hauling them around out here in this damned heat?"

"You didn't kill Paco and Claw, Oates," Lupo said with confidence. "The gunman told us he killed them."

As the two spoke, Anson walked over to where Iron Head sat holding the reins to his and Lilly's horses and reached out for them. The half-breed turned the reins over to him. Anson walked over beside Lupo.

"I never said we killed them," countered Oates. "But it makes no difference who did the killing. The Mexican government is paying bounty for them, dead or alive. There they are, dead as hell. It doesn't matter how they got that way."

"Bounty money is bounty money, however you want to cut it," said Bobby Freedus. He glared at Lupo and spit with an air of contempt.

Oates gave Iron Head a nod and the half-breed lifted the sacks and pitched them to the ground, close to Lupo's feet. The heads landed with a solid thud. Flies scattered.

"Damn!" said Anson, jumping back from the bloody sacks. But Lupo didn't flinch or back an inch. He stood rigid and kept a firm hold on his horse's reins, keeping the animal from bolting.

"All's I need is for you to sign a statement as a representative of the Mexican government, identifying them," said Oates. "Your word will be good enough in Mexico City, you and the general being such good amigos."

Lupo stared at him.

"I expect that's not too much to ask, us bringing

your horses to you and all," said Oates. Then he added in a lowered tone, "Nobody has to ever hear about how one man outgunned all four of yas. It'll be our secret from now on."

"He didn't outgun us," Anson cut in sharply, his fists clenched at his sides.

"He just as well have outgunned yas," Oates, replied to Anson, keeping his eyes riveted on Lupo as he spoke. "I'd as soon a man shoot me as strip me of my guns and transportation."

"I will identify Paco Zuetta and Claw Shanks for you when we reach Chihuahua. It is the nearest town where they can pay you the bounty," said Lupo.

"Chihuahua? Damn," said Oates, "that's five or six days back and forth. We hadn't intended on riding back just yet. There's still wanted men to be hunted out here. Jake Goshen's men are scattered everywhere along the border. We need to stay on them."

"Chihuahua. That is my condition, take it or leave it," Lupo said flatly. "I know we will all three sleep better along the trail knowing that you have an interest in our arriving there safely."

Squatting, Lupo opened one of the bloody bags, then the other. He looked in at the blue-black faces as he held his breath and squinted against buzzing flies. Recognizing the two outlaws, he stood and stepped back from the feed sacks, dusting his hands together. "It's them, all right," he said, making a face of disgust and revulsion.

Oates sat silent for a moment, ignoring Lupo's remark, but considering his offer. Realizing it would be pointless to argue the matter any further, he said, "All right, damn it. We'll ride with you fellows to Chihuahua, if that's what it takes for us to get paid." He turned to Iron Head and gave a nod toward the two feed sacks. "Toss them heads away from here. The quicker we can get rid of them two stinking bastards, the better."

Iron Head slipped down from his saddle, picked up the two sacks and heaved one after the other out onto the sandy ground. As the half-breed remounted his horse, Oates gave a toss of hand toward the two bags and said, "So long, Paco. Adios Claw. . . . Hope both you sonsabitches find hell to your liking." He turned back to Lupo and said in a tone of authority, "Mount up. Let's get started. We've got a long ride ahead of us."

Lupo ignored Oates, not about to start taking orders from him. He looked at Wallick, Anson and Lilly and nodded for them to mount up. As he swung up into his own saddle, he said to Oates, "You three ride ahead. We're going to pick up our weapons. We'll meet you along the trail."

"Your weapons?" Oates said with a wry chuckle. "If you're going after the man who did all this to you, we best stick with you. Like you said, we don't want nothing happening to you until we get our money."

"We are not going after him," said Lupo. "By now he is well on his way to the border."

"He said he'd leave our weapons along the trail," Wallick cut in.

Oates gave a wide grin, so did Freedus. Iron Head sat staring with only a thin trace of a smile. "You amaze me, Easy John," Oates said, managing to not laugh in Lupo's face. "The man loosed your animals, shot one of your men and cracked the other's nut for him ... you think he's left your weapons waiting for you?"

"Yes, I think he has," Lupo replied in a firm voice.

"If it's all the same with you, Easy John," said Oates, "I propose we ride along while you collect those guns, just in case we have to keep this *one* man from eating you *four* boys alive."

Chapter 5

On the trail back up into the rocky hillside, Lupo and Oates led the others until they reached a spot less than a mile from where they had been set afoot and weaponless. Slowing his horse, Lupo looked up at the edge along the higher trail before them. Realizing what a perfect stretch of trail this would be for an ambush, he looked back at Booth Anson.

"Anson, you and Wallick ride ahead, scout this trail for us," he said.

Oates smiled to himself, knowing the only reason for sending men ahead along this trail would be to draw any gunfire that might lie in wait. Anson knew the same thing, and he gave Lupo and Oates both a scowl of resentment as he and Wallick pushed their horses forward and passed them along the trail. "Wait for us where you find our weapons," Lupo called out to them as the two rode away.

Anson didn't answer. Wallick gave only a wave of his hand in acknowledgment. Riding away, Anson said to Wallick under his breath, "Can you believe this? He

might just as well come out and tell us we're both ex-
pendable, far as he's concerned."

"That's not why he sent us," said Wallick. "He just
wants to make sure there's no—"

"Aw, hell, smarten up, Wilbur," said Anson, cutting
him off. He gigged his horse's sides and sent it up into
a quicker gait.

"I'll try," Wilbur said in earnest, shrugging and then
gigging his horse in order to keep up with Anson.

When the two had ridden three hundred yards
ahead of the others on the narrowing trail, Anson
turned in his saddle and said to Wallick with determination, "I ain't going to Chihuahua, and I ain't returning to Mexico City either, Wilbur."

"You ain't?" Wallick stared at him, his dull eyes trying to understand. "But they'll slap you back in that
iron collar if you don't go back."

"No, Wilbur . . ." Anson took a deep breath and
tried to keep patient with Wallick's slow-wittedness.
"They can't collar me if I'm *not* there. You see, the only
way they could collar me if I *am* there . . . or you either,
for that matter."

"You do what suits you, but I'm going back," said
Wallick. "I'm not taking any chances."

Anson looked at him, too puzzled by his words to
know how to reply. After a moment, Anson shook his
head and said, "We did what was asked, Wilbur. We
brought him this far. We would have shown him deep
into Texas had he wanted to ride on. But now he's wanting to turn back to Mexico City. What does that mean for
us? Do we get thrown back in jail because we didn't
track the whole Goshen Gang across the border?"

It was too much for Wallick to sort out all at once. He pondered and wrung his head back and forth with a puzzled frown. "Now I don't know what to think. Maybe you're right," he admitted.

"You're damned right I'm right," Anson said with conviction. "Ma Anson raised no fool. I'm staying far away from that iron collar. They want me, I'll be across the border, cooling my hocks. If you want to stick with me, you're welcome to."

"You mean make a run for Texas or somewhere?" asked Wallick.

"Jeez, yes, Wilbur," Anson said in frustration. "What have we been talking about here?"

"What'll we do over there?" Wallick asked dully, nodding ahead as they rode along.

Anson stared at him for a moment. Then he kept a patient voice and said, "Never you mind for now. But I've got plans, Wilbur, you can count on it. When they took that collar off me, they let lightning out of the bottle."

"Lightning in a bottle!" Wallick laughed. "That's funny, Booth. I like that you're always saying funny stuff like that."

"Whoa, Wilbur, look here," Anson said, veering his horse to the side of the rail ahead, where their rifles and revolvers lay piled on a rock. "I'll be damned. He did leave our guns for us, just like he said he would." Anson slid down from his saddle and looked all around warily. "Keep watch for a trick of some kind," he said in a whisper.

Wallick stopped his horse and looked all around the craggy hillside above them. Anson snatched up his

Colt right away, checked it and found it unloaded. "The sonsabitch stripped my bullets." He shoved the Colt down into his empty holster, then picked up his rifle and checked it. "Empty! Damn it," he cursed, looking back and forth along the hill line above them.

Wallick slid down and picked up his guns and checked them. "Mine to," he said. He reached for Lupo's revolver, but Anson said, "To hell with it. They're all unloaded. Let's get out of here before we get ourselves jackpotted again."

"This is going to make Lupo madder than hell," said Wallick, dropping Lupo's revolver back onto the rock beside Lilly's weapons.

"I've not yet seen Easy John get mad about anything and, believe me, I have scouted him out just to see how far I could go," said Anson. He grinned, stepping back into his saddle and turning to the trail, slipping his rifle down into its boot. "Anyway, I don't give a damn how mad he gets, I don't expect to ever see his face again."

Wallick swung up into his saddle, leaving the other unloaded guns lying on the rock. "You mean all them times you needled him, it was just to see what it would take to make him mad?"

Anson gave him a smug look and said, "Let's just say, I like to know the boiling point of any man holding my collar and chain." He gigged his horse forward.

"You sure are something, Booth," said Wallick, gigging his horse along beside him.

"Stick with me, Wilbur," said Anson. "You ain't seen half of what I'm up to." In moments the two had ridden out of sight, leaving dust from their horses' hooves hanging in the still-hot air.

Shortly after the fine trail dust had settled, Lupo, Oates and the others rode up and stopped, looking down at the rock where the remaining weapons lay in the glittering sunlight.

Gazing after the two fresh sets of hoofprints leading off away from them, Oates said, "Looks like that scout of yours might have had a pressing engagement elsewhere."

Bobby Freedus chuckled to himself.

Lupo only hung his head, staring down at the hoofprints, seeing a double X stamped into the front shoes of both horses. Then he breathed deep and gazed off in the direction Anson and Wallick had taken. Riding up beside him, Lilly stepped down from his saddle and began picking up his and Lupo's weapons and checking them. "I can't say that it comes as any surprise to me," he said to Oates, handing Lupo's revolver up to him.

"Gracias," Lupo said quietly, taking the gun and shoving it down into his empty holster.

"Well, I don't know what you expected, Easy John," Oates gloated to Lupo, "taking a handful of jailhouse rats and thinking they would hunt down one of their own kind." He glared at Lilly as he made the cutting remark. He spoke with a hand on his holstered gun butt.

Lilly ignored Oates and asked Lupo, "Does this change anything? Are we still headed for Chihuahua, or back to Mexico City, or are we going after Anson and Wallick?"

Oates cut in, "If it was me, I'd go after them and swing them from a scrub oak. You can't let people do you that way. Word gets around, Easy John—you ought to know that."

"What about your bounty?" Lupo asked quietly, as if already knowing the answer.

"Sign some paperwork for me to take," said Oates, "like I wanted you to do to begin with."

Lupo smiles slightly to himself and turned his horse back on the trail. "We go to Chihuahua," he said.

"What? And let these two get away?" Oates asked, finding it too incredible to believe.

"They won't go far," said Lupo. "They are not hard to follow." He didn't mention the stampings on the horses' shoes, although the double Xs were clear enough if a person wanted to concentrate on seeing them.

"You act like you almost wanted this to happen, Easy John," said Oates, still using the name that Lupo did not seem too happy with. Narrowing his brow with a look of suspicion, he called out as Lupo rode away, Lilly right behind him, "You didn't have things planned this way, did you?" He gigged his horse along behind Lupo, Iron Head and Freedus right behind him.

"No," Lupo said without looking back, "I did not plan on them running away. But I would have been a fool had I not considered the possibility."

Beside him, Lilly gave him a closer look as they rode on side by side. "What's he talking about, having this planned?" he asked quietly between the two of them.

"Nothing. He is simply letting his mouth air itself out," Lupo replied sidelong without looking at him.

"What did you mean, they wouldn't be hard to

find?" Lilly asked with a trace of his Scottish accent. "If we're through out here, why can't they ride on? Why can't we be shed of them? We're better off without them anyway, are we not?"

"You ask me four questions without taking a breath, Mr. Lilly," said Lupo. "Which one would you most like me to answer?"

Lilly's lips clenched shut. "Whichever suits you, sir." He stared straight ahead.

Lupo said patiently, "They will be easy to follow because both of their horses wear store-bought double X shoes from Arizona Territory."

"Oh?" Lilly gave him a curious look. "Did you plan it that way when you brought the three of us horses?" As he asked, he looked down at his own horse's hoofprints behind him.

"Planned or unplanned, it is a fact, and we will use it when the time comes to find them," Lilly said. "Then he said, "Do not bother to look. Your horse is not wearing double X shoes."

"Oh," said Lilly, feeling better for some reason. He relaxed in his saddle.

"Yours is wearing three Starbach shoes with a single star stamped on the front edge of them."

Lilly grumbled under his breath, recalling how his horse had slipped a shoe a week earlier. He'd had one forged and replaced outside of Sonora. "Blast it all," he murmured to himself. Then he said to Lupo, "I thought you and I had formed a trust between us these weeks on the trail."

"We have, Mr. Lilly," said Lupo. In an offer of explanation he said, "It does not matter whether I had the horses shoed in such a manner. Would you not have taken note of such a thing yourself?"

"I didn't take note," Lilly offered. "But from now on I will."

Lupo gave only a slight smile, still staring straight ahead as they rode on.

Lawrence Shaw didn't know at what point the endless Mexican badlands beneath the speckled barb's hooves became Arizona Territory. He did not even consider the question. Yet he recognized the small supply town when its rooftops and tent points rose up slowly from the sand lying in the distance before him. He also recognized the tiny black speck that he'd spotted an hour earlier as it moved toward him at the head of a rising column of dust.

As the black speck turned into a freight wagon drawing closer, pulled by three mule teams, Shaw had directed the barb with a tap on his knees and led the other animals into the broken shade of a family of saguaro cactus. There he slipped down from his saddle and waited, resting his animals until the buckboard drew closer.

When the wagon slowed down as it approached him, Shaw stepped out onto the hard beaten path of wheel and hoofprints, his hands at his sides without his rifle. His gesture brought the wagon forward until it stopped less than thirty feet away.

"Hello the trail," the shotgun rider called in a husky, but unmistakably female voice. Shaw watched the lanky figure in a ragged tan riding duster stand up facing him, shotgun in hand. "Are you a damned road agent? If you are, you're in for a rude awakening." The woman's gloved hand pushed a floppy hat brim up from her forehead. Her other hand held the cocked shotgun to her shoulder.

Shaw didn't answer as he stepped forward slowly.

"That's close enough," the woman warned. The driver sat rigid on the seat beside her.

"She asked you a question, Mister," the driver said in a gravelly voice. "Are you a thief?"

"If I was I wouldn't be robbing an army supply wagon, would I?"

"That's a point to consider," said the woman, the shotgun still raised and ready.

"People rob most anything these days," the driver said through a face covered with a thick white beard.

"That's true too," the woman conceded, keeping a stony gaze on Shaw.

"Why was you waiting here for us?" the driver asked bluntly.

"Who else is back there?" the woman asked, gesturing toward the shade where the mule and horses stood.

Shaw answered the woman first. "There's nobody else. I wouldn't be fool enough to walk this close to a scattergun if there was a dozen men backing me."

The woman seemed to consider the logic of it.

To the driver Shaw said, "I needed to rest my animals. I saw no other shade between here and Banton."

It made sense. The driver almost nodded in agreement.

But the woman wasn't finished. "What happened to that one . . . ? You kill him?"

"No," said Shaw, "I found him dead, in a cave up in

the hill country." He gave a jerk of his head back toward Mexico. "He's been dead quite a while, from his looks."

"You don't say . . ." The driver craned his neck a little and gazed toward the blanket-wrapped body lying over the mule's back. "Who is he?"

"I don't know," said Shaw. "I'm hoping somebody in Banton can tell me. I've got a notion he's from there."

"Why's that?" the woman asked, lowering her shotgun an inch as she gazed inquiringly toward the body. "We get our share of drifters through here."

"He's no drifter," said Shaw. "Ride forward. I'll show you what I found beside him."

The driver and the shotgun rider looked at each other as if for approval. Then the woman stepped down from the wagon and walked forward while the driver put the six mules forward at a slow walk. "You best have no evil in mind, Pilgrim," the woman warned Shaw, looking him up and down, trying to discern any ill intent.

"None," Shaw said. Walking ahead of the woman and the wagon, he reached the speckled barb and took down the worn leather doctor's bag from his saddle horn.

"Watch your step, Mister," the woman cautioned him until he turned with the bag clearly in his hands and held it out to her.

"Oh my," the driver said, recognizing the medicine bag right away. He stopped the walking mules, wrapped his traces around the brake handle and hopped down from the wooden seat.

Chapter 6

———

Shaw stepped back and watched the woman and the wagon driver. The expressions on their faces told him they both knew who the weather-beaten leather bag had belonged to. Her sense of caution gone, the woman walked past Shaw as if he weren't there. Instead of taking the leather bag he offered her, she ignored it. She stood at the side of the mule and hesitated for a moment. Then she reached out a gloved hand and uncovered the decomposed face beneath a fold of dusty blanket.

"Janie, is it him?" the driver asked as he walked over quickly and stood beside her.

The woman made a face and said, "Hell, Ed, I can't tell who it is, or even what it is."

The driver studied the face for moment before making up his mind. Finally he turned away, shaking his head sadly and said, "Hell yes, it's got to be Doc Edelman." He took the leather bag from Shaw and turned it back and forth in his big calloused hands.

"Why's that?" Shaw asked.

Touching the bare spot along the top frame the driver said, "Right here it used to have a brass plate that read, J.E. MD. Something must've happened to it, I reckon." Shaking his head sadly, he said, "You are the bearer of terrible news, Mister . . . ?" He paused for a reply.

"I'm nobody," Shaw said, not feeling any need to introduce himself. "I'm just a rider passing through, seeing to it this fellow makes it home to his family." He reached out and took the dusty bag from the driver's hands. "I'll turn him over to the sheriff in Banton, if there is one," he said.

"There's not," said the shotgun rider as the driver handed the bag back to Shaw. "There was, but he drank himself to death six months ago." She gave Shaw a critical look up and down and added, "There's a lot of that going around, I hear."

Shaw felt her accusing gaze.

"*Complications* from drinking too much is what killed him," the driver corrected her. "At least that's what the doctor said."

"The doctor?" Shaw asked, glancing at the bag back in his hands. "You have another doctor in Banton?"

"No," said the driver, "but once we saw Doc Edelman wasn't likely to be coming back, his wife commenced taking over, seeing to it his patients didn't go neglected. She's more or less filled his shoes."

"The poor woman is going to take this hard," said the shotgun rider.

"Where should I take the body?" Shaw asked, already realizing that without a sheriff the next likely place would be the town doctor.

"The Edelmans have a place off the trail south of Banton," said the shotgun rider, giving a nod south. Then, with a look toward the mummified face beneath the blanket, she added, "It's Widow Edelman now, I reckon." She studied Shaw up and down skeptically. Then she looked at the driver. "One of us ought to take leave here and ride over with him. It would help Lori Edelman, seeing a familiar face."

"Do you feel safe enough, riding with this stranger?" the driver asked in a lowered tone that Shaw could still hear.

"Are you being funny, Ed?" the shotgun rider shot back at him gruffly, with no attempt at keeping her husky voice down. "If you are, then by God we'll both go. Save you any undue fretting over my safety."

The driver considered it for only a second, then replied, "No, you go ahead on, Janie. Catch up to me along the trail. These staples need to get to Fort Carrick as soon as possible." To Shaw, he said, "Mister, I'll warn you not to give this woman a hard time."

"You needn't warn me," said Shaw. "Like I said, I'm here to take this fellow home; then I'm gone."

"Figures," the woman murmured under her breath.

"What's that supposed to mean?" Shaw stared at her.

"Not a damn thing," the woman said in her husky voice, sounding irritated with him for no reason that Shaw could fathom. "Come on, Mr. *Nobody*. Let's you and me get this sad business done."

Shaw didn't move. He stared at her, then at the driver. "All right, just call me Lawrence. I didn't mean to be rude."

"We understand, Mr. Nobody," the woman said

with an edge of sarcasm. She gave him another critical once-over and said, "Any fool can see you're coming off a hangover bigger than the state of Missouri. I'm surprised you can remember any name at all."

Shaw offered no argument. He knew he looked like a down-and-out drunk, his dusty, battered top hat, his ragged poncho.

"Don't be so hard on him, Janie," the driver cut in. To Shaw he touched his battered hat brim and said, "Mr. Lawrence, I'm Ed Baggs." He swept a hand toward the woman and added, "This ornery creature riding shotgun is Janie. I expect we ought to know one another's names, since you're riding together to the Edelman place."

"The *Widow* Edelman's place," Jane corrected him, still giving Shaw a hard stare. "Thanks to Mr. *Lawrence's* terrible discovery."

Shaw ignored her and turned to his horses. "The quicker we get started, the quicker we'll get this done," he said.

Over the next hour Shaw and the woman looked back from time to time, watching the freight wagon turn back into a black dot as they rode away from the trail. Finally the wagon topped a low rise on the desert floor and disappeared from view, leaving only its wake of dust in the air. Riding one of Shaw's spare horses, the woman turned to him and said, "So, Mr. *Nobody*, is Lawrence your first, last or only name?"

Shaw didn't answer. Instead he stared straight ahead and asked in retaliation, "Is Janie your first, last or only name?"

"Fair enough." The woman nodded. "Janie is my *only* name. Leastwise it's the only name I give answer to." She paused, then added, "Although some of my *good* friends call me JC."

"JC . . ." Shaw pondered it.

The woman cut him off quickly, saying, "But you're not one of my good friends, Mr. *Nobody*. It's Jane to you . . . or Miss Jane, whichever you prefer." She looked him up and down. "Now, what about you? Is Lawrence your first, last or only name?"

Shaw didn't want his name to be recognized. "It's my last name," he said.

"Oh? Then what's your first?" she asked. But before Shaw could respond, she cut in and said, "No, wait, don't tell me. I like *Nobody*." She looked him up and down with her critical gaze and added, "It just suits you. Mr. *Nobody* Lawrence." She gave a flat smile of satisfaction with herself.

Good enough . . . Shaw let it go at that. He didn't care what this woman called him. He had no desire to be around her, or the town of Banton, any longer than necessary. Changing the subject, he asked, "How long has the doctor been missing?"

"Hell, it's been near a year, I calculate," the woman replied after a moment of thought on the matter. "He went to visit some sick Mexican children this side of the border and never made it home. His horse and buggy came back without him. Right off, we figured Mexican bandits got him. But his wife held out hope he'd be back someday, even as the rest knew better." She paused and said, "You've shot that hope all to hell for her now, I reckon." She looked Shaw in the eye and gave him a dry smile. He was beginning to realize that this woman meant no harm. She was just abrasive and cynical. She couldn't help herself, he decided.

"I doubt it was Mexican bandits," Shaw offered, paying no attention to her unpleasant manner.

"Oh, and why is that, Mr. *Nobody*?" she asked, her bad attitude still holding strong. "Are you some kind of expert on Mexican bandits . . . ? 'Cause if you are, you ought to go report to the army. They're looking for bold men who can—"

"Bandits would have kept the horse and buggy," Shaw said, cutting her off.

"You sound awful cocksure of yourself," she said, not giving up, yet sounding as if she believed what he'd said made sense. "Come to think of it, the horse was no worse for wear after a long ride like that. I remember thinking it looked to be in pretty good shape." She studied Shaw's face. "Anything else you'd like to enlighten me on? I'm all ears here."

"I found his body in a cave," Shaw said. "Why would bandits bother dragging him there?"

"Maybe they didn't drag him there, Mr. Know-it-all," she said. "Maybe he was wounded and managed to get there himself before he died."

"Could be," said Shaw. "But there was set of boot prints. It looked like somebody dragged him there and left him." He looked at her, seeing that she had settled down and started taking an interest in what he had to say.

"I can't imagine who would want to harm poor Doc Edelman," she said. "All he ever did was try to cure everybody that needed curing. What kind of world is it when a man like that gets himself killed and dragged away to rot in some godforsaken cave?"

Shaw offered no commentary on the condition of the world around them. He rode on in silence until they topped a rocky rise where the sand had given way to a stretch of rocky soil and sparse patches of spindly wild grass. Beside him, the woman rose a bit in the stirrups and gazed down into rocky valley split by a narrow winding creek.

Seeing only a small buckboard sitting at a hitch rail out front of a large clapboard and adobe house, she said, "It looks like there's only one patient there right now. That'll make things a little easier." She nudged the horse forward. Shaw followed, leading the mule with the body over its back.

Halfway down the long hillside, the two watched an elderly couple walk a child from the porch of the house to the buckboard out front. The man helped both the woman and the child into the wagon; then he climbed up and took the traces. As the buckboard rolled away, Jane gave a look out along the winding valley trail below. Upon sighting four riders along the trail she said, "Uh-oh, looks like we ain't as lucky as I thought we were."

"Who's this?" Shaw asked, the two of them riding down toward the valley floor.

"This is some ne'er-do-wells who work for the late doctor's stepbrother, Bowden Hewes. Everything good the doctor was, Bowden ain't," she said, with an almost-worried look on her face. "And these men of his are worse then he is, if that's possible." She paused, then said, "Ah hell, they've seen us."

On the valley trail the four horsemen had slowed almost to a halt and stared up at them. Then, with a thunder of hooves, they raced forward toward the place where the two trails would intersect. "Get prepared for a razzing of some sort," Jane said sidelong to Shaw. "Whatever you do, keep your head and don't let them see you make a move for your gun."

"Hmmm . . . ," Shaw murmured, gazing at the riders with detached interest, his rifle already lying across his lap.

She gave him a look. "I ain't kidding, Mr. Nobody," she said. "You best take these men serious if you value your life. Let me do all the talking."

Value your life. . . . Shaw almost smiled. "The talking is all yours," he said calmly.

As the four horsemen made a slight turn upward onto their trail, Shaw reined in. When he did, the woman stopped beside him. Seeing the first man lead the others toward them from fifty feet away, Janie whispered to Shaw, "This one is Jesse Burkett. He's the worst of the bunch. Remember, don't let them see you—"

"I heard you the first time," Shaw whispered, cutting her off.

"Well, now, boys, lookie here," said the tough-looking Burkett to the men riding a step behind him, fanning their slow walking horses out into a half circle around Jane and Shaw. "It's JC herself, the loveliest dove west of St. Louis." Shaw noted the mocking insincerity in the man's voice, and his insulting manner.

Jane sat still, her shotgun across her lap, but neither of her hands on it. She was used to this kind of treatment from this sort of man, Shaw decided. "We don't want no trouble, Jesse," she said, trying to keep her voice calm, but failing at it, Shaw noted.

"Ah, 'we don't want no trouble,'" said another man sitting his horse back a few steps, "the magic words of the true coward."

The other two men chuckled darkly.

Shaw stared flatly at the second man.

"We come here on a sad piece of business," Janie said, ignoring the remark. "This concerns Bowden Hewes too. He'll want to hear about this right away." She nodded back toward the body lying across the mule's back.

Behind Burkett, the other three men looked over at the blanket-wrapped corpse and gave one another a guarded but knowing glance. Shaw saw it and put it way for later contemplation.

"I'll decide who needs to hear what out here," said Burkett. "That's what Bo Hewes pays me to do." He jumped his horse forward and stopped just short of plowing between her and Shaw.

The woman jerked back in her saddle but managed to keep her horse in place. Shaw sat staring quietly without so much as a flinch at the man's gesture. Burkett noted Shaw's lack of concern and said to Janie, "Who is this stupid looking jake?"

"This is Nobody, Jesse," said Janie. "Just some drifter who found Doc Edelman's body and brought it here. That's why we're headed down to the Edelmans' place."

"Oh? Nobody, huh?" Burkett turned from Janie to Shaw, his horse's sides against Shaw's horse, deliberately crowding him. "I don't like nobodies." He stared at Shaw, searching for any sign of fear he might have conjured up in him. He saw none. But he continued. "If that's the doctor's body, how do we know you didn't kill him? Maybe you brought him here hoping for a little reward money, some token of appreciation from the family?"

Shaw sat silent, staring right back with a blank expression.

"You can tell Doc has been dead a long time, Jesse," said Janie. "Nobody here just come upon the body and brought it to Banton—"

"Shut up, woman, or whatever you are," said Burkett, cutting Janie off. He stared at Shaw. "I want to hear the words come from his own mouth."

"I—I told him not to talk," Janie said.

"You *told* him not to talk?" Burkett chuckled, then stuck out a gloved hand to Shaw. "Maybe you'd best give me that Winchester, Nobody, before you end up hurting yourself."

Shaw stared at him blankly and wrapped his hand around his rifle stock as if prepared to raise it.

"Uh-uh," said Burkett, stopping him. "I meant give it to me *butt first*."

No one saw the weapon come up from Shaw's lap; they only heard the sudden sickening thump of a rifle butt against flesh and bone. "*Jesus!*" Janie exclaimed in shock as Burkett flew sidelong from his saddle and across her lap on his way to the ground. His blood and broken front teeth splattered her cheek.

"Whoa!" she shouted, sitting back hard on her reins to keep her startled horse from bolting away. As

Burkett tumbled over her, he'd knocked her shotgun from her lap. It landed beside him on the rocky ground. Beside her, Shaw hadn't missed a beat. After force-feeding Burkett his rifle butt, he'd swung the rifle around, cocked, pointed and ready, aimed at the chest of the nearest man in front of him. He still hadn't said a word.

Janie collected herself quickly. With Burkett down, dead for all she knew judging from the sound and impact of the blow, and the other three men stunned for the moment, she found herself and her new associate holding the upper hand.

"Keep 'em covered," she said to Shaw, taking on a commanding tone. She slipped hurriedly down from her saddle, grabbed her shotgun and raised it to her shoulder, cocking it.

Chapter 7

Jesse Burkett lay in a limp heap on the ground, his ruined mouth agape, blood running freely down his cheek. Broken front teeth, both upper and lower, lay strung across the ground like a discarded handful of cracked corn. Jane stepped away from the knocked-out Burkett in time to hear the next man, a California gunman named Max "the Ax" Cafferty, say to Shaw, "You best take note, there's still three of us facing you."

Jane stood braced and ready, waiting to hear a response. But upon a quick glance up at Shaw, seeing he wasn't going to reply, she cut in. "Not for long there won't be. You're next Max the Ax." She put a sarcastic twist on the man's name. "Then you, Collie Mitchum... you too, Bennie Ford." She cut a sharp glance to each man in turn, using her shotgun barrel to single them out.

"You don't have us caught by surprise," said the Ax to Shaw. When Shaw didn't answer, he said to Janie, "Is something wrong with this one? Is he a mute or something?"

"I told him to keep quiet," Janie said, grasping their upper hand more firmly, taking over as much as the situation would allow. "He does whatever I tell him to. I say a word, he'll kill all three of yas."

The gunman studied Shaw's flat, menacing expression. Shaw had made his move on Burkett so fast that none of the gunmen had seen it coming. It had been a sudden blur. Max thought about it. A man that fast and accurate with the butt end of a rifle would be no less fast and accurate with the firing end, he decided. He tried to form a cordial smile, but it came off stiff and insincere.

"Hey, how did all this come about?" He shrugged, making sure he kept his hands away from the Colt on his hip.

"Well, let's see," said Jane, as if giving it all some thought. She was clearly in charge now, Shaw thought, observing in silence. "Oh, I know," she said. "I bet it started when you four peckerwoods came riding in like hell boiling over and Mister No-Front-Teeth Burkett here started throwing his weight around." She gestured a nod toward the knocked-out Burkett.

Max had to take whatever she threw at him for now. He and the other two had been caught cold. He wasn't about to lift iron toward this stranger who seemed all too at home spilling a man's teeth and swinging a rifle around in search of his next target. The silence was all the more unsettling. "Jesse is too hotheaded for his own good," he said, his tone softening.

"Is that what you call a keen observation?" Jane asked with a bemused look. She still bore a splash of

Burkett's blood on her cheek, and his teeth scattered about near her scuffed boots.

"What do you want from us, Miss Jane?" Max asked, shedding his pride. He warily eyed Shaw's face, seeing nothing but sudden death in his calm eyes.

"Toss your guns," Janie said firmly, with no room for discussion on the matter.

The three men lifted their guns, both pistols and rifles, and pitched them to the ground. "There, all gone," said Max, trying to put a lighter spin on the situation, but seeing no change in the eyes of the man holding the rifle aimed at his chest. "Can we take Jesse and go now?"

"Uh-uh. Say the magic words first," said Jane.

"What?" Max looked at a loss.

"You know, the *magic words*," Janie said. She tightened her grip on the shotgun stock with a bitter snarl to her lips. "Say them, you son of a bitch!" she growled.

"Go on, Max. Say it. Let's get out of here," Collie Mitchum said quietly behind him.

"All right." Cafferty took a deep breath and said to Jane in a humble tone, "We don't want any trouble, Miss Jane."

"Aw, heck, Max the Ax," the woman replied with a crooked but friendly make-believe grin, "we never really thought you did." But her smile went away as sudden as it had appeared as she gestured her shotgun barrel down at Jesse Burkett. "Now, get this bloody no-good bastard out of my sight before I change my mind and blow his fool head off."

Shaw watched in silence. He kept his rifle pointed at Max Cafferty as the other two men slipped down from their saddles, hurried over and dragged Jesse Burkett back to his mount. When they had loaded Burkett upward onto the horse like a sack of feed and let him slump forward onto the animal's neck, one of them led him away.

"Can I move now?" Cafferty asked Shaw. But Shaw gave no reply.

"Can you move?" said Jane, grinning crookedly. "Well, hell yes you can move. Move on out of here. Don't come for them guns until we're far enough away that we can't smell you." She took a step forward, shouting, "Now let's see the four of yas start getting smaller, *mas pronto!*" Only when the four riders were headed back along the valley trail at a quick pace, Burkett bobbing loosely in his saddle, did Jane turn to Shaw and say playfully, "You can talk now, Mr. Lawrence."

"Obliged," said Shaw. He lowered his rifle.

"That beats about all the hell I've ever seen," Jane said, sounding put out with him now that the men were out of hearing range. "Why didn't you do exactly like I told you to do?"

"You said keep quiet, and I did," Shaw countered. "You said don't let him see me make a move for my gun. He didn't." He uncocked his Winchester, wiped his hand across the butt and slid the rifle down into its boot.

"No. The lousy bastard never saw what hit him, that's for damn sure." Jane looked at him pointedly, forcing herself not to smile or appear overly friendly. "I had you pegged as some sort of drifter, and a low-down drunkard. Now I ain't so sure about it. Who are you anyway, *Mr. Lawrence*?" She emphasized Mr. Law-rence, instead of calling him *Nobody*.

Shaw didn't answer. When he'd heard the two men raising Burkett from the ground beside him, he'd kept his eyes on Cafferty, but he'd heard the slightest sound of coins jingling as they dropped to the ground. Now that the men were gone, he turned and slid down from his saddle and searched the dirt. *There it is. . . .* He picked up a gold coin along with a short bone-handled pocketknife.

He studied the coin and shoved it into his pocket before the woman had a chance to see it. Another of the stolen gold coins, he told himself. He opened and closed the pocketknife and put it away. Turning to his speckled barb, he busied himself as if checking the horse's saddle cinch.

The woman stepped into her saddle, walked her horse around and looked at him. "What the hell are you doing, anyway?"

"Nothing," Shaw said. He patted his horse's side and stepped back into his saddle. Considering the two coins, he wondered whose pockets they had fallen from, Burkett's or the two men moving him.

"Stop fooling around and let's get on over to the Edelmans' place. If Lori Edelman happened to look out and see any of that, she'll think we're all a bunch of damned savages."

"I wouldn't want her thinking that," Shaw said in a flat tone, wrapping the mule's lead rope loosely around his gloved hand. He put the gold coins from his mind for the time being. But his ride to Banton was starting to turn more and more interesting.

When they had lined their horses side by side, Shaw leading the mule, they stopped for a moment and stared off at the disappearing riders through a rising dust. "We made a pretty damned good pair, wouldn't you say?" Jane asked proudly, crossing her gloved hands on her saddle horn for a moment.

"A pair?" Shaw said quietly.

She looked embarrassed. "Hell, you know what I mean. We put those birds in their place. That's all I was getting at." She straightened in her saddle and jerked the horse around toward the Edelman house in the distance. "I hope we haven't gone and stirred up a hornet's nest, you busting Jesse Burkett in the mouth the way you did."

Shaw rode up beside her. "He struck me as a man long overdue for mouth busting," he said. "What kind of work is this Bowden Hewes in, that he needs men like Burkett and Max the Ax?"

She looked at him as they rode along. "What do you care? You're just passing through."

"Just curious," Shaw said, tugging his top hat down onto his forehead.

"Hewes is in cattle," she said. "Leastwise, that's what he likes for folks to think. Personally, I have my doubts. I think he's one of them who likes taking money from one side of the border and moving it over to the other, if you know what I mean."

"I understand," said Shaw. He was thinking about the coins, wondering if there might be some connection between Hewes and the Goshen Gang.

"But I wouldn't get *too* curious if I was you," said Jane. "Like as not you'll be running into Hewes' men again before you leave these parts. They're not exactly the kind to forgive and forget."

"What about you?" Shaw asked. "Will they be out to get you over what happened out here?"

"They might be," she said, taking on a cavalier attitude. "But I don't give a damn. I'm a big girl. I can take care of myself."

Shaw didn't pursue the matter. He rode on in silence, leading the mule and the blanket-wrapped corpse.

When they rode into a sandy front yard spotted with spindly wild grass and yellow blooming barrel cactus, a tall, handsome middle-aged woman stepped out onto the porch to meet them. Standing at the porch edge she eyed the blanketed corpse as she said down to Jane, "Is—is everything all right, Janie? I happened to look through the window. I saw the four men riding up to you. Were they Bowden's men? I couldn't tell from here."

"Yes'm, they were Hewes' men," said Jane respectfully. "It was Burkett, Cafferty and a couple others." She reached up and removed her hat the way a man might do in the presence of a lady.

"Burkett . . ." The unknowing widow gazed off in the direction the four men had taken. "I hope they weren't abusive," she said. "I know Burkett can be such a loudmouth and a bully."

Jane offered her a crooked smile. "Well, he was a little mouthy upon arrival, but he was unusually quiet when they left." She gave Shaw a glance, then, noting his top hat was still on his head, she frowned and gestured for him to remove it, which he did. "This is Mr. Lawrence," she said.

"Mr. Lawrence," the woman said with a curt nod. Her eyes gave him a quick once-over, and she managed to mask any unpleasantness behind a short, courteous smile. But Shaw knew she had tagged him as a drunkard and a vagrant at first glance. He knew the look, no matter how hard a person tried to hide it. At first glance the woman had no use for him, he told himself. *Well, so be it. . . .* He was here only to bring a dead man home. By nightfall he'd be in Banton.

"Well, then, what brings you two out this way, Jane?" the woman asked as she turned her eyes from Shaw back to the blanketed corpse. From the tremor in her voice it was clear that she already had a pretty good idea.

"I'm afraid we have some bad news, ma'am," said Jane. She slid down from the saddle and took a step back toward the mule.

"Oh no," the woman murmured under her breath, as if bracing herself as she stepped forward down off the wooden porch.

Jane accompanied her to the mule, where the woman stood back and watched as Jane reached out a gloved hand and threw back the edge of the dusty blanket. Shaw had slipped down from his saddle and stood behind Lori Edelman. After a long look at the dried sunken skin that had once been her husband, she turned rigid for a moment. Then she swooned a bit to one side. Shaw saw her going faint and he moved quickly, catching her by her shoulders and steadying her until Jane arrived and took the woman in her arms.

"Easy now, Miss Lori," Jane said in a soothing tone. "You've held up well this past year or more. Don't go soft now."

"Yes—yes, you're right, Jane," the woman said, trying to strengthen her voice as she spoke. "It's not something I haven't been prepared for all this time." She took a deep breath, then asked, "Where, who . . . ?" She didn't finish her question, but she didn't have to.

"Mr. Lawrence here found him," Jane said. "He was kind enough to bring him with him to Banton."

"Oh . . . ?" She turned toward Shaw. He saw her opinion of him reshape itself right before his eyes. "Mr. Lawrence, I—I don't know what to say. I can never thank you enough for what you've done."

Shaw nodded humbly and made no reply. She still saw him as a drifting drunkard, only now she seemed to have surprised herself seeing that he had done something only a decent person might have done. But he didn't care. He'd done what he felt he needed to do, decent person or no, he told himself.

Chapter 8

After Shaw carried the mummified body around the back of the house and laid it out of the heat in a small root cellar, he watered the animals at a trough while inside the house Jane consoled the doctor's widow. After a while, Shaw looked up when he heard footsteps cross the porch and saw Lori Edelman walk toward him, a cloth kerchief in her hand. He could see that she had been crying, but he also saw that she carried herself with a bearing that said she had her emotions under control.

"Mr. Lawrence," she said, with a recomposed air about her. "I am grateful to you for bringing my husband home. May I offer you some sort of reward for your trouble and your thoughtfulness?" It was not a question, rather the first step in a polite offer. She could only assume that he expected something in return.

"No, ma'am," he said, surprising her.

"But I insist," she said. "I know it must have been an inconvenience—"

"Ma'am, please," Shaw said, cutting her off. "I'm

not as destitute as I look." He tried to soften his words with a thin smile.

"I didn't mean to imply that you are destitute. I am simply trying to show my appreciation."

"Your thanks is more than enough," Shaw said.

The widow took a deep breath, realizing his response was sincere and final. "You are a gentleman, Mr. Lawrence."

"Obliged, ma'am," he said. He stood gazing into her eyes, knowing she had more questions she needed to ask about her deceased husband. She did.

"Jane—that is, *Mrs. Crowly*," she said, correcting her informality, "told me you found my husband Jonathan's body in a cave west of the border?"

Jane Crowly. He would have to remember that, he thought. "Yes, ma'am, I did," he replied. He'd remember the doctor's first name, too. "I happened upon the cave in the midst of hard rain, otherwise I might never have crawled into it."

"I see . . ." She shook her head slowly at the long odds of a stranger finding her husband in a cave and bringing his body home. "I had given up any hope of ever seeing him alive. His horse came home pulling his empty buggy. . . ."

"Yes, ma'am, Jane told me everything," he said, offering her a reason to not repeat the painful memory.

But she wasn't finished. She reflected on something, then said, "As long as I had not seen his body it made a difference of some sort. I suppose I used it as an excuse to hang on to thinking he might still be alive, somewhere, somehow." She sighed. "Today, all that ends."

"Yes, ma'am, I hope it's for the best," Shaw said quietly.

She seemed to draw a surge of determination. "It will be, I'm certain. Although now I find myself faced with the decisions a widow must make."

"I'm sure you're going to be fine." Shaw wanted to ask questions about the doctor's stepbrother, Bowden Hewes, but he knew that right now was not the best time or place.

Hearing Shaw as she walked around the corner of the house, Jane stepped over beside the widow and took her hand. "Yes, she will be just fine. She has been a strong woman ever since Doc disappeared. She's not going to go weak on us now. I'm going to stick close enough to see to it."

"Jane, you have been a dear," said Lori Edelman.

"And I'm going to keep right on being," Jane replied in her husky voice. "You won't have to worry about Bowden Hewes pushing you into anything you don't want to do."

The woman looked a little embarrassed, and said, "Please, Jane. I'm certain Mr. Lawrence doesn't want to hear my predicament. I have imposed my life on him enough as it is."

"Nonsense, Miss Lori," Jane said. "I know he'll want to hear what you just told me in the house." She turned to Shaw. Seeing the curiosity in his eyes, she said, "Bowden Hewes has been pressuring her to marry him ever since Doc disappeared."

"Now, Jane," said Lori Edelman. "After all, Bo is Jonathan's brother."

"*Step*brother," Jane corrected her.

"Still, he has expressed his intentions," Lori Edelman said. "It is the accepted practice. He is within his right to ask."

"But you said he's been trying to force you to take up with him since a month after Doc's buggy showed up empty."

"Yes, it's true," said the widow. "At first I put him off because it was too soon after Jonathan's disappearance. Lately I've said it's because I have no proof that Jonathan wasn't coming back. Now," she added with dread in her voice, "I can no longer think of an excuse."

"Tell the son of a bitch you don't love him," Jane cut in gruffly.

"I'm afraid love is not a matter to be considered, Miss Janie," said Lori.

Jane continued. "Then tell him his feet stink too damned bad for any decent woman to ever be able—"

"You need no excuse, ma'am," Shaw found himself saying, cutting Jane off. "You just tell him *no*."

"If only life were that easy," the widow said. "If only matters were so cut-and-dried." She gazed out across the wavering desert as if the answer to her problems might lie somewhere in the fiery vastness of it. Then she seemed to resolve her problem for the moment. She turned to Jane and said, "Enough about me. I'm going to prepare us a nice dinner."

"Oh no, ma'am, Miss Lori," Jane said, "we wouldn't dare impose ourselves. I need to catch up with Ed as soon as possible. He doesn't travel well without a shotgun rider beside him."

"I insist," said Lori Edelman. "It will soon be nightfall. I won't have you traipsing out across the desert after dark." She looked back and forth between the two of them. "I have plenty of room. You must spend the night and get started first thing in the morning." She said to Shaw, "Mr. Lawrence, will you be riding back with Jane, or staying for a while in Banton?"

After finding the other two gold coins in the dirt where he'd cold-cocked Jesse Burkett, Shaw had made up his mind. He intended to spend some time in Banton, see what he could find out that might be helpful once he met up with Dawson and Caldwell.

"I expect I'll stay a while, ma'am," he said, "if there's some work I might do here to support myself." He had no interest in work of any sort, other than to finish sweating out the remaining whiskey lingering in his system. He could use some money, but it wasn't the most important thing to him, he thought.

"There's not much work in Banton, I'm afraid," said the widow. "But I have a long list of work that needs to be done around here to keep this place from going to seed. I can't pay much, but there's a room and board in it. Interested?"

"Yes, ma'am, interested and obliged," he said, without hesitation, glancing around the place. This situation could suit his purposes. He would be close enough to Banton that he could ride into town any day and look things over.

"You better be on your best behavior while you're here with my friend, Mr. Lawrence," Jane said, wagging a warning finger.

"I will be," Shaw said. He sensed something at work here that he didn't quite understand. Some secretive purpose had passed between the two women. Now that

he'd seen it, he realized that everything he'd heard the
two women say since Jane walked around and joined
them had sounded loosely rehearsed. They had a reason why they both wanted him here, he decided.

He was certain it had something to do with Bowden
Hewes pressuring the widow to become his wife. But
he'd have to wait and see. It wouldn't take long, he
thought. Jane Crowly was too outspoken to keep the
matter to herself.

After a night of fitful sleep in a small outbuilding behind the house, Shaw joined the two women at a long
makeshift table in the front yard. Sunlight had crept
up above the eastern horizon when Shaw sat down to
a plate of skillet-fried eggs, jowl bacon, chimenea-baked
biscuits and bubbling-hot gravy. "After the day you
had yesterday, we decided to let you sleep late," Jane
said as the three seated themselves.

"Obliged," Shaw said in a gravelly morning voice.
He picked up a cloth napkin lying beside a cup of
steaming black coffee. An oil lamp sat burning in the
middle of the wooden plank table, offering a circle of
light in the lingering morning darkness. Shaw looked
at Lori Edelman and nodded good morning.

Lori returned his nod with a short but pleasant
smile, and said, "Miss Janie, will you say grace for us?"

Jane quickly swallowed a bit of bacon she'd already
taken and bowed her head only an inch. *"Mucho gracias*
for all the grub, Lord," she said, not in a disrespectful
manner.

"Amen," said Lori and Shaw in unison.

Jane raised her eyes and looked at Shaw. "Juanita

the cook is gone off across the border, delivering herself another grandbaby," Jane said. "So Miss Lori was gracious enough to prepare this big fine breakfast all by herself." She grinned glowingly. "Ain't that just wonderful?"

Shaw looked at her, still emerging from a sound sleep and said, "Yes, wonderful." He sipped his coffee and watched and listened. Jane offered no more on the matter, as if realizing he was not an early-morning talker.

Shaw ate slowly and with no great enthusiasm, the way a man eats when his appetite has not fully recovered from a long, hard drinking spree. As he ate he felt Lori Edelman's eyes on him, and he knew that she understood what she was looking at. He knew he still awoke with red-rimmed yellow eyes. His hands were not steady upon first rising. Neither his taste nor his stomach was yet what they should be.

Did it show? Of course it showed, he told himself. He consciously eyed his hand holding the coffee cup up to his face. There was a faint tremor there that a person like Lori Edelman would no doubt see. Even Jane Crowly saw it, he reminded himself. *Hell, everybody saw it.* . . . He sipped the coffee and set down the cup.

Shaw listened but contributed very little to the polite breakfast banter. Lori Edelman herself spoke very little, the grief of the past year being brought back to the surface after seeing her husband's decomposed body. Jane Crowly tried to keep up a light conversation. But with little help from Shaw and the widow, breakfast finally ended in cordial silence.

"Well, morning is wasting," Jane said, standing and

wiping her mouth on a cloth napkin. Shaw and Lori Edelman stood up beside her. When the two had thanked the widow appropriately, they walked to where the horses had spent the night in a small barn. "I'll bring this barb back here to you on the return trip to Banton," she said, swinging the blanket, then the saddle over the little bay's back and cinching it deftly.

"I might not be here by then," Shaw said, watching her eyes for a reaction. "I might be staying in Banton myself by then."

"Oh?" She looked up from her task.

Shaw gestured his hand around the place and said, "I can't see much needing to be done around here, can you?"

"A job is what you make of it," Jane said, a bit knowingly, he thought.

He made no reply. Instead he watched as she lifted the reins to the barb after having slipped the bridle bit into its mouth. "Anybody asks about this horse, is there anything I should know?" she asked, wanting make sure for herself that the horse was not stolen.

"I'm not a horse thief, Miss Janie," Shaw said.

"Aw, hell, I know you ain't," she said, sounding ashamed for questioning the matter. "But you have to admit, you don't look like a man who'd own two horses and a mule. It's good to know how a horse got where it is. Can keep a fellow from stretching hemp."

"I understand, Miss Janie," Shaw said. He gave a slight grin.

"And you don't have to call me Miss Janie anymore," she said, her voice softening. "Far as I'm concerned, you can just call me Janie."

"Not JC?" Shaw asked.

She returned his slight grin. "Not yet, but we'll see how it goes," she said. "I am still impressed as hell at how you smacked Jesse Burkett in his choppers. I loved every minute of it."

"My pleasure, ma'am," Shaw said, touching the brim of his battered top hat. He nodded at the barb horse. "Both of these horses came out from under a couple of wanted outlaws. That one belonged to a Mexican, Paco Zuetta." He gestured toward the speckled barb standing nearby. "That one was Claw Shanks' horse."

"Mercy," said Jane, recognizing both names. "You didn't come upon their horses easily, I'm speculating."

Shaw had to let her know, he thought, in order for her to watch out for herself. She would be traveling in country full of outlaws who knew one another, who recognized horses, saddles, boots, anything that linked their kind together or identified outsiders. "I killed them," he said flatly.

"You killed them?" Jane stood staring at him, questionably at first. She looked him up and down again, as if she might have missed even more than she'd thought the last time she'd done so. "Are you—? Are you a bounty hunter, Mr. Lawrence?" she asked with hesitation. Shaw could see she was beginning to have second thoughts about him staying here with Lori Edelman.

"No," Shaw said. "There was a time when I was what you might call a hired gun." He gave a light shrug. "But that time is long past for me. You needn't worry about Miss Edelman being here alone with me. I am not a man who mistreats women."

"I think I already sensed that much from you, Mr. Lawrence," she said in a gentler and more sincere tone, the likes of which he had not yet heard from her.

Shaw nodded. "You can drop the *Mister* and just call me Lawrence."

"I'm obliged, Lawrence," she said. Then her gentle tone changed. "But I have to warn you if anything happened to her—"

"I understand," Shaw said, stopping her threat.

They turned and walked the bay out of the barn into the first rays of sunlight. When she had stepped up into her saddle, she looked off as if considering something. Then she looked down at Shaw and said, "So, what do you think of Miss Lori?"

"She seems a fine woman," Shaw replied quietly.

"She's a sad woman right now," said Jane, looking closely at him, "but a fine woman nonetheless. It would be a damned shame to see such a fine woman end up with the likes of Bowden Hewes, don't you think?"

"I can't say," Shaw replied. "I've never met the man."

"Oh, but I bet you will meet him," Jane said, pulling on her gloves and adjusting the reins in her hands.

"I'll reserve my opinion of him until that time," Shaw said.

"You're every one of yas a bunch of damned fools," Jane said gruffly, seeming exasperated with him all of a sudden.

Shaw just looked at her.

"All of you *men*," she said. "None of yas knows what's good for yas."

"Stop matchmaking, Janie," Shaw said bluntly. "I told you I think she's a fine woman. What more can I say?"

"Oh, she's a fine woman," said Jane. She leaned down slightly in her saddle and tugged her floppy hat down onto her forehead. "Tell me something, Lawrence, if she's such a *fine* woman, why the hell are you already talking about leaving, staying in Banton?"

Shaw only stared in stubborn silence.

"Lord God," Jane said, gazing off in exasperation. She shook her head and slapped a gloved hand roughly onto her crotch. "I wish I was a man, just so I could show all you wooden-headed sonsabitches how to act."

"Careful what you wish for," Shaw said. He stepped back and raised a gloved hand above the bays' rump.

"What the hell is that supposed to mean?" Jane asked in a half-angry, half-joking voice.

Shaw didn't answer. He slapped the bay's rump and sent it lopping away onto the rocky valley floor.

Shaw waited for a moment, staring out behind her, running things through his mind. When he turned and walked back toward the house, Lori Edelman had walked around from the side of the house and met him in the yard. "Well, Mr. Lawrence, shall we begin?" she asked.

He noted a difference in how she looked at him. It was as if she no longer regarded him as some drunkard and drifter. Why the change . . . ?

"Yes, ma'am," Shaw said. He stood as if awaiting her first bidding of the day.

"First of all, I—I want you to help me give Jonathan a proper burial . . . here in the front yard, so I can see his grave from my bedroom window." She turned toward the house and added, "Come with me. I'll show you the view. You can help me decide."

Chapter 9

At the bedroom window overlooking the front yard, Shaw stood beside Lori Edelman, his battered top hat in hand, and gazed out across the sandy, rock-filled valley floor. The only shade near the weathered house was that of a tall saguaro cactus and the bare bough and branches of a burled and twisted desert oak. It took Shaw a second to realize that his help was not needed in picking a spot for her husband's grave. But hadn't he known that to begin with? he asked himself.

Of course you did . . . , a voice inside his mind replied. He could recall no time in his life when a woman invited him to her bedroom that he did not clearly understand her intentions at the start. His recent bout with whiskey might still have him a little off his game some, he thought, but not that badly—never that badly.

He turned to look around at the widow and found her standing very near, so near that he started to step back in order to give her more space. But then he stood firm, knowing that had she wanted more space she would have taken it. "Ma'am . . . ?" he said, asking what she wanted from him.

He gazed steadily down into her eyes in silence until she said, "I heard you and Jane speaking in the barn."

"Oh?" He held his gaze.

"I wasn't eavesdropping," she added quickly, "simply walking past to gather some kindling for the chimenea."

She glanced away, then back to him. "Anyway, I heard you say you killed two outlaws along the trail here?"

"Yes, ma'am," he said. "They would have killed me if I hadn't."

"Yes, I understand how things are here," she said. She remained close, only inches between them. Too close, for a woman in mourning, Shaw told himself— for a woman standing with a man in her bedroom, her husband's mummified corpse lying in an outbuilding.

"I just wanted you to know that I heard," she said quietly. "Jane told me last night how you handled Jesse Burkett. . . ." She let her words trail.

"Do you want me to leave?" Shaw asked, already knowing the answer.

"No, I don't," she said. Her eyes came back up to his. He saw an invitation there. "I'm not judging you. This is a hard, unforgiving land, where men kill one another. I've learned to accept the fact." She paused, then added, "As for Jesse Burkett, a good rap in the mouth sounds like just what the doctor ordered." She gave a trace of a smile. "And I *am* the doctor."

"Yes, ma'am." Shaw nodded. Now he understood why her gaze had softened earlier, why she'd seemed to begin viewing him in a different light. Like many people, whether they would admit it or not, Lori Edelman took comfort in knowing there was a man like him nearby in a place as fierce and deadly as these high desert plains.

She reached out, took his hands and drew him against her, guiding his arms until they knew she wanted them around her. Raising her face to his, she closed her eyes. They kissed long and deep, revealing to each other that it had been far too long for either of them.

When the kiss ended, Shaw whispered against her burning cheek, "Your husband—"

"—is dead," she finished for him. "He has been for a long time. I have grieved enough that my account is paid in full."

Shaw noted a determined tone to her voice, as if she refused to suffer any more than she had already. "I understand," he said, recalling how the death of his beloved wife, Rosa, still haunted him day and night.

"I hoped you would," the widow said. She led him to her bed as she reached up and loosened the drawstring of her blouse.

Shaw watched her undress. Only when she stood naked before him did he reach up, pull off his ragged poncho and toss it and his hat sidelong onto a chair. The woman looked at the big Colt standing holstered low on his hip. In contrast to his worn and ragged clothes, the gun and its leatherwork glistened, clean, sleek and well maintained.

"I'm only passing through," he said. He pulled out of his shirt and tossed it on the chair.

"I know," she said.

Shaw heard the urgency in her voice. He caught a faint short gasp from her as she watched him loosen his gun belt and pull it from around his waist as if uncoiling a snake. He stepped forward, close to her, close enough to feel the heat of her against his bare chest. "So long as you know," he said quietly. He draped the gun belt over the corner of the headboard. The bone-handled Colt stood like a deadly sentinel above the clean white pillows.

When he'd fallen asleep, he'd done so with Lori Edelman dozed against his chest. But when he'd felt her stir beside him, he'd awakened for a moment to see her standing beside the bed. "Rest," she'd whispered, gathering a housecoat at her waist and shoving her hair back from her face. "I'll be right back."

He drifted back to sleep, and awoke again when she'd returned and held a water gourd to his lips. "Here, drink this," she whispered.

In a moment he was back asleep. When he awakened again the sun had moved over low onto the western horizon and he realized how long he had been lying there. As soon as the realization struck him, his eyes opened and his hand went to the gun hanging only inches above his head.

"Don't worry, it's still there," she said, sitting at a vanity brushing her long auburn hair in a mirror.

"Have . . . I been asleep all day?" he asked hesitantly, still feeling only half-awake.

She smiled coyly. "Off and on," she said almost in a whisper. "Don't tell me you've forgotten everything?"

He thought about it. He remembered now, the two of them, there in the big bed. "No, I remember it now," he said. "It just took a minute." He didn't try to get up, but rather scooted himself up onto a pillow for support. He lay naked beneath a thin blanket. "What did you give me to drink?"

"Just something to make you rest," she said. "No alcohol or opiates, just some herbs I had on hand, mixed with some cool water." She stood up, walked over and sat down beside him on the bed. "You looked like you needed it. How do you feel?"

"I haven't felt this good in a long time," he said, and he meant it. He looked at the chair where he had tossed his clothes. The clothes were still there, only they had been washed and sun-dried and lay neatly folded and stacked.

"Good," she replied. She placed her hand on his chest above the blanket. "It's plain to see that you've been through a rough time lately." She tried to speak delicately about his condition.

But Shaw would have none of it. "I've been drunk, down drunk," he said bluntly. "There's no need in me trying to cover it up. Like you said, 'it's plain to see.'"

"I didn't mean to upset you, Lawrence," she said.

"You didn't," he said in a softer voice, managing even a slight smile in reflection on their lovemaking. "Believe me, I couldn't be more pleased." He pulled the blanket aside and swung himself up onto the edge of the bed beside her. "I have to say, this was not what I expected."

"I hope you don't think me a terrible person," she said, "poor Jonathan lying dead, not even in the ground yet, and me taking liberties with the man who brought him home to me."

Shaw looked at her. "No, I don't think you're a terrible person." He thought about himself and how he had reacted when he'd learned his wife was dead. "People do what they do to keep from going crazy sometimes."

She gave him a closer look. "You sound like you know from experience."

"Yes, Lori, from experience." He didn't want to talk about his precious, long-dead Rosa, not while seated naked beside a woman on her bed, her husband's remains waiting in an outbuilding while Shaw had made love to his widow. "They say experience is the *worst* teacher," he added.

"The *best* teacher, is what they say," Lori corrected.

"Best . . . worst." Shaw gave a wry grin and a short shrug. "What the hell do *they* know anyway?"

Lori gave a slight smile in response, reached over and brushed a lock of hair back from his forehead. "If you ever want to talk about it," she said, "I'll listen without judging, I promise."

"That's the best offer I've had for a long time," Shaw said. As he spoke he reached up and took his gun belt down from the corner of the headboard and laid it beside him.

"I mean that sincerely," Lori said.

"So do I," Shaw replied. Slipping the big Colt from its holster, he checked it deftly and closely. "And I'll keep your offer in mind."

He cocked and turned the cylinder with his thumb, feeling and listening to the sleek action. He looked at her as he slipped the Colt back loosely into its holster, then stood and stepped over to the chair, where his clean clothes lay.

"I took the liberty . . . ," she said, regarding the clean trousers, which he raised, inspected and stepped into.

"Much obliged," Shaw said, buttoning the trousers at the waist. "Now let's take a couple of minutes and talk about why I'm here," he said.

Lori looked surprised and confused. "You're here because you brought Jonathan—"

"No," Shaw said, pointedly, cutting her off. "I mean, why am I *here*, in your bed?"

She looked even more surprised and confused. "I—I don't know how to answer. You said yourself, 'People do what they do sometimes to keep from going crazy.'"

"I know what I said," Shaw replied. "But you didn't invite me to your bed when you still thought I was just some harmless drunken saddle tramp who happened upon your dead husband."

"Whatever are you talking about?" Lori asked, standing and walking away from him, not facing him.

"I'm talking about you overhearing Jane Crowly and I talking about how I killed two outlaws and her telling you how I handled Jesse Burkett. It was after all that when I became a whole other person to you, one fit for your admiration, and *affection*." He gestured a hand toward the disheveled bed.

"All right, perhaps I had no respect for you when I saw you as a drunken saddle tramp standing in my yard. I was grateful to you for what you did, but that was all." She stood rigid and stared away from him.

"The rest . . . I don't know why. If learning that you're a dangerous man had anything to do with it, perhaps it did. But if it did, it was without being *consciously* aware of it."

Shaw heard her voice turn tearful. He eased down and walked to her from behind and put his hands on her shoulder. "Look, I'm sorry. I should not have brought it up. I'm a gunman. In my world people use one another. Nobody offers anything without expecting something in return."

"That's not just your world, Lawrence," she said quietly. "I'm finding that to be the case in my world as well."

"All I'm saying is, if you're expecting something in return, let's be honest about it, put it out on the table, so to speak." He paused, then said, "I'm not above being used. None of us are, most especially those of us who can admit how much we've used others."

She turned, facing him; he dropped his hands from her shoulders to her waist. He saw a welling of tears in her eyes, but now they had stopped as quickly as they'd started. "It's Bowden Hewes."

"I had a feeling it was," Shaw said. He held her not at arm's length, but not against him either.

"You don't know what it's been like with him," Lori said. "Every time he comes here he gets more insistent. I have put him off as best I could. But I know how he's going to be when he finds out that Jonathan is dead."

"You could leave here," Shaw said, just to find out how committed she was to this place, this weathered house in a rocky valley along the edge of a blazing desert.

"This is my home, Lawrence," she said, "and these are my people. I'm their doctor now, their only doctor. They need me."

"And you need them?" Shaw interjected.

She looked at him.

"I mean, since you're not a doctor, at least not like your late husband. This is one place where you can carry out the profession without the credentials."

"Yes, that's true, I suppose . . . if you chose to look at it that way," she said. "I am every bit the doctor Jonathan was, credentials or no."

"I see." Shaw nodded. She had convinced herself of her situation. Nothing he said was going to alter her thinking in any manner. "You think that my being here with you might put off Bowden Hewes?" he asked. "You figure that just the presence of another man will send him on his way, out of your life?"

"Yes, it would," she replied firmly, as if she had given it much thought and had convinced herself.

Shaw gave her a pointed and knowing look.

She relented but only a little. "I mean, yes, it could . . . it should," she said, bravely defending her position.

"It could, it should," Shaw said, "but what if it doesn't?" He watched her eyes closely. "What then?" He knew where this was headed, whether she *consciously* knew it or not.

"I don't know *what then*," she said, looking away from him again. "I only know that I have a profession and a home, and my own way of life here. I must do whatever it takes to protect that. I cannot allow myself to be overpowered by someone like Bowden Hewes."

"Do you want him dead?" Shaw asked flat out, tired of sparring over the matter.

"Kill him?" She looked startled by the very mention of such an act. "No, nothing like that," she said. "I mean, I'm certain things would never go that far." She paused, then asked with hesitancy, "Would it?"

"By now Hewes knows what I did to his man, and he knows why I came here. So I expect we'll be finding out soon enough," Shaw said.

"Don't think that I really want you to kill . . ." Her words trailed.

"Forget I mentioned it," Shaw replied. "Maybe I'm still not thinking straight from all the whiskey I've poured through me." He knew there was no use going over it again. He was here, sleeping with a woman Bowden Hewes considered his own. He had struck the first blow by rifle-butting one of Bowden's riders. Likely as not, it wasn't a matter of whether he *would* kill Hewes, he told himself. It might only be a matter of *when*.

PART 2

Chapter 10

Bowden Hewes and his top gunmen had been traveling back to his sprawling ranch in Fire River Valley when his front riders spotted Max "the Ax" Cafferty, Collie Mitchum, Bennie Ford and Jesse Burkett riding toward them at a loping pace. Burkett flopped back and forth in his saddle, still a little addled and half out of his head from the hard lick he'd taken. His lips were still swollen to twice their size, and as purple as overripe plums.

Watching the four approach across a stretch of rolling sand hills dotted with sparse wild grass and barrel cactus, a Wyoming gunman named Ned Gunnison said under his breath to the two men riding alongside him, "Bo ain't going to like them riding out to meet us. He told everybody to lay low 'til we get back and get things set up." He stared past the rise of dust behind the four riders, looking to see if they'd been followed.

"Jesse rides like he's been wetting his whistle. Maybe all four of them are drunk," said one of the men beside him, a man named Carl Pole.

"That ought to make for an exciting day," Gunnison said dryly.

The third man, a young Irish American named Danny Grimes, nodded toward one of two covered wagons rolling along the trail behind them. "Want me to wake Bo up, so's that we can watch the fur fly?" he said with a devilish grin.

"I expect we might just as well," said Gunnison, watching the four riders draw nearer.

But as the four turned and looked back toward the heavily loaded wagons, they saw the four-horse teams come to a halt. "I'm betting Foster already woke him," said Grimes.

At the first big wagon, Bowden Hewes stepped out from behind the front flap and down onto the ground, an open canteen in his hand. His black tie hung loose around his neck; his shirt collar lay open. He carried a black flat-crowned hat in his other hand. From behind the first wagon the driver of the second wagon hurried down from his wooden seat and unhitched a saddled horse from behind his wagon. He came running forward, leading the horse to Hewes at a trot.

Without a word of thanks, Hewes put his hat on, took the horse's reins, swung up into the saddle and booted the big silver, black-legged bay forward. He arrived among the three front riders as Max and the others drew closer, slowing to a walk, then to a halt.

"Bo, I know you said lay low, and we did," Max called out from thirty feet away, waiting for word from Hewes before coming any closer. "But we've had a hell of a thing come up all of a sudden."

"Get in here, Max," Hewes called out with a jerk of

his head. Looking at Burkett, he said to Gunnison beside him, "Is that son of a bitch drunk?" But getting a better look at Burkett, seeing his battered, swollen face, Gunnison winced and replied, "If he ain't, he should be. Looks like somebody fed him a boot for breakfast."

Carl Pole muffled a chuckle. A cold stare from Hewes silenced him. Then Hewes looked closer at Burkett's face as the riders drew to another halt ten feet in front of them. "Jesus, man," Hewes said, examining Burkett's grotesque purple mouth. "Someone should have warned you about sneaking up behind a range mare."

Pole snickered again, but this time it was all right with Hewes.

Jesse Burkett raised his face and tried to speak, but it sounded like a man talking over a mouth full of chewed potatoes.

Eyeing Burkett closely, Hewes asked Max, "What the hell did he say?"

"I don't know, Bo," said Max, shaking his head. "Something about killing the sumbitch who done this to him."

"Who *did* do this to him?" Hewes asked. Then, before Cafferty could answer, he asked, "What the hell are you doing out here? I gave orders."

Cafferty said, "I know you did, Bo, and believe me, I thought long and hard before coming out here. But I've news that can't wait."

"Yeah?" Hewes stared curiously. "Then let's have it before it becomes old news."

"They found your brother's body," Cafferty said. "We run into Jane Crowly. Her and some drifter was on their way to the Edelmans' with the doc's body. I knew you'd want to know, so I took a chance and we came on out."

"Jane Crowly, damn her twisted female hide," said Hewes. "She's always sticking her lousy nose where it don't belong."

"But she's not the one who found the doc," said Cafferty. "It was some half-wit mute, looks like he fell out a whiskey barrel. He's the one who did this to Jesse. He butt-smacked him straight in the mouth—harder than I ever seen a man hit in my life."

Burkett made a guttural sound that drew their attention to him. "I . . . never . . . saw . . . a . . . thing," he said in a muffled tone, taking his time to try and form the words with his split and swollen lips.

"The fact is none of us really saw it," said Cafferty. "But I saw a blur; then I saw a rifle pointed at my guts. The sonsabitch had us cold. He took our guns, else we would have shot him full of holes for what he done—"

"Hold it," said Hewes, eyeing Burkett, then looking back at Cafferty. "Some *half-wit*, as you call him, did this to Jesse, than held the rest of you at gunpoint, took your guns?"

Cafferty's face reddened. "You had to see it to believe it, Bo," he said. "He was faster than anything human I ever seen. Now that we got our guns back, far as I'm concerned I'll ride out to the Edelmans' and splatter his brains all over the yard. All you got to do is say the word."

Hewes just looked at him. After a moment of contemplation on the matter, he asked the four sitting in front of him, "None of yas ever saw this man before? You saw nothing familiar about him?"

They shook their heads, Burkett doing so extra slowly to keep from moving his pain-throbbing face.

"But you did see Doc Jon's body?" He looked from face to face.

"Well, no, not what you'd call *per se*," Cafferty said cautiously. "But Jane said it was the doc. I expect she'd know."

Hewes stared at him, his grim expression growing darker as Cafferty spoke. Finally he said to Cafferty and Burkett, "Both of yas get out of my sight before I empty this gun in your bellies." His black-gloved hand wrapped around the butt of a big Smith & Wesson revolver strapped to his thigh.

Cafferty and Burkett jerked their horses away from the other two and raced out of sight over one of the rolling sand hills. When they were far enough away for comfort, Cafferty jumped down from his saddle, took a few deep breaths and leaned against his horse's side. He took a few more deep breaths to calm himself. "Hell, I knew he was going to take this bad," he said. Burkett sat in his saddle in silence, his face throbbing harder after riding away at a hard run.

Back at the wagons, once the two were out of sight, Gunnison shook his head and asked Hewes, "What do you want us to do about this man?"

Hewes murmured aloud to himself, "Of all the damned times for this to happen." He gazed away into the distance in the direction of the Edelman house.

"We can go calf rope this jake by his ankles and drag him back to you, if that suits you."

"No, that's not the way for now," Hewes said, still giving everything some thought. "We need to keep things cool here until we're finished with the gold." He glanced back at the heavily loaded covered wagons with a look of concern. "All right, here's the deal," he said to Gunnison, "you, Pole and Mackey come with me." He turned to Bennie Ford. "Once I'm out of sight, go tell Cafferty and Burkett to get back on here. The four of yas escort this equipment the rest of the way. Start setting it up in my barn."

"Sure thing, Bo," said Ford.

Hewes stared at him as if in afterthought. "Did everything happen like Max said?" He raised a gloved finger for emphasis and warned, "Don't lie to me, Bennie, or I'll cut your tongue out."

"Yeah, Bo," said Ford, a meek, worried look coming onto his face, "it happened just about that way. The man was fast, and it wasn't the first time he ever swung down on a man—you could tell by how he handled himself."

Hewes looked at the other rider. "Collie?" he asked in a firm tone.

"He was not a half-wit like Max said," Collie Mitchum ventured. "This ragged top-hat wearing bastard knew his way around a rifle butt."

"What would you call him, then?" Hewes asked, staring at him.

"Me?" Mitchum looked at Ford, then back at Hewes and said without fear of reprisal, "From what I saw, I'd call him a son of a bitch."

Shaw had finished digging the grave in the yard before the sun had reached its highest, hottest point in the sky. When he'd returned to the barn, he carried his shirt thrown over his shoulder, along with his gun belt. At a plank workbench inside the barn, he hung the shirt and gun belt on a row of wall pegs beside his ragged poncho and the battered top hat.

As he wiped off his sweat with a cloth the widow had sent with him for just such a purpose, he heard a menacing voice say from within the dark shadows of the barn, "Make one false move, Senor, and you will die! Now raise your hands, *pronto*!"

Shaw turned his attention slowly toward a Mexican who had slipped out of a stall and stood holding an ancient flintlock pistol out at arm's length. The man stalked closer and stopped ten feet away. In a shaft of light at the open rear barn door, Shaw saw a burrow standing with its head lowered. Past the burrow stood a sweaty desert barb.

"Oh . . . ?" Shaw said calmly, taking his time, looking the man up and down. "Everybody dies." He studied the gun closely, noting the cocked hammer, but seeing no flint in the striker.

The man looked surprised by Shaw's lack of fear. "Do not test me, Senor. I am not bluffing," he said firmly. "I will shoot you dead."

"Not with that gun, you won't," Shaw said with confidence.

The man fidgeted in place, looking suddenly unsure of himself. "Why—why do you say that?" he asked, his face looking nervous beneath the brim of his wide straw sombrero.

"No flint," Shaw said, though he raised his hands chest high, complying with the man's demand.

The man almost sighed with regret, as if to admit

that Shaw had him cold. The ancient pistol slumped in his hand; he caught himself and jerked it quickly back up. But before he'd collected himself, Shaw's Colt was out of the holster, cocked and pointed at him.

"Was that your only plan?" Shaw asked quietly.

The man looked dumbstruck by how quickly he'd lost what he'd thought was the upper hand. "*Si.*"

Shaw nodded. "Uncock it and put it away," he said.

The Mexican sighed again, but did as he was told, shoving the big bulky pistol down into his waistband beneath his own poncho.

"Who are you and what are you doing here?" Shaw asked. He resumed wiping himself down with the cloth in his free hand while he held the Colt aimed at the Mexican.

The Mexican had instinctively raised his hand chest high, yet he defiantly tilted his chin and said, "No, Senor, it is I who must ask who *you* are, and what are *you* doing here?"

Shaw began to sense that the man had good reason for being here. He lowered the Colt an inch. "I brought the body of Dr. Edelman home to his wife."

"Dr. Edelman is dead?" The man crossed himself and gave a sorrowful look. "I should not be surprised," he said, "but it is still a sad thing to hear."

"That's why *I'm* here. Now your turn," Shaw said, the Colt still in play.

"I am Raul Hernandez," the man said, calmer and with a better disposition now that Shaw had offered an explanation for his presence here. "*Mi suegra*—the mother of my wife works for the Edelmans. I escorted her back from a visit at my home." He nodded in the direction of the border, then toward the rear of the barn. "Mama Juanita," he called out in English. "You can come in. It is all right."

A short elderly Mexican woman entered the rear barn door, and Shaw lowered the Colt another inch. She hurried forward, also making the sign of the cross, and said with a troubled look, "Dr. Edelman is dead?"

"I'm sorry to be the one to tell you, ma'am, but yes he is."

She adjusted a scarf about her head and shoulders and said, "I must go to Senora Edelman right away." Shaw stepped to the side and watched her walk past him. Then he turned back to Raul, the Colt hanging loosely in his hand.

"Senor, I must apologize for letting us get off to such a bad start," Raul said. "It is regrettable."

"No apology necessary, Senor Hernandez," Shaw said. "I realize this is dangerous country." He let the hammer down on the Colt, turned and shoved it down loosely into the holster. In turn he took his shirt from the peg and slipped into it.

"Please call me Raul," the Mexican said with a curt bow of his head.

"Please call me Lawrence," Shaw said, buttoning the bib of his shirt. Shoving the shirttail into his trousers, he lifted the gun belt from the peg, swung it around his waist and buckled it all in what appeared to be one smooth stroke. "I understand congratulations are in order." He lifted the Colt a half inch and dropped it back loosely into its holster. Raul watched intently, taking note of the deft expert manner in which Shaw went about his task.

As if snapping back from watching with rapt attention, Raul said, "Huh? Oh yes, my baby daughter." He straightened and said, "*Gracias.*"

"You must be very proud," Shaw said as a matter of form. He bent and tied the holster down to his thigh.

"*Si*, I am very proud," said Raul. "I have been proud for eight years in a row." He held up eight fingers. "I have four sons, and now four daughters." He gave a pleased but tired smile. Then he looked away toward the house, seeing Lori Edelman go inside from the porch with Juanita's arm around her. "How is Senora taking her husband's death?" he asked quietly.

As Shaw straightened up from tying his holster down, he turned toward the house with him. "I'd have to say overall she's holding up pretty well," he said, careful not to reveal that anything had happened between him and the widow in either his words or his actions.

"Good," said Raul as Shaw turned, facing him. As if dismissing the matter, Raul looked around and asked, "Where is the doctor's body?"

"Over there," Shaw said, nodding toward the outbuilding fifty yards from the barn.

"I must stay and pay my respects, and help you bury him," said Raul. He looked at Shaw as if seeking his approval.

Shaw only nodded.

"But first I must bring my horse and *mi suegra*'s burrow in out of the heat and give them some water and feed," Raul said.

Shaw watched him walk away. He knew it wouldn't be long before everyone far and wide knew about Lori

Edelman and himself. But he wasn't going to be the one who let the news out, he thought. Taking his poncho from the wall peg, he slipped it over his head, took down his top hat and carried it as he walked to the small outbuilding where the doctor's body lay waiting.

Chapter 11

Owing to the condition of her husband's body, Lori Edelman asked that Shaw and Raul simply wrap it in an additional blanket for burial. After doing so, Raul brought a dusty plank from a short stack in the rear corner of the barn. He laid the bundle of hide and bones on the plank and tied the two together with strips of rope, giving the blanketed skeleton some rigidity when the time came for them to lower it into the ground.

At the graveside, Lori Edelman stood closer to Shaw than he thought was appropriate. He saw that both Juanita and Raul took note of it, yet he made no effort to move as the widow gripped his forearm and looked down at the body one last time. Stooping, she continued holding his arm as she scraped up a handful of sandy soil and let it pour down onto the body. Straightening, she stepped back as Juanita and Raul both crossed themselves and stood with their heads bowed. She gave Shaw a sidelong glance that asked him to say a few words over her husband.

His hat in his free hand, Shaw took a breath and searched for something good to say about this man he'd never known, whose wife he'd slept with, to a God he had not always believed in.

"Uh, Lord . . . ," he began with uncertainty. He stalled for a moment, and in doing so he looked up from beneath his lowered brow and saw that Raul was watching and listening with a doubtful look on his face.

Before going any further, he caught a glimpse of four riders coming into sight from the base of a short rock hillside across the valley floor. At the same time he felt Lori Edelman squeeze his forearm again, this time tighter. "Wait, please. Here comes Bowden Hewes. I must allow him to pay his respects."

"Yes, ma'am." Shaw almost sighed in relief. He turned his gaze to the riders, then to Raul, noting a look of concern come to the Mexican's face.

Watching the riders draw nearer, Shaw nodded toward Juanita and said quietly to Raul, "Why don't you take *su suegra* inside the house, let her rest awhile."

"But I am not tired, Senor," the elderly woman said, holding her head scarf gathered at her throat. She gave Shaw a curious look, then looked to Lori Edelman for guidance.

"Yes, please, Juanita," said Lori, "go on inside and rest."

"Rest? But I—" the woman started to protest.

Raul stopped her. "Aw, but you know so well how tiring this noon heat can be, *mi suegra*," Raul said, understanding Shaw's intent. He stepped over, looped an arm around Juanita's shoulders and began ushering her toward the house. "I will return immediately," he said over his shoulder to Shaw.

"No, Raul," Shaw said calmly. "Why don't you sit this out too? I had a little run-in with Hewes' men. He might not be in a friendly mood."

"Oh, I see . . ." Raul gave a concerned look toward the riders, then quickly accompanied his mother-in-law out toward the house.

Shaw stood in silence beside the widow as the riders rode into the yard. Only when Hewes was close enough to see her do so did Lori drop her hand from Shaw's forearm. Shaw did not fail to notice her gesture or how she had timed it just right for Hewes' benefit. "Let me handle this," she whispered without taking her eyes from Bowden Hewes.

"It's all yours." Shaw cut her a sidelong glance and took a short step away from her, just in case he suddenly needed elbow room.

Hewes stopped his horse ten feet on the other side of the grave. Ned Gunnison, Carl Pole and Devlin Mackey spread their horses out a few feet behind him. Staring at Lori, Hewes said in a half-angry, half-injured tone, "Would you bury my brother without so much as a word to me?"

"I thought you were still away on business," Lori said cordially.

Shaw listened. He gave the three other mounted riders a once-over, then turned his gaze back to Hewes, realizing that the big man was avoiding his eyes.

"I was away," said Hewes to Lori. "But I was on the trail home when some of my men rode out to meet me.

They told me about Jonathan." He jerked a nod toward Shaw without looking at him. "I take it this is the man who found him?"

"Yes, it is," Lori said in the same cordial tone of voice and bearing. "This is Mr. Lawrence." She looked at Shaw and continued the introduction. "This is Bowden Hewes, my late husband's brother, the one I told you about."

Shaw looked at Hewes and waited for any sign of acknowledgment. Hewes ignored him. He glanced at the grave, then stepped down from his saddle and walked over to its edge. Looking down, he took his hat off and shook his head. "Did he happen to tell you what he did to Jesse Burkett?" Hewes asked Lori, staring down at the blanket-wrapped body.

"Jane Crowly told me," Lori said. "It sounded like Burkett was up to his same rude, bullying behavior." She managed a thin, guarded smile. "I understood that Mr. Lawrence here merely corrected him."

"*Mr.* Lawrence, huh?" Hewes gave her a dubious look, as if knowing there was no need for any formality between her and this stranger. But before she could reply, he asked sharply, "Did that filthy *she-male* happen to mention that poor Jesse had two teeth knocked out and three more broken?"

"Yes, *Miss Crowly* told me," she shot back. "And refrain from that sort of bawdy house language in my yard, Bowden. I expect better from you, here at my husband's graveside. Besides, Jane is a friend of mine. Are you suggesting something untoward about me, as well?"

"Of course I'm not," said Hewes, quickly backing off of the subject of Jane Crowly. "I only repeat what I've heard everyone else call her."

"And those who do are wrong," Lori said with finality on the matter. "If you say anything else bad about her, I shall have to ask you to leave."

Shaw stared in silence. The three riders behind Hewes had settled into position. They returned Shaw's stare.

Hewes' thick jaw tightened, but he kept silent about Jane Crowly. He gave the widow a harsh look, yet there was something almost apologetic in his eyes. Then he looked away from Lori and stared down into the grave, his hat brim crumpled in his tight fist. After a moment he changed the subject, saying, "Is this all *my brother* gets, a blanket? Not even a coffin?"

"Your stepbrother . . . but *my husband*," Lori said coolly. "Yes, it's all he gets. There's barely enough of him left to wrap in a blanket, let alone a coffin." She laid her hand back on Shaw's left forearm. Shaw felt awkward. But he didn't move away. "Aren't you going to ask Lawrence about how he found *your brother*, Jonathan? Or does it not matter to you?"

Hewes looked up from the grave; an angry glare came to his eyes. "Of course it matters to me," he said harshly. He turned his gaze to Shaw and said, "All right, Mister, where did you find my brother?"

"I found him in a cave across the border," Shaw said, offering no more courteousness than he'd received. He fell silent.

Lori removed her hand from his forearm. Shaw was grateful.

Hewes stared at him for a moment as if in contemplation, then asked, "Was there any foul play in evidence?"

"None," Shaw said flatly. He watched Hewes' eyes closely for a response for a moment. Seeing no sign of surprise or question, he only stalled for a couple of seconds before he went on to say, as if it might have slipped his mind, "Except for the two bullet holes in his chest."

Hewes' eyes narrowed, knowing that Shaw had just tried to test him.

"I'm obliged you brought my brother home," he said, a bit grudgingly, "in spite of what you did to my man Burkett."

Shaw didn't reply concerning Burkett, but he did give a slight shrug of one shoulder, enough to show the four of them that he had no remorse for what he'd done.

Hewes' gaze went back to the widow. "At least now we know for certain that poor Jonathan is dead," he said. "We can get on with what's right and proper." He turned back to Shaw. "I expect you'll be wanting to move along now, stranger . . . for health reasons." He gave Shaw a menacing look. "I'll be seeing to everybody's welfare here."

"Soon," Shaw said, with no regard for Hewes' subtle threat. "I like to take my time leaving, make sure I didn't miss something."

Stiffening at Shaw's words, Hewes gave a commanding look at Gunnison, who gigged his horse forward a step, the other two moving right along with him. Gunnison stared down at Shaw. "Are you simple-minded, drifter, or maybe you just don't hear so good. What Bo Hewes is telling you is that it's time you high-tailed it out of here before you get hurt. This is Fire River country. It's ours. You know what they say about fire: Step too close and a fellow can get himself burned down mighty easily."

"Let me know where *too close* is," Shaw said, taking a deliberate step forward. He stared at Gunnison, his hand hanging at the edge of his poncho. His big Colt stood out of sight beneath the poncho, but only an inch from his fingertips.

Behind Shaw, Lori Edelman saw things were about to get out of control. "Bo Hewes, how dare you ride in here and let these bullies threaten my guest when I'm trying to bury my husband!"

Hewes relented. He clenched his jaw tight again, and gave a sharp jerk of his head, signaling Gunnison and the others to back off. "This is a funeral. You men step down and help. Take turns with the shoveling," he said gruffly. To Lori he said, "All right, let's get Jonathan laid to rest." He turned to Shaw. "This day belongs to my brother. You brought him here; you've been properly thanked for it. Don't push your luck with me."

"Luck was made to be pushed," Shaw said flatly, appearing to give no heed to any threat Hewes and his men had tried to present to him. He watched the men step down from their saddles and walk to where a shovel stood stuck into a mound of dirt beside the grave.

When the last shovel of dry, rocky dirt had been pat-ted down, Shaw, Lori Edelman, and Juanita stood at the graveside and watched Hewes and his men mount up and ride away. Only when they were out of sight did Raul walk down from the house with a long shotgun in the crook of his arm. "You had no need to worry. I kept you covered, Senor," he said to Shaw.

"Obliged," Shaw said. "But I don't want you getting tangled up in any trouble I might have with Bowden Hewes and his bunch."

"I am not afraid of Bowden Hewes," Raul said, not understanding that Shaw wasn't talking about being afraid. "I have broken horses on his ranch for him many times. Neither him nor his men frighten me."

"I saw that plain enough," Shaw replied, "but you and your family still have to live in these parts after I'm gone." He gestured a nod toward Juanita. "I don't want to cause you trouble later on."

"He did not see me"—Raul shrugged with a pleasant smile—"and I will be gone back to Mexico tonight."

Rather than push the matter and make the man feel bad, Shaw decided to let the matter drop for now. He gazed off toward the drift of dust Hewes and his men's horses had left standing on the still air. When Lori stepped over near him, he noted that this time she didn't lay her hand on his forearm—no need to, he thought, now that Hewes had seen all she wanted him to see. . . .

Along the trail leading away from the Edelmans' and across the valley floor, Bowden Hewes rode on in a dark brooding silence. Behind him the three other men looked at one another, knowing Hewes could fly into a killing rage at any moment. Finally, as they neared a

fork in the trail that turned east toward Fire River, Ned
Gunnison ventured up beside Hewes and offered him
a shot from the bottle of whiskey he'd rummaged from
his saddlebags.

Hewes took the bottle, turned up a long swig and
handed it back to Gunnison. He blew out a breath,
wiped a hand across his lips and said, "Ned, we've got
a lot riding on us getting that equipment home and set
up. Can I count on you and those two to take care of
this ragged-ass saddle bum, get him out of my hair for
good?"

"Say the word, it's done, Bo," Gunnison replied.
"We don't need any outsiders hanging around right
now. Far as we know he could be the law."

"The law? Ha, I doubt it," Hewes said, with a harsh
chuckle. "This man is a drunk, or he has been anyway.
No self-respecting lawman would let himself get down
this low, not if he wanted to stay alive. He wouldn't be
able to cut it in this country."

"Yeah, you're right, he's not a lawman, this saddle
bum," Gunnison said, considering it. He didn't want to
disagree with Hewes while he appeared to be in such a
bad mood. "What do you want us to do, hang around
close, catch him when he leaves the place? Make sure
there's no trouble around the Edelman place?"

Hewes thought about it for a moment. "Maybe a little trouble close to home is just the thing it would take
to jar Lori back to her senses. Maybe she needs to be
reminded that a woman needs a man like me around to
take care of her." He gave a flat grin.

"Hell, we can kill him and stick his head on a gatepost out front, if that's what you want, Bo," Gunnison said, grinning himself.

"Let's not get crazy here, Ned," said Hewes. "After all, we're not barbarians, are we?"

"No, we're not," said Gunnison. "But damned if there's not times when I wish we were."

Staring straight ahead, Hewes said, "The three of yas cut around wide and ride back. Get in close. After dark tonight, catch him out front, on his way to the jake or something. Leave him lying in her front yard."

"She'll figure we done it, Bo," said Gunnison.

"That's my whole point, Ned," said Hewes. "She'll figure us for it right off, but she'll never be able to say for certain." His grin gone, his face grew cold and hardened. "It's time she learned not to play these little games with me. She belonged to Jonathan. Now she rightfully belongs to me." He paused, then said, "Mess him up good, Ned. Make an example of him."

"It's done, Bo," said Gunnison. He took the bottle, corked it with the palm of his hand and turned his horse back to the other two riders. When he sidled up to them, he jerked his head toward the trail back across the valley and said, "Let's go, boys. We've got some killing to do."

Chapter 12

———

At dark, after a meal prepared by Juanita in the stone and clay chimenea in the side yard, Shaw stood with a cup of coffee hooked onto his finger. He watched Raul lead his saddled desert barb toward him. Raul, seeing what he took to be a look of concern in Shaw's eyes, said, "Do not worry about me, my friend. I always travel at night . . . and I know how to stay away from all the main trails in this border country."

Shaw only nodded.

"Besides"—Raul swung up into his saddle and adjusted his ragged striped poncho around him—"it would be easier to catch a fox than it would be to catch me."

"All the same, be careful," Shaw told him.

"All the same, I will," Raul said, a smile on his face in the light of a three-quarter moon. He touched his fingertips to his bare forehead and said, "*Adios, mi amigo.* It has been interesting meeting you. I will have much to tell my wife about this trip." Then he turned his desert barb and heeled it toward the valley floor, a bag of food hanging from his saddle horn, his sombrero off and drooping on his shoulder from the end of a rawhide tie.

"*Adios*," Shaw replied, returning Raul's gesture with his right hand. He watched the Mexican's desert barb move away at a walk.

Shaw kept a broad watch on the dark valley floor long after Raul had been swallowed up into the purple night. He did not look around when he heard the front open and close from across the yard. Nor did he turn when he heard Lori's light footsteps move across the yard toward him. Instead he called out quietly, "Over here."

"Oh, there you are," she said after a moment, seeing Shaw standing beside the tall saguaro cactus like some lone stoic sentinel given care of the night. "Did you see Raul off?"

"Yep." Shaw still didn't turn as he heard her walk up beside him. He felt her slip her arm into his. He finished the last sip of coffee.

"Lawrence, is everything all right?" She had noted his quietness throughout dinner.

"Yes, I'm good," he said, opening conversation. "What about you?"

"I'm good," she said, sounding happier and more relaxed than he'd heard her sound since he'd arrived. "I don't know about you, but I think everything went very well."

Shaw knew she was pleased with the way both of them had handled themselves. Without facing her, he gave a thin half smile. "Yeah, everything went all right." Then he asked quietly, "Did you get the sort of response you were hoping for from Bowden Hewes?"

"I—I don't know what you mean," she said with a puzzled tone. "I wanted him to see that I am not alone out here. I wanted him to understand that he has no hold on me. Did I do something wrong?"

Shaw only shook his head slowly. "No, you didn't do anything wrong. But don't get too excited. We haven't seen the last of that man. He thinks he has a rightful claim on you. I believe he intends to have you one way or the other."

"I know," she said, "but having you here buys me some time. It gives me room to think while I figure out how to best handle the situation."

"If that's all you need, I'm happy it worked out for you," he said.

"What about you, though?" she said, snuggling against his shoulder. "Weren't you simply magnificent out there, the way you refused to take any bullying off on Ned Gunnison!"

"I am not a man easily buffaloed, Lori," Shaw said, recalling the many times in his life he'd watched a gunman fall in the dirt street before him. It was nothing for him to get excited about. He hadn't surprised himself.

"Well, I'm excited enough for both of us," she said, her head on his shoulder. Then she turned her face nearer to his ear and in a lowered voice said, "Do you know what all of this excitement makes me want to do?"

Shaw gave a suggestive smile. "I hope it's something involving us both."

"Play your cards right and I'm sure it does," she whispered playfully. She ended her words against his lips. They kissed long and deep. When it ended, she reached down, took him by his hand and led him toward the house with a sense of urgency. On the way they walked past her husband's fresh grave. *As if it's not there*, Shaw told himself.

At the first sound of hoof striking stone on the narrow trail coming toward them, the three riders stopped and froze in place, listening intently. Within a moment they began hearing the rise and fall of shoed hooves moving along at a walk. Ned Gunnison lowered the bottle from his lips and whispered sidelong to Pole and Mackey, "Easy boys. I ain't never been this lucky in my life."

The three nudged their horses silently off the narrow back trail and stepped down from their saddles.

"This way, Ned," Carl Pole whispered, gesturing toward a thin game path leading up into the rocky hillside above the trail.

They led their horses quietly to a flat spot on the hillside. Sliding their rifles from their saddle boots, they left their mounts standing and continued upward on foot. They looked down and saw the single rider in the purple moonlight. "What was it you said about *lucky*?" Mackey whispered to Gunnison with a whiskey-lit grin.

"Damn, it's the drifter sure enough," said Pole almost in disbelief, making out the silhouette of the poncho on the bare-headed rider below them.

Gunnison had put the bottle away, but now he jerked it out of his shirt, yanked the cork and took a long swig. Letting out a whiskey hiss, he handed the

bottle to Pole and said, "Boys, the first shot's mine.
Then you can both make buzzard bait out of what's
left." He raised the rifle butt to his shoulder and took
careful aim, almost straight down on the top of the
rider's head.

"He ain't going to know what hit him," Mackey
whispered, the whiskey bottle in hand.

Pole and Mackey both watched and waited. After a
moment, they looked at each other. "What are you
waiting for?" Pole asked Gunnison. "Shoot this sucker.
Let's get on home."

"Damn it, I can't," said Gunnison, letting the rifle
slump.

"What the—?" Mackey stared at Gunnison as if he'd
lost his mind.

"By God, I can," Pole said, cutting Mackey off.
Without wasting another second, he jerked his rifle up
to his shoulder and cocked it. "I ain't squeamish."

"Damn it, no!" Gunnison whispered harshly. He
knocked Pole's rifle barrel down. "Didn't you hear Bo
say to mess him up real good?"

"I damn near forgot," said Mackey.

"So did I," said Gunnison, "but I caught myself." He
glared at Pole. "*Squeamish . . . ?*"

Pole looked frightened. "I wasn't thinking real
clear," he said.

"You ever call me squeamish again, you'll be in hell
before you get it said."

Mackey said, "Bo also wanted us to leave him lying
dead in the dirt, in the Edelman yard." He looked back
and forth between them. "What are we supposed to
do, kill him and drag him all the way back there?"

"That's damn well what we're supposed to do," said Gunnison, already rising into a crouch and heading for the horses. "Come on, let's go do what we said we would."

On the trail, Raul rode along quietly. Moments earlier he had heard a muffled sound high up in the rocks above him; yet after listening closely and hearing nothing more, he soon dismissed the matter. It was only when he'd reached a point where the trail made a blind turn that he realized he'd made a mistake.

"Well, well, *drifter*," said Gunnison, him and Pole sitting atop their horses in the center of the narrow trail, their rifle butts propped on their thighs. "Looks like you picked yourself a bad night for sightseeing."

Raul stopped his horse quickly and half turned it, ready to give it his boot heels and bolt away. But he saw the third dark figure behind him, on foot, standing center trail. "You ain't going nowhere," said Devlin Mackey, his rifle at port arms. He'd waited silently in the rocks along the side of the trail until the lone rider had passed.

"For a man who wasn't in a hurry to leave today, you sure seem ready to cut on out of here right now," said Gunnison. He raised his rifle and took aim.

"Wait, Ned! *Por favor!*" Raul shouted loudly, seeing the mistake the three were about to make. "It is I, Raul Hernandez!"

"Jesus! Hold your fire, Ned," said Mackey, recognizing Raul's voice and seeing the Mexican more clearly from his angle. "This ain't the drifter. This is that Mex, the one Bo hires on to break horses for him!"

"Raul?" said Gunnison. He lowered his rifle an inch.

Raul said hurriedly, "You can damn well believe it is me! What are you doing out here? You almost shot me!"

"Aw, hell, we didn't even come close," Gunnison chuckled. "Ain't you ever heard, 'A miss is as good as a mile'?"

"*Si*, I have heard it," said Raul, realizing what they were up to out here in the dark, but not letting on. "Only I don't think you would have missed me, not from this close."

"No harm done, anyway," said Gunnison. "I say we forget this ever happened." He'd laid his rifle across his lap. "We're out here hunting a skunk for Bo Hewes, if you must know," he said, finally answering Raul's earlier question. "What are you doing out here?"

Raul answered honestly. "I brought my wife's mother to the Edelmans' hacienda. She was visiting with my family while my wife had a child."

"Another little beaner, eh?" said Pole. "How many does that make, forty or fifty?" He laughed.

"Don't pay this fool any mind, Raul," said Gunnison. "I congratulate you."

Raul overlooked Pole's remarks. "Gracious," he said to Gunnison.

Mackey stepped over to where he'd left his horse standing out of sight. He led the horse back and said to Raul, "If you brought your mother-in-law to the Edelmans', you must've been there when we near had a run-in at Doc's funeral service."

"*Si*, I was there," said Raul, knowing it was not a good idea to lie. He wasn't going to mention that he'd been inside the house holding a shotgun, prepared to let go a blast of buckshot if it had become necessary. "I saw everyone out in the yard."

"Why wasn't you out there?" asked Pole.

"My mother-in-law felt ill. I had to take her inside." He paused, then added, "To tell you the truth, I thought there was going to be trouble." He gave a sheepish grin. "I do not go around sticking my nose where it does not belong."

"In other words, you was scared," Pole said bluntly with a nasty grin.

Raul gave a slight shrug. "If you want to know, *si*, a little scared. I have worked for Bowden Hewes. I know how he can get. I thought there was going to be some shooting."

"There was going to be," said Mackey, "if Bo hadn't stopped us."

"There still is *going to be*," said Pole. "We're on our way back right now. We're going to shoot some holes in the drifter's belly, maybe tie some barbwire around him, drag him around in the dirt . . . see how tough he is then."

"You talk too damned much, Pole," Gunnison said.

"So what? Raul here ain't going to repeat nothing, are you, Raul?" Pole said. "Who's going to listen to a Mexican?"

Raul just stared at him. After a moment he said calmly, "I've got to go."

"Hold up, Raul," said Gunnison, feeling the whiskey cloud his thinking a little. He let his rifle barrel lower until it pointed toward the Mexican. "I think you best stick with us awhile."

"I must get home," Raul said. "I have much to do

there." He started to turn his horse away. But Mackey grabbed the bridle and stopped the animal.

"The only thing you *must* do is what we damned well tell you to do," Mackey said.

Raul looked from Mackey to Gunnison and Pole, who sat staring, both of their rifles pointed at him. "We like you, Raul," Gunnison said in a warning tone. "Don't make us get stout on you." He stepped his horse forward. "I want you in on this. Call it my way of keeping you quiet about us killing this bummer."

Raul had already made up his mind. Once away from these three, he would circle around and ride a fast pace back to the Edelmans'. Raul a gave tug on his reins, hoping to get Mackey's hand off the horse's bridle. "I told you I have many things to do."

Pole gigged his horse forward, beside Gunnison. "You can't do none of it if you're dead, can you?"

Raul fell silent, seeing he was in a bad spot. He could smell the whiskey on them from ten feet away. "I want no part of this. The man has done nothing to me."

"Maybe he hasn't, *Ra-ul*, but *we will*," said Pole with a mocking grin. "Now lift that poncho; let's make sure you're not packing iron."

Raul raised his poncho slowly, the handle of the flintlock pistol showing above his waistband. He gave a short, guarded gaze in the direction of the Edelman house, as if judging the distance.

"Whoa now, look here," Pole said to the other two. "It's a good thing we checked. What if Raul here decided to ambush us all three on our way—"

He stopped talking as Raul jerked the big clumsy gun up and cocked it toward his face. "All of you back away!" Raul demanded. As he spoke he felt Mackey turn loose of his horse's bridle and take a cautious step sideways.

"Take it easy, Raul," Gunnison warned. "Don't do something you're going be sorry for."

"I am riding away from here. Do not try to stop me if you value your lives," Raul said.

"Hey, you've only got one shot," said Pole, his rifle still aimed loosely at Raul from ten feet away.

"And by the saints, I will put it in your head," Raul said, "if you try to stop me."

"Give him room, boys," said Pole, seeing the Mexican meant it.

"All right, Raul, you win," Gunnison said, backing his horse but keeping his rifle cocked and his thumb over the hammer. "Ride away. Let's act like none of this never happened."

Raul backed his horse, the flintlock still out at arm's length and cocked. But as he started to turn his horse, Gunnison shouted, "Drop him," and all three rifles exploded in rapid succession.

Two shots lifted Raul and flung him from his saddle; the flintlock pistol flew from his hand. "I got him!" Pole said proudly. "So did you, Ned!" He stepped forward where Raul lay writhing in the dirt. "You missed him, Mackey, sure as hell."

"I didn't miss him," Mackey said, "you did."

Gunnison and Pole slipped down from their saddles and led their horses toward the downed Mexican as they levered fresh rounds into their rifle chambers. Raul managed to pull up onto his side and tried to drag himself farther away, blood running from two holes in his chest. His paint horse had spooked and raced away along the dark trail.

"Like hell I missed," said Pole.

Gunnison stooped and picked up the flintlock and turned it in his hand. "Damn, this gun wouldn't have fired if he'd wanted it to." He stood over Raul and put a boot down on his back to make him stop crawling. "What the hell was you thinking, pulling a fool stunt like this?" he asked. "We wasn't going to do anything to you, just make sure you kept quiet."

"I . . . warned . . . him," Raul gasped, blood running freely from his lips. "Now . . . he knows . . . you are . . . coming. . . ."

"What did he say?" Mackey asked, still stinging from missing his shot.

"Said he *warned him*—talking about the drifter, I guess," Gunnison said with a shrug.

"Oh yeah?" Mackey said down to Raul. "Take this, then." He fired a round into Raul's head from only inches away. The Mexican's blood sprayed upward on all three of the riflemen. Mackey levered a fresh round into his rifle chamber and turned to Pole with a fierce stare. "There, did I miss that time?"

Pole gave a dark chuckle, wiping a drop of Raul's blood from the back of his hand. "Naw, but look how much closer you were."

"Mindless sonsabitches . . . ," Gunnison growled at them under his breath. He gazed off in the direction of the Edelman house, knowing that anyone listening was bound to have heard the shots. "The Mex screwed any chance of surprising that drifter into the ground, boys."

Stepping over beside Gunnison and gazing out

alongside him, Pole asked, "So, what are we going to do now?"

"We told Bo we'd kill this fellow for him," said Gunnison. "Do you want to ride in and tell him we failed him?"

"No thanks," Pole said without hesitation.

"Then I expect we best go on with the plan," said Gunnison. He turned to his horse and swung up into his saddle. "You two throw Raul over his horse. We'll take him back to the Edelmans'."

"How are we going to explain him being dead?" Mackey asked.

"We found him dead out here." Gunnison gave a wry grin. "We can always say some Apache killed him."

Chapter 13

————

Shaw awoke with a start and swung up onto the side of the bed. Instinctively he'd grabbed the big Colt standing in its holster at the corner of the headboard. Beside him, Lori Edelman stirred and turned, looking up at him from her pillow. "What is it, Lawrence?" she asked, though she too had heard the distant sound of gunshots.

"Rifle fire," said Shaw. Naked, he stood up and walked to the open window, peering out across the purple-shadowed hills. "Didn't you hear it?" He scanned back and forth in the distance as if he might somehow see beyond the dark shadowed hill lines.

"I thought I did. But I wasn't sure if I heard it or if I was only dreaming," the widow said, rising naked and throwing a sheet around herself. She hastily lit the oil lamp on the nightstand. Then she walked over and stood beside him.

Gazing out in the direction the shots had come from, Shaw considered Raul and said with resolve, "I'm riding out there."

"Why?" Lori said. "We don't know if those shots had anything to do with Raul. For all we know, it might simply have been some drunken cowhands blowing off steam on their way back from Banton." She stared out with him. The purple night lay still and endless beneath a canopy of stars and a half-moon that appeared to rest on its side.

"With pistol shots it might've been some drunken cowhands, but not with rifles," said Shaw. He paused in grave contemplation, then said, "I knew that Hewes and his men might be prowling around. We should have stopped Raul from leaving tonight."

"Raul is a proud man. He wouldn't have stood for us telling him what to do," said Lori. "Besides, he knows this country better than most anyone. He can travel without being seen."

"Yes, but I figure so do Hewes and his men," said Shaw. He'd already turned from the window and reached for his clothes lying on a chair. The widow stood watching. "Anyway, I'm going to make sure he's not in trouble out there."

"I think it's going to be nothing but a waste of time and sleep," Lori offered.

"I hope it does turn out to be a waste of time and sleep," Shaw said in earnest. "But I won't know until I get out there."

"All right, then . . . I'm going too," she said, her decision sounding like retaliation of some sort.

"Uh-uh." Shaw buttoned his fly and sat down and picked his socks up from his boot wells. "I'll make better time alone. Besides, if Hewes or any of his men are out there, I can't risk getting you hurt."

"Bo Hewes' men wouldn't dare harm me," Lori said confidently.

"Maybe not," Shaw said, "but a stray bullet answers to nobody." He pulled on his socks. "I'd feel better if you waited here."

"All right . . ." Lori seemed to have to force herself to comply with him. "But if you're not back soon, I'm hitching the buggy and riding out looking for you."

"There'll be no need for that," Shaw said. He pulled his boots on in turn, then stood up and looked at a pocket watch lying on a nightstand beside the bed. "Raul's been gone a little over three hours. He's taking his time. If I push hard I can cut his time by half."

He took his gun belt from the headboard, swung it around his waist and buckled it. He deftly slipped the Colt from its holster, checked it and spun it back into its leather, all in what appeared to be one sleek quick motion.

The widow watched his hand as if awestricken. Then she said in lowered voice, "There's lot I don't know about you, isn't there?"

Shaw didn't answer. Instead he asked, "How do I get to Hewes' place?"

"No, you don't want to go there, Lawrence, believe me," she said, shaking her head at the idea of it.

"I don't want to go there," Shaw said, "but I want to know where it lays, so I'll know what direction to avoid if I lose Raul's tracks."

"That makes sense," she conceded. "Twenty miles east off the main trail, there's a valley trail leading down to the left. It stops at Río Del Fuego."

"Fire River," Shaw said, translating the words.

"Yes, and once you cross the river everything you touch has Hewes' name branded on it. Once you cross Fire River, any trail you take leads to Bo's ranch." She looked at him closely. "The word is that no stranger has ever crossed Fire River and came back to tell about it."

"Sounds like my kind of place," Shaw said, unimpressed. He bent, wrapped the strip of rawhide around his thigh and tied his holster down.

"Promise me you won't take Bo and his men too lightly, Lawrence, please," Lori said.

"I don't take anybody too lightly, Lori," he said, straightening and adjusting his holster. He stepped over to the wall where his rifle leaned beside the saddlebags he'd taken from Shank's speckled barb. He checked the rifle, slung the saddlebags over his shoulder and picked up his battered top hat.

Lori watched, holding the sheet around her. "I'll just dress and walk you to the barn," she said.

"No," Shaw said firmly. "I can be on the trail by that time."

She didn't argue, instead she stepped closer and gave him a light kiss on his cheek. "Hurry back to me," she said.

"Yes, ma'am," Shaw said, tugging his top hat down and giving a slight tip of the brim.

He quickly saddled the speckled barb, walked it out of the barn and onto the trail starting at the edge of the yard. When he'd stepped up into the saddle and nudged the animal forward, he turned and looked

back at the bedroom window. As he looked back he
saw the lamplight dim until it turned black.

Back to bed and back to sleep, he thought to
himself; and for some reason he wondered just how
much any of this really meant to her. The Widow
Edelman had a striking beauty and intelligence to her,
so much so that it had taken a while before he'd begun to feel her cold detachedness. What they did for
each other in bed was good, but there was nothing
beyond that.

Maybe that's good.... He turned back to the trail
ahead of him and booted the speckled barb up into an
easy run.

The woman felt nothing for him. Shaw knew she
was using him only to make a point to Bowden Hewes.
She saw he was tough and hard to scare. That was
what she needed right then. Had she known he was
Fast Larry Shaw it might have impressed her more. But
she didn't know, he reminded himself.

Had her situation with Hewes pressuring her not
existed, he would never have been invited into her bed,
not in his sore and struggling condition. *But so what?*
he thought. People used one another every day in
every way, didn't they? He raced ahead in the purple
moonlit night, thinking things over as the sound of
the barb's hooves sounded out strong and fast on the
hardened trail beneath them.

After two hours of steady riding along the hill trail
the effects of the whiskey had worn off. Ned Gunnison,
Carl Pole and Devlin Mackey had sobered and turned
surly and ill tempered with one another. When Pole

slowed almost to a stop at a narrow turn in the trail, Gunnison turned in his saddle and looked back. "You best keep up, Carl. We're not going to nursemaid you this whole damned trip."

Pole gigged his horse forward with a snarl, leading Raul's paint with Raul's body tied down over its back. "I've been leading this dead man the whole way. I don't see why we're taking him back with us."

Mackey and Gunnison didn't answer.

"I don't see what our damned hurry is, either," said Pole. "The drifter ain't going nowhere. So we end up killing him at midmorning instead of at the crack of dawn. Who cares?"

"I care," said Gunnison, staring straight ahead, Mackey riding alongside him. "If the drifter heard the gunfire, we don't want him skinning out of there, and cause us to miss killing him altogether."

"But for all we know he didn't even hear the rifle shots," said Pole, catching up to them, and riding on Gunnison's other side.

"A man like this drifter heard the gunshots," said Gunnison. "What do you say, Devlin?" he asked Mackey, looking for support.

"Oh yeah, the drifter heard the shots, no matter how fast asleep he was," said Mackey. "We'll be lucky if he ain't hightailed it out of there by now. He might be tough, but only a fool would take a stand not knowing how many guns were coming after him."

"There, you see?" Gunnison said to Pole. "Listen to us; you might learn something."

"Yeah." Mackey grinned tauntingly. "Nobody needs to stay stupid all their life."

Pole gave him a dark glare but kept quiet as they rode along. An hour later the three stopped at a thin runoff in the rocks lining the trail beside them and let the horses drink while they filled their canteens with cool water. Mackey and Pole dropped down in the rocky sand to rest. "We should have brought along more whiskey," said Pole, taking out a bag of chopped tobacco and rolling himself a smoke.

As he worked on his fixings Raul's horse finished drinking and wandered a few yards farther along the trail. Pole didn't try to stop the horse.

"There goes Raul," Gunnison observed, watching the paint horse.

"He ain't going far," Pole said with a shrug, knowing he could collect the horse and its dead rider when they rode on.

"We might just get some whiskey when we get to the Edelmans'," Mackey said, sprawling backward on the ground with his hat pulled low over his eyes.

"Doc always kept a bottle or two in his desk," said Gunnison, still standing, leaning back against the rock where the runoff water ran down in a thin stream. "I expect the widow might still keep one there." He gazed off along the dark trail in reflection. "If that drifter ain't already taken it over and drank it up."

"I bet Doc's whiskey ain't all the drifter has taken over," said Mackey, his voice muffled under his hat. "I can see him rooted up between the widow's long white thighs as clear as a bell."

"I can see you dead *'clear as a bell'* if Bo gets wind of you saying something like that," Gunnison warned.

Pole puffed on his cigarette and listened to the two of them.

Mackey chuckled under the hat brim. "No reason for him to ever know I said it, is there?"

Ned Gunnison didn't answer. Instead he stared off along the trail, his ears piqued toward the sound of hooves coming toward them.

Hearing no reply from Gunnison, Mackey tipped his hat up enough to look at him and said, "Well, is there?"

"Shhh, hush up, damn it," said Gunnison. "I hear a rider coming."

Mackey sat up and shoved his hat back down onto his head. He and Pole looked at each other and listened intently for a moment. "If that's the drifter, he sure as hell didn't *hightail* it out of there, did he?" Pole said to Mackey. The two stood up and hurriedly dusted the seats of their trousers, Pole's cigarette hanging from his lips.

"Hold it! Whoever it is, he's stopped!" Gunnison said, keeping his voice lowered. Hearing the hooves clack to a quick shuffling halt on the trail, he crouched and squinted in the darkness for a better look. "You two get across the trail and take cover, before he sees you and lights out of here! Pole, kill that damned cigarette!"

Pole dropped his cigarette and crushed it beneath his boot heel. He and Mackey hurried off the trail, pulling their horses along with them. "I got a feeling if it's him, he ain't likely to be lighting out of here," said Pole sidelong to Mackey.

"Get ready," said Gunnison. "If it's him, we're taking him down, here and now." He ducked out of sight into the rocks alongside the trail, rifle in hand. Across the trail the other two did the same.

Thirty yards ahead, Shaw sat as still as stone atop the speckled barb, listening and staring intently for any further sight or sound coming from the darkness ahead of him. He had seen a faint glow of cigarette for only a second. But a second was all it took.

No sooner than he'd stopped the barb to sit and listen, he'd heard the rustle of boots and the scraping of the horses' hooves as the two gunmen had pulled the animals to cover. *All right*, he told himself, *somebody is there. Someone heard me coming.* . . . Silently he slipped his rifle up from its boot and nudged the barb forward at a slow walk.

From their cover behind rocks along the edge of the trail, Mackey and Pole listened to the soft clop of hooves moving toward them. "Stupid sumbitch thinks we can't hear him," Mackey whispered, cocking his rifle hammer slowly and quietly, getting himself ready. Beside him Pole did the same. Keeping their eyes on the dark trail, each of them raised their rifle butts to their shoulders.

Across the trail, Gunnison sat waiting, watching, his own rifle resting over a rock in front of him, cocked and ready. But just as he could make out the dark shadowy figure clopping forward in the black purple night, he saw the speckled barb's empty saddle and said in a raised voice to Mackey and Pole, "Hold your fire, boys. It's just a stray horse wandering along."

Mackey let out a relieved laugh, stood up and said loud enough for Gunnison to hear him, "A damned stray? What's the odds on that? Looks like some poor sumbitch must've got himself thrown and—"

Shaw's first rifle shot nailed him in the center of his chest and sent him flying backward, dead before he hit the ground.

Chapter 14

———

"He's killed Mackey!" Pole shouted, jumping to his feet and firing blindly. Across the trail Gunnison had seen the streak of gunfire coming from the middle of the path ahead of them. Rising slowly from behind the rock, Gunnison took aim at the dark outline walking toward them. But before he got his shot off, Shaw's second bullet sliced through him and sent him backward, his rifle flying from his hands.

Hearing Gunnison let out a loud grunt and hit the ground hard, Pole fired three more wild shots before Shaw's rifle honed in on his muzzle flash and shot him dead.

After a silent moment Shaw walked forward, emerging out of drifting rifle smoke and the purple darkness like some apparition from a netherworld. He led Raul's paint horse by its reins, the Mexican's lifeless arms swinging back and forth with each step of the animal's hooves.

A few feet ahead of him Shaw saw Gunnison lying back against a rock, trying with all of his waning strength to lever a round into his rifle chamber. A large circle of blood covered Gunnison's chest, and more pumped out in a braided stream with each beat of his heart.

"I . . . knew it was you . . . drifter . . . you sonsa-bitch," he said haltingly. His blood-slick hands could not get a grip on the rifle and make it do his bidding. Finally his right hand gave up on the weapon and went to the big Dance Brothers revolver on his hip. But by the time he'd managed to get a grip and slide the pistol up from its leather, Shaw was less than three feet from him and kicked the pistol from his hand.

"You killed Raul for no reason," Shaw said flatly, his tone not revealing how bad he felt about it. He had his rifle cradled in the crook of his arm. His Colt was in his right hand, cocked and loosely pointed.

"He made . . . his choice," Gunnison said. "Damned fool pulled . . . a worthless gun . . . just to warn you." Now that he knew his rifle and pistol were of no use to him, he clutched his shattered chest with both hands. Blood spilled from between his clasped fingers.

Shaw couldn't help but wince at hearing what Raul had done. It had been foolish of the Mexican, yet he didn't want to think of it as a foolish act, not here, not now. Raul had performed an act of heroism in order to save his life, or so the brave Mexican must've thought. That was the only way Shaw wanted to think of it right now.

Stooping down beside the dying gunman, Shaw pulled out the gold coin he'd found in the dirt the day he'd rifle-butted Jesse Burkett. "You ever see these kinds of gold coins before?"

"No . . . never," Gunnison said, yet his expression told Shaw he was lying. "You ain't . . . just some . . . no-account drifter, are you?"

Shaw didn't answer. He reached out and ran his hand down into Gunnison's pocket.

"You're already . . . picking over . . . my bones?" said Gunnison, his voice getting weaker as he spoke. "Are you the law?"

Shaw still didn't answer. He pulled out two gold coins from Gunnison's trouser pocket and looked at them in his palm. "Why are so many of these stolen coins showing up among Hewes' men?" he asked.

"Yep . . . you're law. . . . I can smell it." Gunnison chuckled with blood running down from his lips and added, "Now, go to hell . . . lawdog." He spit dark blood at Shaw.

"I'll find the rest of the stolen coins across Fire River, won't I?" he asked, knowing whatever he had to ask he'd best do it quickly. Gunnison was fading fast.

"So what . . . if you do?" Gunnison gasped and managed a belligerent grin. "You won't know . . . what you're looking at." He chuckled again, this time coughing more blood as he did so.

"What do you mean by that?" Shaw asked, leaning in closer.

"I mean . . . I mean—" Gunnison gasped. He never finished the words he'd tried to start. His head tipped back and to one side, and his eyes stared upward blankly into the dark heavens. Shaw stood and pocketed the gold coins and walked slowly, his Colt hanging loosely in his hand.

It's time to get back to work. . . . He was sober, he had spent some time resting, getting his wits back. He'd brought the doctor's body home and slept with his widow. *What more can a man ask for?* he thought, with a grim opinion of himself. He looked at Raul's body and shook his head slowly. While he and the Widow Edelman had slept together warm and naked, a good man had died.

Moments later, he had dragged each of the dead gunmen to their horses and tied them down over their saddles. As the first glimmer of dawn light spread in a silvery line on the horizon, he made up a lead rope to the four-horse string, stepped up atop the speckled barb and rode east, following the hill trail until it came to the fork Lori had told him about.

Turning onto a narrower trail, he rode onto a wide valley floor. Across the rocky, sandy valley he rode, until the trail stopped at a low wide river that snaked away north into a stretch of hills the color of rusty iron and strewn with blue-green cactus. To the south the river ran between deeper banks and disappeared out of sight. "Fire River," he said aloud.

Stepping down, he separated Raul's paint horse from the string and tied its reins to a spindly cottonwood. Stepping back into his saddle, he led the three horses into the river and across, the depth of the slow-running water never reaching above the horses' bellies.

On the other side of the river, Shaw stepped down and tied the three horses in a loose line, then slapped their rumps, sending them galloping forward on a trail leading off over a rolling hillside. "See you soon, Bowden Hewes," he said. He remounted the barb and rode it back across river. He unhitched Raul's paint horse from the tree and rode away in the direction of Banton, leading the dead Mexican behind him.

Across Fire River, the three horses walked along the winding trail like some bizarre funeral procession, their heads lowered in the heat of the day. When the string topped a short rise and headed down onto a wide draw, two range guards looked up from where they sat atop their horses watching a small herd of cattle graze on sparse clumps of wild grass.

"Well, bust my jaws," a red-bearded Nebraskan outlaw named Terrence Web said, his wrists crossed on his saddle horn.

"Mine two," said the other man, a younger outlaw named Billy Scott. He pushed up his broad hat brim as if to afford himself a better look. "That's Ned Gunnison's horse in the lead. Did you think that's Ned strapped over its back?"

"I'd be inclined to," said Web. "What about you?" He gave the younger gunman a dubious look.

The younger outlaw's beard-stubbled face reddened under Web's critical gaze. "Come on," he said, gigging his horse with his spurs. "Let's gather them up and take them in. Mr. Hewes ain't going to like this."

"You don't think so?" Web taunted, gigging his horse alongside him.

An hour later, out front of Hewes' large adobe, log and stone hacienda, two riflemen straightened up from leaning against a gait in the rail fence surrounding the yard. "Who the hell are these two bringing in?" one rifleman asked the other.

"I don't know," the other man replied absently, "but they sure ain't in none too good a shape."

Moments later, inside a large barn behind the hacienda, Bowden Hewes, a gunman named Dean "Quick Draw" Vincent and a portly outlaw named Thomas Finn turned from watching a crew of Mexican workers assist some of his gunmen in erecting a tall iron smokestack that reached up through a newly cut hole in the barn's roof.

"What the hell is this?" Hewes growled, seeing several of his gunmen gathered around Terrence Web and Billy Scott as the two led the three-horse string toward him.

The men stopped a few feet away. Web called out above the sound of the Mexican's hammering on the iron fittings overhead, "Bo, we got bad news. Ned, Pole and Mackey are all three dead." He made room for Hewes to come forward and take a look for himself.

Hewes, Vincent and Finn walked from horse to horse, looking at the bodies. "Sweet Jesus," Hewes murmured in a gruff voice, a thick black cigar clenched between his teeth. "Where'd you find them?"

Web had grabbed a handful of dusty hair on each of the corpses and raised their faces for Hewes to identify. "A couple of miles from the river," said Web. He dropped the last dead face and dusted his gloved hands together.

"I hope these three ain't your best, Hewes," Vincent commented. Web looked Dean Vincent up and down, not recognizing him.

"This is Dean 'Quick Draw' Vincent and Thomas Finn," Hewes said to Web and Scott.

"I've heard of you," Web said to Vincent, trying to look unimpressed but still eyeing him closely. He took note of the big bone-handled Colt on Vincent's hip.

"Hear that, Tommy boy?" Vincent said to Finn. "He's heard of me."

"Good for you, cowpoke," Finn said to Web. He and Vincent turned back to Hewes. "Does this change anything? I need to know before I send Finn back to Jake and the gang."

"Not at all," said Hewes. "I hate losing a man, but losing even three doesn't stop a parade, does it?"

"Not to me," said Vincent, "and not to Jake and the rest of the boys." He nodded toward Ned Gunnison's dust-covered body. "I knew Ned up in Colorado. He was no light piece of work." He looked at the other two dead men and said, "Who do you suppose done them in?"

"I know who done them in," Hewes said. "It's some damn saddle tramp who found my brother's body up in the hills." He didn't want to go into detail of the situation between himself and his brother's widow.

"Some saddle tramp, huh?" said Vincent, sounding doubtful. He looked at Finn, then back at Hewes, and said to him, "Maybe you ought to see if he's looking for work and hire him. He appears good at trimming numbers."

Hewes ignored the suggestion. "He's a dead man when I see him." He turned to his men. "Round everybody up." He said to Vincent, "This son of a bitch is holed up at my dead brother's house. We're going to ride over there and kill him."

"He's at your dead brother's house?" Vincent said with a bemused look.

"Yeah," said Hewes, "he found my brother's body and brought it home to the widow."

"He's holed up with your brother's widow?" Vincent gave Finn another look, then said to Hewes with a smug, knowing grin, "That sounds interesting." He looked back around at the Mexican work crew and at the large iron chimney reaching up through the opened roof. "I'm wondering if I should send word to Jake, tell him we'd best hole up for a while on getting this thing done. It appears you might have a lot of personal problems plaguing you here."

"No," Hewes snapped, "we're going right on with our plans. If you think that saddle bum is holding me up, you're wrong. Jake Goshen knows I'm good for taking care of business." He turned a confident gaze to Finn. "You tell him we'll have this set up and ready by the time him and the rest of the boys get here."

Finn nodded, but he looked to Vincent for approval.

"Tommy's going to ride back and tell Jake and the boys to bring the gold on in," said Vincent. He looked all around the large barn at the work going on. "But I ain't leaving right away. I'm going to stick with you and your men. We're going to find this so-called saddle tramp and make sure he doesn't kill all your men and put you out of business."

In a dingy service room above the Red Dog Saloon, Booth Anson stood shirtless, a soiled and bloodstained bandage on his healing shoulder wound. He held a foamy mug of beer in his hand; his sweaty hair lay plastered to his wet forehead. Watching out the window as Shaw rode in leading the paint horse and the dead Mexican, Anson called out over his shoulder to Wilbur Wallick, who lay stretched out on a bare feather mattress spooning cold beans from an airtight container.

"Get over here, Wilbur," he said. "You won't believe this."

Next to Wallick a naked whore cursed in a sleepy voice when she felt the whole bed squeak and bounce as Wallick got to his feet and walked to the window. Looking down beside Anson, Wallick saw Shaw step down from the speckled barb at a hitch rail. "I'll be damned, it's him, big as life! Look, he's toting a body around with him."

"It won't be long before somebody'll be toting his dead ass down the street," said Anson. He pressed his hand to the bandaged shoulder as if gauging how much longer before it would completely heal. "Get your boots on, Wilbur. We're going to follow him around some, see what he's up to."

"Right, Booth." Wallick hurried and set the airtight container of beans on a nightstand, then reached for his boots. "Think we ought to wake Mean Myra and tell her we're leaving?"

"If she doesn't see us here, she'll get the idea," Anson said.

"But what if we still owe her some money?" Wallick asked.

"Jeez, Wilbur," said Anson, just looking at him, not knowing how to answer.

From the bed the woman's muffled voice said, "I already been paid, unless you both want to give me a little something extra." She rolled onto her back and propped her back up against the iron bars of the headboard.

"Cover yourself, Myra," said Anson. "You look rank as hell lying there like that." He reached for his own clothes piled on the grimy floor.

"Oh, I look rank, do I?" Mean Myra Blount reached over beside the can of airtights, picked up a bag of tobacco and rolling papers. "I must've looked like a warm apple pie when I *uncovered*," she said in a knowing tone as she rolled herself a thin smoke and ran it in and out of her red-smeared lips. "You sure couldn't get your fill—"

"Shut up!" snapped Anson. "That's not the kind of thing I like talking about."

Mean Myra chuckled, reaching for a match and lighting her cigarette. "Throw me my dress," she said.

Anson picked up her dress from a chair and pitched it over to her. She spread it over herself and continued smoking and watching Anson dress. "Who did you see ride in down there, if you don't mind my asking?"

"The sumbitch who shot me," Anson said, sitting down on the edge of the bed to pull on his boots, barely using his right arm beneath his sore and healing shoulder.

"So you're going to kill him?" the dark-haired young woman asked. She idly twirled a strand of hair as she smoked and talked.

"Oh yes, you bet I am," said Anson.

"I might just get dressed and come along, watch it for the sport of it," she said.

"Oh, I might not be killing him today," said Anson. "It depends on how things look when I find him. If I get a good chance, I'll take it. If not, I might wait until my shoulder's all the way right."

"I see," Myra said, settling back as if she had doubts it would ever happen.

"No, you don't see," said Anson, catching the skeptical tone. "He's dead, he just ain't found it out yet. Soon as I can swing some iron at him, he's going down face-first." He stood up and stamped his boots into place on his feet, looked down at her and said, "You don't believe it, you come along and take a look-see."

"I might," Mean Myra said, blowing out a thin stream of smoke through her perched lips. "Let me know when you get ready to do it. I don't want to get all dressed for nothing."

Chapter 15

A gathering of curious onlookers had watched as Shaw spun the speckled barb's reins to an iron hitch rail out front of the town barbershop. He hitched Raul's paint horse beside the barb, untied Raul's body and dragged him off the saddle and over his shoulder. A few of the onlookers standing closer tilted their heads at an odd angle in order to get a better look at the dead Mexican's face as Shaw walked past them.

"Sorry, Raul. I should have covered you up," Shaw murmured to the corpse as he stepped away to the open shop door. In a bottom corner of a window a sign read: FINAL ARRANGEMENTS.

At the door, the town barber, who had been watching, stepped aside and gestured Shaw in. "What happened to Raul?" he asked straightaway, staring at the body as Shaw stopped in the middle of the floor and turned and looked at him.

"You know this man?" Shaw asked.

"I sure do. That's Raul Hernandez," the barber replied. "He used to do odd jobs around town some, off and on. His mother-in-law cooks and keeps house for the Edelmans." He gestured Shaw toward a door, then stepped ahead of him and opened it for him.

"I know," said Shaw, walking through the door. "I met him at the Edelmans' hacienda. He was on the trail home from there when somebody killed him." Seeing a long wooden mortuary table in the middle of the room, Shaw lowered Raul over onto it.

"You were at the Edelmans'?" The barber looked at him even closer now. "Then you must be the drif . . ." His words trailed as he eyed Shaw's ragged, dusty poncho and battered top hat. "That is, you must be the *fellow* who found the doctor's body, too."

"Yeah," Shaw said cynically, "I'm good at finding bodies lately. How'd you know about that?"

"Jane Crowly and Ed Baggs took the news of it all the way to Fort Carrick. It made it back here by wire. This is a strange newfangled world when what a person says a hundred miles away makes it home before they do." His eyes widened a bit. "Word is you knocked Jesse Burkett's teeth out!"

Shaw only nodded. "I want to make sure Raul gets seen to properly." He gestured a gloved hand around the room and said, "Looks like you're well equipped for the job."

"Yep, I'm the man you want for this," said the barber. "I'm the only Chicago-trained professional around." He motioned toward a sawed-off shotgun hanging on a wall peg with a tin star dangling from a strip of raw-hide. "I'm also the town's acting peace officer until we get ourselves a real sheriff."

Shaw gave him a patient stare.

"Right," the barber said, giving a nervous little cough to the back of his hand. "Anyway . . ." He looked at Raul's dead, dust-covered face appraisingly, noting the gaping bullet holes in him. "Shave, haircut, washed, dressed and in the ground for six dollars— that's in a place we've got staked off especially for a graveyard. Mexicans are buried right alongside the rest of us." He winked and added, "Of course, off a little to one corner, if you get my meaning."

Shaw gave him a hard stare for a long moment, then said, "Get it done."

"Right away, sir," said the barber. "I'm Wheatis Buckley at your service." He looked at Shaw as if expecting a name in return.

"Call me Lawrence," Shaw said. He reached down into his pocket and came up with money for Raul's burial.

"My pleasure, Mr. Lawrence," the barber said, taking the money as Shaw dropped it into his clean, poised hand. His hand snapped shut quickly as if this stranger might change his mind. "Now, what about yourself, sir, if I may inquire?" he asked. "Will you be getting a shave and a haircut today?"

Shaw didn't answer. But when he turned to walk out of the shop he saw three men standing across the street, staring toward him through the open door. He stopped and said to the barber, "Yeah, let's do that too, while I'm here."

"A wise decision if I may say so," Wheatis Buckley said, noting Shaw's two-day beard stubble and the long dust-covered hair gathered beneath the battered top hat brim.

Shaw took off his top hat and hung it on a hat rack before seating himself in the barber chair. As the barber stepped forward with a clean shawl to spread over him, he said to Shaw, "You may also hang your gun belt there if you wish."

Shaw just stared at him.

"Yes, well . . ." The barber spread the shawl over him, tied it loosely around his neck and adjusted the chair back into the shave position. "I hope this water is hot enough to meet your approval." He took a wet shaving cloth from a pan of hot water, wrung it and covered Shaw's face with it. Beneath the warm cloth, Shaw relaxed and closed his eyes for a moment as Wheatis Buckley twirled his shaving brush in a shaving mug and worked up a thick, soapy lather. "So, how was the ride here?" he asked, making conversation out of force of habit.

Shaw didn't answer.

Across the dirt street one of the three men said to the other two without taking his eyes off Shaw, "I can't say I've been all that fond of Jesse Burkett." He gave a short, nasty grin. "But there are times you feel like shooting a man just to watch him die."

"Willis, you're cold as ice," said a gunman named Parker Maddox, who stood beside Bert Willis, the two of them leaning back with a boot raised against the front of a building. "I don't know about watching him *die*. But I know Bo would be mighty grateful to us if we shot a few holes in this trail-bird."

"There's something familiar about him to me," said the third man, a Texas gunman named Fred Cooder, who had ridden up from Eagle Pass a month earlier to work for Bowden Hewes. He had taken a step forward as if for a better look across the street and through the open barbershop door once Shaw had removed the top hat. "I just can't place the man."

Willis gave another short grin and straightened from against the building now that the stranger was seated and leaning back with his face covered. "If you're going to *place* him, you best be doing it quick." He adjusted his gun belt on his hips. "He's about to leave this world with a clean face . . . but unshaven." He started across the street. The other two flanked him a step behind.

Maddox looked over at Cooder and said, "Well? Any luck yet?"

"No," said Cooder, "but I've seen him before somewhere; I know I have."

"All you Texans claim to know one another 'til one of you gets caught in congress with a sheep," said Willis with a sidelong look.

Cooder ignored the remark, concentrating more intently on the stranger in the barber chair as the three continued across the dirt street.

Inside the open door, Wheatis Buckley saw the three gunmen advancing toward his shop. "Oh, dear," he said to Shaw in a guarded tone, "here come three men who work for Bowden Hewes—pals of Jesse Burkett, no doubt." The sound of the shaving brush clicking around in the soap mug had stopped. "What should I do?"

"Go on with it," Shaw said beneath the wet shaving

cloth. He reached up with a fingertip and rounded a peephole in front of his right eye, just enough to look at the men when they stepped inside and spread out.

"My goodness, *my goodness . . . ,*" the barber whispered nervously, the brush in his fingers going back into its spin around the inside of the shaving mug.

"We saw you ride in with the dead Mex, Mister," Willis said, standing the closest to Shaw.

Shaw sat in silence watching the man through the peephole in the shaving cloth.

After a second, Willis said, "Did you hear me, stranger?"

"No," Shaw replied. The barber stopped working up the lather and took a step back when Shaw's left forearm came out slowly from under the shawl and moved him away.

Willis was taken aback at the reply, but only for a second. He cut a glance to the other two men, then said to Shaw, "You're not from here, so I best let you know—"

"I'm from here," Shaw said. "Born here, raised here, been here all my life." He reached his hand up slowly and pulled the wet cloth from his face.

Maddox started to speak. "Stanger, you ain't from—"

"He's being funny with us, ain't you?" Willis said to Shaw, cutting Maddox off.

Cooder winced, recognizing Shaw now that the shaving towel was off his face. "Oh hell."

"Did you think it was funny?" Shaw asked the gunman in a flat tone, adjusting the leaning chair back into its upright position. He could see the look on Willis' face grow darker, and heard the scrape of his boots on the floor as Willis spread them shoulder width apart.

"No, I didn't think it was funny," Willis said, his voice growing tighter, going into a growl. "You're the sumbitch from the Edelmans'. You busted up a friend of ours, Jesse Burkett. We don't allow no-account saddle bums to injure one of our own around here. We think we need to chop you off at the ankles."

Shaw just stared at Willis. He'd seen the stunned look on the face of the gunman standing to Willis' right. The man had recognized him; Shaw knew that look. Now the question was, would the gunman recognizing him cause him more, or less, of a problem when the shooting started. Less, Shaw decided, judging the man's pale, frightened expression. All right, Shaw decided, it was the man in front of him first, then the man to his left.

"I suppose it won't help any if I apologize," Shaw said, having it all worked out and ready to put into action.

Willis let out a dark chuckle. "Hear that, boys? He wants to apologize."

Cooder tried to speak. He said in a low, cautious tone, "Willis, hold up. I know who this is." He spoke faster. "This man's from Somos Santos, Texas. He's known as Fast Larry—"

"Shut up, Fred," Willis snapped, cutting him off without glancing toward him.

Shaw didn't take his stare away from Willis.

"I say it's too damned late for any apologies, stranger," Willis said. A nerve twitched in his jaw; his fingertips twitched with it.

Shaw saw it coming; he didn't wait for it. "I believe you're right," he said calmly. With a blaze of fire, the barber shawl flew up from Shaw's lap. One blaze, a second, then a third.

The terrified barber dove for cover as screaming bullets took over his small, tidy shop. Willis caught the first shot in his chest just as he made a grab for his revolver. His boots left the floor as the impact hurled him backward through the large shop window in a spray of blood and shattered glass. He landed backward against the iron hitch rail with a heavy twanging sound, then pitched forward onto his face. His forehead cracked hard on the edge of the plank boardwalk, raising a puff of dust. But he didn't feel it. Behind him the spooked horses reared against their hitched reins.

Before Willis had even begun his backward flight, Maddox took the second shot straight through his broad forehead. His hat flipped up in front like some sort of parlor trick as the bullet blew out the back of his skull. His eyes crossed in a sharp angle as he slammed the wall and spun along it three times, spraying blood and matter on his way until he seemed to spin down to the floor.

Shaw's third shot caught Fred Cooder dead center and rolled him along a shelf, knocking out barbering tools, combs and bottles of lilac water and witch hazel. His gun flew from his hand, hit the floor and went off. The stray bullet hit a clock on the wall and sent it exploding into pieces.

The Texan landed with a grunt, followed by a long moan. From a rear corner, the barber's striped cat had jumped straight up five feet into the air from a deep sleep at the first sound of gunfire. The animal hit the floor in time to race straight across Cooder's bloody back and out the shattered front window, leaving a line of a single red paw print behind. It stopped across the dirt street and sat and licked blood from its raised front paw.

Still seated in the chair, Shaw patted out a flame on the shawl in his lap. "Are you all right, barber?" he asked.

"I—I—No, for God's sake. No! I'm not all right, sir!" He stood up, clearly shaken and felt all over himself for any wounds, even though the shots from Shaw and the one misfire from the dead gunman had been the only four shots fired.

"Then I suppose you won't be finishing my shave and haircut?" Shaw asked, shoving his Colt back down into its holster. Outside onlookers came forward with careful trepidation, staring all around at the bodies as the speckled barb and the paint horse settled back down at the iron hitch rail.

"Look at my shop," the barber said, spreading his hands in despair.

Shaw stood and walked to the peg where his top hat hung. "I'll just come back another time," he said courteously.

The barber stared at him in awe. "What did this one call you?" He pointed a shaking finger down at Fred Cooder's bloody back. "I—I heard him. He said you're known as—"

Shaw stopped him with a hard stare. Changing the subject altogether, he said, "Where's the best place to stay in Banton?"

"You-you're going to be staying here a while?" The barber didn't seem to believe his own ears. "Mr. Lawrence, when Bowden Hewes gets wind of what you did to his men, he'll be coming for you with all the gunmen he can round up! You can't stay here! It'd be suicide!"

The barber didn't know the half of it, Shaw thought, thinking about the three dead gunmen he'd sent riding in to Hewes' place earlier that day. He looked off along the street toward a weathered clapboard hotel a block away. The building afforded a good view of the main street running in both directions.

That would do when the time came, he told himself. For now, he had brought Raul's body here for a proper burial and sent the dead gunmen to Hewes as a message. It was time to see what Hewes was up to in his stronghold on the other side of Fire River.

When the shooting had begun, Booth Anson and Wilbur Wallick had been walking toward the barbershop. Having watched Shaw walk inside moments earlier, the two had then seen the three gunmen enter the barbershop only to see one of them come flying through the shattered glass. "Jesus!" Anson had said, hearing the other rapid gunshots and watching the cat come racing out across the street. "Keep walking, Wilbur," he said in tight voice.

Turning quickly on his heel and heading back in the opposite direction, Anson ducked his head, fearing he'd be seen. Beside him Wallick said, "Don't we want to go have ourselves a look-see?"

"Just keep walking, Wilbur," Anson said, his head even lower. Onlookers ran along the boardwalk toward the barbershop, then slowed almost to a halt as they neared the body lying in the street by the hitch rail. "We've got to make sure we do this thing right."

At the barbershop, Shaw stepped outside in time to look along the street and catch a glimpse of the two before they ducked back into the saloon. Recognizing them from the trail, he nodded to himself and walked toward the hotel. Banton could get awfully hot for him in a hurry, he told himself. But then he let out a breath and thought about it.

Hell, what did he care . . . ? He wanted to find out what he could about Hewes and his men and the gold coins before he went off searching for Dawson and Caldwell. Maybe it would make up some for him getting drunk and disappearing for the past month. He hoped so, he thought, walking to the hitch rail. He gathered both horses and walked them toward a sign that had a red painted arrow on it pointing toward the town livery barn.

He gazed off to the southwest, past the distant hills and past the border. Somewhere, Dawson and Caldwell were out there, tracking down Jake Goshen's gang. It was time the three of them got back together and got down to business, he told himself. But first he had a trip to make, back out across the sand hills to Hewes' stronghold. He had a feeling something there would tell him more about the gold coins.

PART 3

PART 3

Chapter 16

Crayton Dawson stared down at the gunman Jefferson Sadler lying dead at his feet, then lifted his gaze along the deserted street of the ghost town at another outlaw's body lying sprawled dead amid sand and sage brush. Past the corpse he saw his partner, Jedson Caldwell shoving a wounded man along in front of him.

"This one is Kermit Bedlow," Caldwell called out. "He says he wants to talk to us. Right, Bedlow?" He gave the bearded man a nudge with his rifle barrel.

"It's not Bedlow, *gahl-damn* it, Undertaker! It's Bead-low," the outlaw corrected him, clenching his bleeding forearm as he stumbled along the street. "You ought to know more about a man 'fore you stick a bullet in him."

"What did you just call me?" Caldwell asked, stopping the outlaw a foot away from Dawson and giving the wounded man a hard glare.

The man looked worried. "I called you Undertaker; ain't that what everybody calls you?" He turned his scared eyes from Caldwell to Dawson. "Hell, I meant no harm by it. I'm in no position to be giving you any guff."

"That's all right," Caldwell reassured him. He looked at Dawson and asked with a bemused expression, "Have you heard anything about this?"

"I heard it mentioned a couple of times," Dawson said, reloading his still-smoking Colt as he spoke. "I expect it must've taken hold. Do you object?"

"No, I suppose not," Caldwell said. "It seems strange though. I went to mortuary school, took my training and got all my paperwork, but nobody out here ever called me much of anything. I take on a badge and shoot it out with some outlaws and now I'm the Undertaker."

"Hard to figure," Dawson said, closing the gate on the big Colt and dropping it into its holster.

"You mean you really *are* an undertaker?" Beadlow asked, giving Caldwell a strange look, still gripping his wounded arm.

"I studied to be one," Caldwell said.

"But you're not now," Beadlow said with relief in his voice. "That's good. I'm thinking a man would be taking a heap of bad luck on himself getting shot by an undertaker. I figured it was just a nickname, you know, from all the gunplay you've been in around here."

"Enough said on the matter," Caldwell replied. He took off his derby hat, brushed sand dust from its brim and put it back on. "Tell Marshal Dawson here about Jake Goshen's whereabouts." He pulled off his fingerless black gloves and stuck them down into his vest pocket.

"What about my arm?" Beadlow asked. He was clearly testing the lawmen, seeing what he could manage to get for himself.

"What about it?" Caldwell asked. He'd already planned to sit the outlaw down and tend to his wound. But not right now, not now that Beadlow had tried using it as an item of barter.

"What about it?" Beadlow looked incensed by Caldwell's lack of concern. "Hell, I'm bleeding something awful here! I need patching up."

"You'll get it," Dawson cut in. "First we're going to talk about Jake Goshen and the rest of his gang. We know you're not one of his close circle, so don't waste our time lying. Just tell us what you know."

Beadlow tightened up. "I'm not telling you a gahddamn thing until we get settled on what's going to happen to me if I cooperate with yas."

"Fair enough," said Dawson. "You're going to jail if you cooperate with us. You're wanted in Arizona Territory for bank robbery, train robbery, horse stealing and assault on a peace officer."

"But we wasn't even in the US of A when you fellows started chasing the four of us. You had no more authority there than a wild goose."

"We won't tell if you won't," Caldwell put in.

"That's real funny, Undertaker," said Beadlow, getting surly all of a sudden. "But since you two have got nothing to offer me, I ain't telling neither of yas a gahldamned thing." He jutted his chin toward Dawson. "How's that, Marshal Dawson?"

"That's fine," Dawson said calmly. Then to Caldwell he said in a firm tone, "Shoot him, Deputy."

"Yes, sir," said Caldwell. He raised his big Colt from his holster, cocked it and leveled it at arm's length, the tip of the barrel only an inch from Beadlow's sweaty forehead.

"Whoa! Wait! Hold on, Deputy!" said Beadlow. He turned loose of his wounded arm and held his bloody hand up.

"Some last words you want to say, Beadlow?" Dawson asked rigidly.

"Last words? Hell no, but I got something to say sure enough," said the frightened outlaw. "I never seen anything that can't be bargained on a little. What kind of lawmen are you? You went meddling down there where you don't belong. . . . Now you're ready to kill a man only because he's trying to build a softer spot for himself?"

"Is that all, Beadlow?" Dawson asked. He gave Caldwell a nod of approval.

"No, wait, that's not all," Beadlow said hurriedly, seeing the resolved look on Caldwell's face behind the long gun barrel. "What do you want to know? I'm giving it all up." He looked back and forth between the two and saw them ease down. "I can't say it's fair though," he growled under his breath.

Dawson ignored his comment; Caldwell lowered his Colt, uncocked it, but held it ready, letting Beadlow know that shooting him was an option still hovering close at hand. Reaching into his trouser pocket, Dawson pulled out one of the German gold coins and showed it to the outlaw. "One of you four spent this in El Zorro Rojo Cantina the other night."

"Stanley, you checkered-shirt-wearing son of a

bitch," said Beadlow, cutting a sharp glance off toward a trail of dust rising in the distance. "He wasn't supposed to be spending any more of that German gold, and he knew it. Now he's the only one to get away. Here I am shot, and Sadler and Holliway both dead."

"He's not getting far," Caldwell said. "But right now we want to know everything you can tell us about the gold and about Jake Goshen."

"We'd been seeing the stolen gold everywhere the past few months; then it started drying up," Dawson said. "What happened? There was too much for it to all have been spent that fast on whores and whiskey."

Beadlow seemed to consider it for a moment; then he sighed in submission and said, "All right. What you saw was just some of the men's cut of it—some holdover you might say, to keep everybody drunk and satisfied for a while. The biggest part of it, Jake and his partners held on to, until they figured out what to do with it." He gave a tight dirt-streaked grin. "I don't think any of them expected to come into that much money all at once."

"His partners?" Dawson asked. "Who are you talking about?"

"I don't know them myself, but I heard talk," said Beadlow. "Jake ain't running his gang all by himself. He's got partners, men who know how to cover this much money without it looking like what it is. I heard loose talk that one of them might be Cheyenne Smith. But I wouldn't swear to it."

"Cheyenne Smith is a gambler and a dandy," said Caldwell. "He doesn't consort with outlaws. . . . Doesn't have to, from what I've heard."

Beadlow paused in consideration, staring at them. Then he said, "Do you two know how big a bunch this is you've been trying to lock horns with?"

"We've got an idea," said Caldwell. "We've killed five of them in the past three months . . . put seven more behind bars."

"See?" Beadlow pointed out. "That's why they call you Undertaker. But that's not even a start. With this much gold involved, Jake has every outlaw from here to Missouri coming to ride with him. He's bigger than the James-Younger Gang."

"Next question," said Dawson. "Where will we find Jake Goshen, Dean Vincent—the big guns of the gang?"

"Ordinarily you wouldn't find *any* of them," said Beadlow, "leastwise not around these parts." He paused and asked, "Any chance of me getting a bed, maybe a room with a barred window in it?"

The two lawmen stared at him until he gave in and shrugged.

"All right," he said. "Rumor has it that Jake, Vincent and Leroy are sticking together real close right now, trying to get this gold situation settled. I wish I could send you straight to them, so's Quick Draw Vincent could shoot your eyes out. But I don't know where they are."

"Take your best guess," said Dawson. "You four were headed back across the border. Was that to lead us into a nest of Goshen's men, get some odds in your favor?"

"Well, sort of," said Beadlow. He hesitated.

CROSSING FIRE RIVER   173

"Come on, Kermit. Tell us where you were taking us," Caldwell persisted.

"We was headed up into the hill country north of Banton," Beadlow said. He nodded toward the distant rise of dust. "That's where Stan Booker is headed. There's a big camp made up there. It's been there ever since the robbery in Mexico City." He gestured down at the fresh blood running down his forearm and dripping steadily into the sand. "I won't be able to tell you anything more if I stand here and bleed out."

"Fix his wound up, Deputy," Dawson said. "We'll talk some more on the way to jail."

"What jail might that be?" Beadlow asked as Caldwell walked toward his horse to get some bandaging from his saddlebags.

"Fort Carrick," Dawson said. He directed the outlaw toward a rock and had him sit down for Caldwell to tend to the wound. When Caldwell came back, he tore Beadlow's shirtsleeve open and began washing and inspecting the bullet hole.

Dawson walked away along the empty street, toward the body lying in the dirt. He gazed off across the rolling sand hills, through the endless wavering heat. Somewhere out there he knew he'd find Lawrence Shaw if he searched hard enough, he thought. Fort Carrick might be a good place to start looking.

By the time the two lawmen and their prisoner rode into Fort Carrick they'd both talked with Kermit Beadlow enough to know that he had nothing else of any importance to tell them. Beadlow was a nobody, a man at the bottom of a long list of outlaws who rode with the Jake Goshen Gang. When they'd hitched their horses at the rail out front of a newly constructed log and stone jailhouse inside the fort, Beadlow stepped down, looked at Dawson and made one last try at staying out of Yuma Prison.

"Marshal, what if I told you I know where there's a whole feed sack of those German gold coins buried?" he said to Dawson.

"I'd say you're lying, Beadlow," Dawson replied.

"But what if I say I can take you right to it and put your hands on it?" Beadlow countered quickly, hesitating as Caldwell took him by his upper arm and guided him toward the door.

"Save your story," Dawson said. "Use it to make some friends inside—it might keep somebody from stealing your blanket." He stepped away as Caldwell gave Beadlow a push toward the jailhouse door.

At the door a man stood hatless with a wet cloth pressed to a purple knot on the side of his head. He stepped forward when the two lawmen walked closer and eyed Beadlow up and down. "What are you looking at, peckerwood?" Beadlow asked. "Have you never seen a desperate, hardened criminal before?"

The man turned his reply away from Beadlow and said to Dawson and Caldwell, "Indeed I have. I was waylaid by one today. I had my horse and my water stolen from me. I had to walk fourteen miles in the heat, bone-dry. I thought this might be the scoundrel who did it to me."

"No," said Caldwell in Beadlow's defense, "he's been with us all day." But before reaching past Beadlow and opening the door, Caldwell asked, "Was the man who robbed you wearing a checkered shirt?"

The man's eyes widened. "Hell yes, he was! Did you come upon him? He's riding my red roan and leading his worn-out horse behind him."

"No, we didn't see him on our way here," Dawson replied for Caldwell as the deputy and the prisoner walked inside, "but we're planning to catch up to him as soon as we drop this man off. The man you're talking about got away from us this morning. I expect he ran his horse out by the time he reached you. Which way did he go?"

The man said, "He was riding due east toward the old Apache trail around the fort. I came to in time to see his dust. The way he was riding, he'll likely run out of transportation again before the day is over."

"Unless he robs somebody else," Dawson replied, gazing off across the wavering desert floor beyond the fort.

After the lawmen had turned Beadlow over to the guards on duty, they stayed only long enough to see that he was locked safely behind bars. Then they rode out of the fort and made their rounds of all the drinking establishments, both weathered shack and ragged tents that surrounded the fort's perimeter.

"Nothing," Caldwell said, stopping at the last, the dirtiest and lowest-looking saloon of the bunch. "You don't suppose something bad has happened to him, do you?" he asked Dawson, who stood beside him. They had led their horse the length and breadth of the squalor.

Looking around, Dawson said, "You mean something worse than this?" He shook his head. "No, I don't think so. Drunk or sober, Shaw has a way of taking care of himself."

Across a rutted wagon path from them, a mere skeleton of a woman walked out of a small tent wearing nothing but a dingy gray towel over her bare shoulder. She carried a tin pan of wash water in her hands, which she threw out into the dirt. Before she turned and walked back inside, the two lawmen saw her give them a drug-encumbered smile and cup a thin blue-veined breast toward them. Needle marks stood out, red and scabbed over in the crook of her badly bruised arm.

"What makes him do it?" Caldwell asked, not really expecting an answer, not really wanting one.

Dawson only looked at him for a moment—they both knew Shaw's reasons and there was no need to discuss them. "He's not here. Let's ride," he said grimly.

Chapter 17

From their wagon seat, Jane Crowly and Ed Baggs had seen the lone rider racing across the rolling sand hills in front of them. He rode a desert trail that stretched waterless for miles and circled east of Fort Carrick, the sort of trail a man traveled only when he did not want to be seen or followed, Jane and Ed both thought, watching him. The rider left behind him a tall rise of dust that had barely settled a half hour later, when their wagon rounded the string of low hills he'd disappeared behind.

"Hold up, Ed," Jane said, spotting the rider lying facedown in the sand. "It looks like this damned fool has broke his neck." The rider's worn-out horse stood spread-legged ten yards away.

"Looks like he come near killing his poor cayuse first," Baggs added, stopping the wagon and pulling back the brake handle as Jane picked up a small rubber-coated water bag and jumped down. She walked forward, her shotgun in hand.

Jane looked back along his trail, judging where he'd

come from and speculating why he'd been in such a hurry. When she stood over him, her shotgun ready if she should need it, she said down to the rider's back, "Hey, idiot, are you dead or alive?"

After a silent moment she reached out with the toe of her boot and gave him a sharp nudge. "What's the deal?" Ed called out, walking over to her from the wagon.

"I was right, he must've broke his fool neck—" Jane's words were interrupted by a rasping voice speaking into the sand, saying, "Wa-water . . ."

"Well, I'll be damned; he's alive," said Jane. She and Baggs looked at each other in surprise.

Squatting down to the fallen horseman, Jane rolled him over until his bare head rested on her crooked knee. "Here, hero, drink this." She held the uncapped water bag to his dry, dusty lips and poured a small trickle of tepid water into his mouth.

The smell of the water caused the exhausted horse to stagger over to her. "Poor critter," Baggs said. "A man ought to be whipped, treating a horse this way." He picked up the rider's hat lying on the ground, dusted it and poured some water into it for the parched animal. On Jane's knee, the rider strangled a little, coughed and perched his lips for more water.

"Hold on, idiot," Jane said, "I didn't take you to raise. This water's got to last us to Banton." Yet even as she protested she poured another thin trickle into his mouth.

Squinting up at her in the glaring sunlight, the man swallowed another sip and managed to say in a breaking voice, "Who . . . are you folks?"

"We're not Apache," Jane said. "The way you were riding, it looked like you thought you had a whole nest of them stirred up and coming after you." As she spoke, she reached down, slipped his Colt from its holster and shoved it down into her belt.

The man didn't answer. But he took note of his gun being lifted as he scooted up onto her knee a little and looked back along his trail. "Thank God you came along. I was done for," he said in a cracking voice, as if his gratitude had brought him to tears.

"Don't get blubbery on me," Jane said. "You can't afford to lose any tears." She stood up, helping him to his feet with her. "Were you headed anyplace special, or just seeing how soon you'd die out here?"

"Over near Banton," the man said, ignoring her sharp tongue. He stood shakily, his arm looped around her shoulders, and looked at the wagon sitting in the wavering heat. The little bay she'd borrowed from Shaw stood beside the wagon, hitched to it by a lead rope. "I've got folks there."

"I know everybody around Banton," Jane said. "Who are your folks?"

"My folks are"—the man stumbled a step; Jane grabbed him for support, but with a speed Jane hadn't felt him capable of, the man snatched his Colt from her waist, cocked it and shoved it into her flat, hard belly— "none of your damned business, she-male!" he said, his arm tightening from across her shoulders to around her neck. "Drop the shotgun or I'll bust you wide open!"

"Damn it, I knew this was a trap," Jane said, angry at herself for being taken in. "I had to jump down and help this lousy turd." She threw the shotgun aside, disgusted. "What the hell's wrong with me?"

"We don't have time to figure that out," said Stanley Booker. He looked at Baggs, who stood wide-eyed, his hands going chest high instinctively. "You, drop that sidearm and back off."

"Don't hurt her, Mister," Baggs pleaded. "She was only trying to help you."

"Only way she could have helped me was to kill my ma before I was born," said Booker. He shoved Jane away from him. "Both of yas walk away from here 'til you hear me leave. I see either of you look back, I'll put a bullet in both your coconuts."

Jane and Ed turned and started walking away across the desert floor, the sun beating down on them. "If you ever see me try to render a humanitarian act toward another *man*, you have my permission to put your boot straight up my ass, hard as you can stick it."

"I'll do it, too," Ed said, walking stiffly, afraid to turn and see what the outlaw was doing. Noting the water bag in Jane's hand, he said, "He forgot to take our water bag. As long as we've got it, we ain't likely to die." He gave a wink and a grin.

"Jesus, Ed," Jane whispered with a wince, "you need to talk a little louder; he might not have heard you real clear."

Baggs lowered his voice and repeated, "I said, he forgot to take our—"

"Damn it, Ed," said Jane, cutting him short. "I heard you well enough the first time. Why you start whispering?"

"I don't know," said Baggs. He ducked his head and kept walking.

A hundred yards out they ventured to turn and look back when they heard the sound of their wagon horses' hooves pounding away along the hard-packed trail. "Well, there he goes," Ed said. The outlaw rode away hard on the little bay after cutting the team horses loose and shooing them with a slap on their broad rumps. "We'll be the rest of the day gathering these horses, but at least we're both in one piece. . . . No harm done."

"Speak for yourself, Ed," Jane said, sulking, "I'm harmed, damned well harmed. He should just as well have killed me as to humiliate me this way. This is the last time I'll ride shotgun. I ain't fit for the job."

"Hell, Jane, don't be so hard on yourself," said Ed. "This could have happened to anybody." He hitched his trousers up a notch on his round belly and started walking in the direction of the fleeing wagon horses. Jane sighed heavily and walked along behind him.

Dawson and Caldwell spotted the wagon as they rode onto a sand rise and looked out across the rolling hills. But by the time they had ridden straight to the wagon, Jane and Ed Baggs had gathered their horses, hitched them and tied together the leads where Booker had cut them with a boot knife. Booker had taken Jane's shotgun and Baggs' big dragoon pistol.

"I feel naked as a bride," Jane had said, seeing the two riders coming toward them in a rise of dust. Looking all around in the sand, she shook her head in disgust and said, "There ain't a rock around here to chuck at them."

"I'm betting we won't need rocks; guns neither," said Baggs, eyeing the riders as they drew nearer.

"Oh, why's that, Ed?" Jane said sarcastically. "You figure they'll kill us before they get much closer?"

Baggs eyed her and said, "You always expect the worse, don't you?"

"I'm no grinning idiot, Ed, if that's what you're asking," she replied with a frown. "What's got you so optimistic anyway?"

"I ain't optimistic," Baggs said. "But I ain't always expecting some kind of disaster befalling me."

"Expect it? Hell, I count on it, Ed," Jane said. She wiped dust from her face with her shirtsleeve and stared out with him. "I wish I at least had a sharp stick to poke at them," she murmured under her breath. "I hate dying without a fight."

"If you're that concerned they're going to kill us, hop up and we'll light out of here," said Baggs.

"What's the use running now?" Jane said, seeing the faces of the two riders as Dawson and Caldwell slowed their horses. "We can't get away in this damned wagon. All we'd do is piss them off."

"Here they are, and we ain't dead yet," Baggs said sidelong to her as he raised a hand toward the two dust-covered horsemen.

"If you know what's good for you, you'll ride on and leave us be," Jane called out in a threatening tone.

Baggs looked at her.

"It's worth a try," she whispered.

"We're lawmen, ma'am, in pursuit of a felon," Dawson called out. They had been watching Jane and Baggs gather their horses and bring them back to the wagon for the past half hour through sun glare and wavering heat. "It looks like you might have crossed paths with him." He gestured down at the single set of hoofprints leading to the wagon, then turning to two sets as they led away.

"Well, hell yes, of course we saw him," Jane said. In an accusing tone she went on. "If you two hadn't took so damned long getting here, maybe you could have shot the sumbitch before he took our guns and stole my riding horse." She gestured off in Booker's direction. "Now he's got one resting while he's riding another. He'll be harder to catch."

Dawson and Caldwell nudged their horses closer and looked down at the two teamsters. "Sorry about your horse, ma'am," Dawson said, touching his hat brim.

"You don't look none too broken up about it," Jane said. "Anyways, it wasn't my horse. A fellow loaned it to me the other day. I was taking it back to him. Now I can't bear thinking I have to face him, tell him the animal's gone."

"I'm Marshal Cray Dawson, ma'am," said Dawson. "This is Deputy Jed Caldwell."

"Ma'am, Mister," said Caldwell, touching his hat brim toward them in turn. "With any luck we'll catch him and get your horse back for you," he said to Jane.

"I won't miss any meals waiting for it," Jane said in a cynical tone.

"I'm Ed Baggs," said Ed, "and my shotgun rider here is Miss Jane Crowly. Pay no attention to Jane here. She's got a big mad on over that borrowed horse getting stolen from her."

"And our guns, Ed," Jane said. "Don't miss a chance to tell some stranger we got our guns snatched right out of our hands."

Baggs gave a dark chuckle. "Hell, what's the difference he stole our guns? I always say, so long as you're alive, you ain't lost nothing."

"I almost wish I'd catch him before you two do," Jane said Dawson. "I'd love to get my shotgun back and unload it on his worthless ass."

"What's this fellow wanted for?" Baggs asked, staring out as if Booker might come riding back into sight at any minute.

Caldwell took a breath and went into Booker's list of crimes. "He's wanted for murder, forgery, train robbery, cattle rustling—"

"We get it," Jane said, cutting him off. "He's one of them kind, wanted for every low act under the sun."

"Yep, he's one of them kind," said Caldwell.

Jane eyed the soft-spoken deputy's cut-off black gloved fingers, his well-trimmed dark beard, his string tie and brocaded vest. "Wait a minute, I've heard the name Caldwell. You're the one they call the Undertaker, ain't you?"

"Well, yes, Miss Jane." Caldwell looked a little embarrassed. "As it turns out, I am that person, although I only recently learned of it."

Jane planted both hands on her slim hips and looked at the two as if in a new light. "Ed, these fellows are the two lawmen I was telling you about a while back, the ones sent down to clean up the border, if you can believe such a thing is possible."

"That is us, ma'am," said Dawson. "I expect if we didn't think it was possible we wouldn't have taken on the job."

"I meant no offense," Jane said. "The fact is, now that I know who you two are, I'm feeling better about the odds on me ever getting that borrowed horse back. At least I can tell the fellow we've got some high-handed first-class lawmen hunting it down for us."

"You can tell him we will do our best to get the horse back for you, ma'am," Caldwell put in, ignoring the *high-handed* remark.

"I hope so," Jane said, "because the man who lent it to me is not a man I would want to disappoint if I was you."

"Oh, and who is this fellow?" Caldwell asked.

"It ain't so much *who* he is as *what* he is," Jane replied.

"He is one tough *hombre*, by her account of him," Baggs put in before she cold continue.

Jane frowned at Baggs for butting in. "Oh, excuse me, Ed, was you talking? I thought it was me."

Baggs grumbled and fell silent.

"The fellow's name is Lawrence, and I saw him butt whip a gunman who works for one of the most powerful men in these parts."

"Lawrence, eh?" said Dawson. Making the connection, he and Caldwell looked at each other knowingly. "Now, where have I heard that name before?" he feigned with a slight grin.

"I don't know," said Jane, "but that's all the name he goes by. The horse he lent me is one of two horses he took from a couple of wild outlaws who had the misfortune of tangling with him."

"He sounds like a tough *hombre*," Dawson said almost with a sigh of relief. He relaxed in his saddle and said, "Why don't we accompany you two to Banton, since you're both having to travel unarmed."

"What about catching that rascal?" She nodded in the direction Booker had taken.

"He'll keep 'til morning," said Dawson. "This Lawrence fellow is more important right now."

"Why's that?" Jane asked cautiously.

"I believe he's a man we've been searching for," said Dawson.

"He's not in any trouble with the law is he?" Jane asked with a wary look.

"No, ma'am," said Dawson, "he's no outlaw. We're looking for him for other reasons." He and Caldwell stepped their horses aside and gestured the two up into the wagon seat. As soon as the wagon began to roll forward the two lawmen fell in alongside and rode with them across the sand hills in the tracks left by the fleeing outlaw and the two horses.

Chapter 18

———

Shaw sat atop the speckled barb looking down onto the riders from a black slice of evening shade on the rocky hillside. He'd left the paint horse at the town livery, wanting to slip across Fire River and back as easily and quietly as possible. As soon as Hewes and his men had ridden past, he gave the barb a touch of his boot heels and rode a thin trail down out of the hills. He knew where Hewes and his men were going; they were looking for him.

When he reached the shelter of a tree line along Fire River, he waited a few minutes until darkness set in. Then he eased the barb into the shallow water and rode across at a slow, silent walk, the horse moving as if it knew the danger lying ahead of them.

Topping a rise in the direction he'd sent the string of horses with the bodies over their backs, he spotted a campfire glowing in the distant darkness. "We don't want to go there," he whispered to the speckled barb, and he turned the animal wide of the campfire and rode on.

Deeper into a wide valley he spotted more light in the darkness ahead of him. This time the glow came from the windows of the hacienda silhouetted against the purple sky. When he'd ridden closer he spotted a slim crack of light seeping out between two large barn doors. He rode toward it as he drew closer to the hacienda, slipping his rifle from its boot and laying it across his lap.

In the darker shadows of a weathered cottonwood tree, he stepped down from his saddle, hitched the barb's reins and slipped away quietly toward the crack of light, his rifle in hand.

When he reached the large double doors he peeped inside and saw the crew of Mexicans busy at work on the tall iron chimney. On the dirt floor beneath the chimney he saw a large furnace being assembled, its iron door big enough walk into in a crouch. A single armed rifleman sat dozing in a wooden chair leaned back against the wall. Beside the furnace three of the crewmen struggled with attaching a large bellows to an iron frame connected to the furnace's side.

A smelter's furnace? Yes . . . He stared for a moment, just letting the discovery sink in. This was how Jake Goshen and his gang were going to deal with the German gold coins. He had Hewes turning them back into untraceable, unidentifiable gold bullion. He looked all around but saw no sign of any gold.

The coins weren't here yet, Shaw decided. If they were, Hewes would never have ridden away and left that much gold unguarded. Every man who worked for him would be right here, right now. Shaw would never have made it across the river without getting cut down by rifle fire.

There must have been an awful lot of gold stolen to make it worth their while to smelter it down and start all over, Shaw thought, watching the Mexicans labor on into the night, in the light of oil lanterns.

Coming here had answered a lot of questions for him, he told himself, easing away from the barn and back toward his waiting horse. It made sense now why there had been so many gold coins showing up lately. Jake Goshen had let enough gold leak out among a few flunkies to keep the law on both sides of the border chasing its tail. Now he must've decided it was time to deal with the bulk of it.

Hewes had had a stake in the big Mexican National Bank robbery. Just how big of a stake, Shaw had no idea; maybe Hewes' only part of it was to smelter the gold down. But whatever Hewes had to do with the robbery, he would find out soon enough, Shaw told himself, unhitching the barb and stepping up into the saddle. It was time he found Dawson and Caldwell. Goshen and his men would be gathering here soon enough, gold and all. Handing this to Dawson and Caldwell would make up some for all the drinking he'd done.

Turning the barb, he gave it a light touch of his boot heels and sent it away from the hacienda at a slow, silent walk until he was well out of hearing range from the workers in the barn. Then he put the animal up into a gallop and headed back through the darkness toward the banks of Fire River.

Upon crossing the river and stepping down a moment to let the barb shake itself off, he stared down at hoofprints on the ground in the pale moonlight and gazed off toward the Edelman place—the place where Hewes had last seen him. This meant that Hewes had heard nothing yet about the three men Shaw had killed in town earlier that afternoon. If he had, he would have ridden straight to Banton.

Riding farther on, Shaw turned at the fork in the trail and continued following the same hoofprints until he stopped at a spot where the Edelman *haceinda* loomed black against the distant purple sky. He saw the glow of lamplight and firelight flickering in the side yard. But he noted that the house itself was dark except for a lamp that he watched move from window to window as someone carried it through the darkness.

"Let's go, horse," he said, giving the barb a tap of his boots. He put the horse up into a gallop across the low riding sand hills and kept the pace until he reined the animal down a hundred yards from the house.

He hitched the barb's reins around a short, spiky bush and slipped forward quietly until he moved wide around the yard to the other side of the house. Using an empty rain barrel, he climbed up onto a low rear roof and worked his way from roof level to roof level. Finally he eased out onto a wide ledge and inched around it until he stood outside the half-open bedroom window.

From inside the bedroom Shaw head Lori Edelman speaking to Bowden Hewes. But rather than the voice of a woman being pursued and pressured by a man she had no use for, he heard a calm conversational tone that caused him to peep inside as if he didn't believe his ears.

"This is all taking too long, Bo," he heard Lori say, standing against Hewes, the two with their arms around each other.

"Everything was moving along just fine until the drifter showed up with Jonathan's body," Hewes replied into her neck as he nuzzled his face there. "Everything will still move along just fine. Quick Draw Vincent sent his man Finn to tell Jake to bring the gold on in to us. They're waiting, not far from here. Meanwhile, I got something to take care of."

Lori Edelman pulled back far enough to say to his face, "You're going to kill him, aren't you? I can tell by the way you're acting."

"The way I'm acting?" Hewes paused, shook his head and said, "Look at it this way, darling. I wouldn't have to kill him if you had sent him on his way, instead of bedding down with him."

"I—I was lonely and you weren't here for me. And I was more than a little angry and impatient with you, Bo," she offered as if in her defense. "I still *am* impatient with you," she added, stepping away from him altogether.

"But no longer lonely, I take it," said Hewes, gesturing a hand toward the bed.

"Presently, no," Lori said demurely, looking away from him with a trace of a smile. "I have found myself fulfilled for the time being." She touched a hand to her hair. "The drifter was just what the doctor ordered," she added in a teasing and suggestive tone. "You should thank him for taking care of me so well while you were gone to gather the smelting equipment."

"I would kill any other woman for treating me this way," Hewes said in a half growl, half laugh. He put his arms around her from behind and pressed her to him. "I don't know what I want to do worse, wring your neck or make love to you until you scream. Seeing you with the drifter has made me crazy for you. Picturing the two of yas together here has stirred me into a frenzy."

"Right now you'll neither wring my neck nor make love to me," she said confidently, wrestling free of him once again. "There's gold to be melted down. Besides, I'm still angry with you over Jonathan's body. You said you'd take good care of things, that he'd never be found. I'd never have to think about him again." She motioned toward the window, the yard lying below. "I have to see his grave every day, every time I look out the window."

"Once we're through, you can have him dug up and moved out of sight," said Hewes.

"Yes, I suppose I can have that done," she said, stepping away from him as he tried coming near her again from behind. "It would look bad doing it now. But as soon as we're finished with the gold, it must be done."

"But you're not going to be here after we finish with the gold," said Hewes, stopping, giving up on gaining any affection right now.

"Oh yes, that's right. I almost forgot," Lori said playfully. "You'll be taking me to Paris as soon as we have

our share of the gold." She smiled and became recep-
tive of him. She stepped over to him, took his wrists
and placed his arms around her waist.

Shaw had seen enough. He pulled his eyes away
from the window as the two moved closer to the big
bed. He heard the wooden bed frame give out a muffled squeak as he inched back along the ledge and
eased away along the roofline.

Once on the ground, he crept along in a crouch until
he'd made his way past the gathering of men sitting,
eating and drinking at the long table in the yard. Raul's
mother-in-law, Juanita, hurried about with a platter of
food and drink in her hands.

When Shaw stood back beside the speckled barb in
the purple darkness, he took up the reins to the horse
and looked back toward the glowing lamplight in the
bedroom window as a hand trimmed it down. "It figures . . . ," Shaw said quietly to himself, thinking about
the exchange he'd just witnessed taking place between
Lori Edelman and Bowden Hewes.

That was what had been missing between him and
the widow; she hadn't cared anything about him, and
he must've sensed it in spite of all her efforts. He
stepped up into the saddle and turned the barb quietly.
All she had done was use him to keep Hewes jealous
and off balance in his attempt to accommodate her.

This was all about the gold; Shaw had merely stumbled into the right place at the right time, a drunk trying to finish sobering himself up. While every lawman
on both sides of the border had been riding their horses
into the ground chasing down leads, he had wandered
the desert, only to find himself lying in the grateful

arms of a woman whose brother-in-law and *lover* was connected to the gold thieves he and Dawson and Caldwell were searching for.

So be it . . . Nothing like a little blind luck now and then to let a man know he's on top of his game, he told himself, riding on.

In the middle of the night Thomas Finn had split away from Vincent and Hewes and the rest of the armed riders. He'd ridden on as quickly as he could across the rolling sand hills and up into the jagged rocks of the low hills northwest of Banton. When he caught sight of a small campfire glowing beneath a rock overhang, he slowed his horse and veered over long enough to investigate.

"Whoa," he murmured to himself, looking at the tired, shadowed faces huddled around the small fire. He recognized the Mexican lawman, Juan Facil Lupo, Maynard Lilly and the three bounty hunters, Iron Head, Merle Oates, and Bobby Freedus. "Easy John Lupo riding with bounty killers," he whispered under his breath.

His right hand went instinctively to the butt of a big Remington holstered across his belly. He drew the gun, but he had no intention of using it, not here, not now. Knowing the fierce reputation of every man gathered there, he eased backward at a crouch, mounted his horse and rode away as quietly as he could.

A half hour later, at a spot beside a towering chimney rock, he stopped on the thin trail and called out to the hillside lying before him. "It's me, Finn, don't shoot!" he said, loud enough to be heard and hopefully have his voice recognized before a volley of gunfire exploded toward him.

A gruff voice called out from the black-shadowed hillside, "What's the secret word?"

"The secret word? Hold on, fellows!" Finn froze for a moment, then said in a shaky voice, "Hell, nobody told me any secret word."

He heard a rifle hammer cock. He started to turn his horse and bolt away. But a dark laugh came from the shadows. "There's no secret word, Finn. Get yourself on up here," the voice said.

"Yeah, that was real funny, Claude," Finn said in a tight voice.

A gunman named Claude Martin rose from behind a rock and stepped forward, barely visible until he stopped a few feet away from Finn. "I'm just following orders, Tommy," he said. "But you ought to have heard yourself. You sounded like you spilled water in your saddle."

"My saddle's dry," Finn said in a prickly tone, stepping down from atop his horse and leading it along beside the rifleman. "Whose orders were you following, anyway?"

"Jake's orders," said the rifleman. "The only ones I ever follow."

"Is Jake still nervous over having all this gold out in the open?" Finn asked.

From the blackened hillside Jake Goshen said in low growl, "I don't get nervous, Finn, I get mad. You want to see what *mad* looks like on me?"

"Sorry, Jake," said Finn, "I meant nothing by it. I've just a big stupid mouth sometimes."

"Yeah?" said Goshen, stepping forward, three men surrounding him. "Then you best start using it right now. What's going on with Hewes? Is it safe riding in with the gold?"

Finn made sure he shifted any responsibility for what he had to say over to Dean Vincent. "Quick Draw said to tell you to come on ahead. Everything is getting set up and ready to go."

Jake Goshen stared at him in the pale light of the moon. "You don't sound real sure of yourself, Tommy," he said.

"I'm telling you what he said for me to tell you, Jake," said Finn.

"What's going on there, Tommy?" Goshen reached out a gloved hand to Finn's shoulder and squeezed. "I want to know why you're passing this thing off to Vincent."

"Here's the thing of it," Finn said. "On my way here, I come across the camp of Easy John Lupo and the Scotsman. They're traveling with those bounty hunters who work for the Mexican government."

"Those sonsabitches," said Goshen, "they've got no business over here." He frowned. "Did they see you? Which way are they headed?"

"No, they didn't see me," said Finn. "I can swear to that. They look to be traveling the hill trail toward Banton."

"All right, they'll be no problem for us so long as we know they're around," said Goshen. "What else?"

"There's been some trouble between Hewes and his men and some drifter who brought Doc Edelman's body back from the desert hills. Since this bummer showed up, it seems he's been poking the doc's widow. He beat the hell out of one of Hewes' top gunmen and killed three more when Hewes sent them after him."

Goshen gave a puzzled look at the men gathered around him. "You're saying *one* drifter has done all this?" He held up a gloved finger for emphasis.

"That's what Hewes says, just one," Finn answered with a shrug.

"Damn . . ." Goshen considered the matter. Finally he gave a laugh under his breath. "I wonder if he's looking for work." He gave a smile all around to the men. His teeth glistened through his thick black beard.

Finn gave a short laugh of relief. "That's sort of what Vincent said when Hewes told us." He turned more serious. "But Hewes didn't find it so funny. Anyway, Vincent said he'd ride with Hewes and get rid of the man, so's we won't have to worry about anything going wrong."

"That was good thinking on Vincent's part," said Goshen. "It leaves him there where he can keep an eye on things for us." He gave another flashing grin. "It looks like Banton's going to be a hot spot, what with Mexican bounty hunters and lawmen crawling all over town. Lucky for us we'll be laying low at Hewes' place while we melt our gold down. Once it's melted down, there ain't a way in hell anybody can prove it's stolen."

Chapter 19

In the middle of the night Lawrence Shaw stepped down from the speckled barb's saddle at the edge of town and walked the tired horse the rest of the way to the livery barn. From inside an empty store, where they had taken up a lookout for Shaw's comings and goings, Wilbur Wallick watched man and horse walk in and out of the glow of oil pot fires set up at five-yard intervals along the dirt street.

When Shaw and the speckled barb drew close enough to be recognized, Wallick eased over to where Anson lay sleeping on a blanket on the dusty floor. Mean Myra lay sleeping against him. The big gunman shook Anson roughly by his shoulder. "Wake up, Anson. He's back," Wallick whispered. "He's headed this way right now!"

Anson came awake with a start. "Jesus, Wilbur, take it easy," he said in a cross tone. Myra stirred beside him.

"You said wake you when I see him," Wilbur said in an excited whisper.

"I didn't say yank my arm out of the socket," said Anson.

"Did I do wrong?" Wilbur asked dully.

Anson struggled to his feet, snatched his rifle from against the wall and stumbled to the dirty window. Myra stood up and slapped dust from her coat and shook out her hair. Outside Anson and Wallick saw Shaw moving along on foot. "No, Wilbur," he said with a sly little grin, "you did just right." He levered a bullet into his rifle chamber and cocked the hammer.

"Are you going to shoot him right now?" Wallick asked, sounding excited.

"Oh yes. It's time I put this sonsabitch down once and for all," said Anson. "Get Myra over here where she can see it."

"I'm here," said Myra in a lowered tone. "Get to it."

"Wait, there's somebody coming!" said Wallick as Anson started to slide the rifle barrel out through a broken windowpane.

"Damn it!" Anson stopped and looked in the other direction along the dirt street. He uncocked the rifle and lowered it.

"I thought you were going to shoot him," Myra said, clearly disappointed. "Did you freeze up?"

"Yeah, I thought you was going to shoot him too," said Wilbur.

"Shut up, Wilbur, and pay attention here," Anson whispered, ignoring Myra's question.

Stepping out of a dark shadow into the flickering light of an oil pot, Jane Crowly called out to Shaw in a hushed and guarded voice, "Lawrence, wait up. I've got to tell you something. Don't go in there! It might be a trap." She gestured toward the livery barn looming behind the row of buildings as she hurried across the street.

"Slow down, Miss Jane," Shaw warned, stopping and staring at her.

She skidded to a halt in front of him, her hands chest high. "I might have made a big mistake, Lawrence. On the trip back here I went and blabbed my mouth about you to a couple of men claiming to be lawmen."

"Claiming to be lawmen?" Shaw looked past her at the saloon where her freight wagon sat at a hitch rail. Then he looked toward the livery barn. "And they're in there waiting for me?"

"Hear that, you all?" Anson said to the other two, listening through the broken window. "This sonsabitch is wanted!" He raised the rifle to his shoulder and cocked it again. "Anything coming for his hide is ours."

"So shoot him," Mean Myra coaxed.

Wallick watched Anson take aim in rapt fascination. His brow twitched in anticipation of the gunshot. But instead of firing, Anson listened as Jane went on. "Yes they are. They said they're looking to meet up with you." She stared toward the livery barn with him. "I say lurking in the dark is no polite and proper way to meet a man."

"What do they look like?" Shaw asked, already having a pretty good hunch who the two were.

"They said they're the two lawmen that was sent to clear out the outlaws along the border. One is a tall fellow like yourself, and the other is shorter and dressed like a dude. He wears gloves with the fingers cut off, like some damn chimney sweeper. Claims he's the one they call the Undertaker."

"The Undertaker . . ." Shaw gave a slight smile and relaxed a little.

"I thought I best get over here and tell you," she said. "I've been watching for you ever since Wheatis the barber said he saw you ride out." She shook her head. "I hope I haven't brought trouble down on you . . . although I know you're a man who can handle it if I did."

Hearing a sound coming from the direction of the empty building, the two turned toward it. Shaw's hand wrapped around the butt of his Colt. Anson jerked back away from the broken window and hugged flat against the wall. On the boardwalk, Jane and Shaw saw the barber's cat, who stood staring at them with a wary look, as if remembering its last encounter with Shaw and his big Colt.

"Dang cat nearly got itself shot," Jane said. She looked back at Shaw. "Did I screw up something, the way I usually do?" She looked ashamed. "Ed says I'm a calamity walking around waiting to happen."

"It's all right, Jane," he said. "Obliged you came and told me though." He nodded toward the livery barn. She walked alongside him.

When Shaw and Jane stepped out of the dim light of an oil pot toward the livery barn, Anson looked back out and cursed under his breath. "Damn it, I should of shot him while I had him in my sights."

"Yeah," said Wallick, "you sure should have."

"But you didn't, now, did you?" Myra said sarcastically.

Anson couldn't face Myra, but he stared at Wallick coldly for a moment. "That's all right. I know where they're headed. Come on, Wilbur, both of yas, I'm still going to nail his shirt to his chest."

The three hurried out the rear door of the empty building and raced along the alley toward the livery barn. When they slowed to a walk and moved forward in a crouch, they stopped at a crack in the back wall and stood listening intently.

At the front barn door, Shaw stepped inside and said quietly toward the hayloft overhead, "Dawson, Caldwell, it's me, Shaw."

Shaw . . . ? Jane stared at him.

Dawson stepped to the edge of the hayloft in the darkness and said, "How'd you know we're here?"

"Instincts," Shaw said. Behind Dawson a lantern flared to life in Caldwell's hand. A golden circle of dim flickering light filled the blackness.

Looking down at Shaw from the loft and seeing the buckskin-dressed woman beside him, Dawson said quietly, "I see Jane Crowly managed to jump ahead of us and get to you first."

As if having to defend her action, Jane stepped forward and said, "So *the hell* what? I told you this man is a pal of mine. I didn't know whether you was telling the truth or not. I wasn't going to be responsible for him getting ambushed."

"It doesn't matter," Dawson said, trying to put the matter aside. He climbed down a ladder to the straw-covered floor. Caldwell climbed down behind him, holding the lantern up for light.

"Damn right it doesn't," said Jane, refusing to let it go. "Anyway, what the hell kind of friends are yas, sneaking around in the dark like you're up to no good?"

Shaw cut in before either Dawson or Caldwell could answer. "They wanted to see what was going on here before they made their presence known, Jane." He looked at Dawson, then back at her. "That's sort of how we work together."

"Work together?" Jane gave him a curious look. "Are you saying that you're a lawman too?" She looked him up and down. As if he already concluded his answer, she said, "And here I thought you was just a good ole drifter and a drunk."

Shaw looked at Dawson, a little ashamed, and replied to Jane, "That was just my disguise. I've been gathering information about a gang of outlaws all the way across the desert."

Going along with Shaw's explanation, Dawson nodded and said, "Well, I'm glad to see you've been able to drop the disguise."

Outside in the darkness, Anson and Wilbur looked at each other. Myra stood back with a hand on her hip, a look of disgust on her face.

Without a word, Anson lowered the rifle he'd raised and aimed through a wide crack in the barn wall. The two backed away slowly, Myra right beside them, until they got out of hearing. Then the three broke into a run and didn't stop until they reached the end of the alleyway. "Jesus, Wilbur, we've uncovered a swarm of lawdogs!"

"I know, I know," Wallick said with fear in his voice. "What are we going to do? I wish I'd never come along with you across the border. I should have stuck with Easy John and the Scotsman. What do you suppose they're up to?"

Myra stared at them, shaking her head. "The same thing every lawman I've screwed lately has been *up to,* you idiots—the stolen Mexican gold."

Anson and Wallick looked at each other. "I want out of here!" Wallick said suddenly, unable to keep his fear in check. "What are we going to do?" He paced back and forth, his hand on either side of his big head. "What are we going to—"

"Get ahold of yourself, Wilbur!" said Anson, grabbing him and shaking him soundly. "I'll tell you what we're going to do. We're going to go get the hell out of here." He gave the frightened gunman a shove in the direction of the saloon, where their horses stood at the hitch rail. "The gold, huh?" he said sidelong to Myra, who ran along with them.

"Hell yes, the gold," she said. She grabbed the reins to a horse standing a few feet away, seeing a rifle butt sticking up from its saddle boot. "You should've had enough sense to know that."

"Maybe I did know it," said Anson. "Maybe I wanted to know if you knew it too."

"Yeah, right," Myra said skeptically. She jerked the horse away from the rail, helping herself to the animal without hesitation. "Don't mind if I do . . . ," she murmured, swinging up into the saddle as Anson and Wallick did the same. In moments the three were mounted and beating a fast path out of town.

In the barn, Jane and the three lawmen looked toward the sound of horses' hooves fading north along the dirt street. "Drunken cowhands, no doubt," Jane speculated. As soon as the sound diminished a bit, she looked at Dawson and Caldwell, then at Shaw. She asked him, "What did you call yourself a while ago?"

"Shaw. It's my name," Shaw said.

"Oh?" Jane gave him a perturbed frown. "Then who the blazes is Lawrence?"

"That's my name, too," Shaw said. "My name is Lawrence Shaw." He watched her coolly, waiting for recognition to sink in. When it did, Jane corkscrewed her face and said almost to herself, "I'll be damned, Fast Larry Shaw! The fastest gun alive! How the hell did I miss seeing it? I must be the dumbest—"

"I don't go by Fast Larry anymore," Shaw cut in. "I go by Lawrence." He turned to Dawson. "I'm glad you two showed up. There's a lot getting ready to happen around here."

The three stood looking at Jane expectantly until she took the hint and said, "If you fellows will excuse me, why don't I just go see how Ed's making out getting us up another load to Fort Carrick?"

The three nodded and watched her head for the barn door.

"Anything to do with the gold or Jake Goshen and his gang?" Dawson asked as Jane reached out to shove the door open.

"Yep," said Shaw, "I've found out plenty." He

looked from one to the other. "Both the Jake Goshen Gang and the gold are on the way to a place near here, *tonight*. They're bringing the gold with them. They're going to melt it down to keep it from being identified. The man who's got the equipment to melt it down is Bowden Hewes. He's on his way here tonight."

"Hewes, that crooked sumbitch," Jane remarked, stopping at the door.

Shaw turned his words to Jane. "Him and the widow are in it together. Hewes is coming here to kill me."

Jane looked stunned, but she recovered quickly and said, "I hope you know I had no idea any of this was afoot, else I'd have never—"

"I know that," Shaw said, cutting her off. "Nobody is blaming you." He turned back to Dawson. Seeing the confused look on his and Caldwell's face, Shaw said, "I'm going to fill you in on everything before Hewes and his men get here." The three turned once more toward Jane, who stood staring at them.

"All right," she said, "I'm going." She turned and walked out the door grumbling under her breath.

Stan Booker jumped down from the horse with the shotgun in his hand and let the spent animal he was riding stagger away into a sandy draw. Beside him the other horse stood frothed and winded. Both horses had run long and hard without water. The second animal tried to shy away when he stepped up in the stirrup. But Booker would have none of it. He shot a nervous glance back along his trail.

"Hold still, you flea-bit cayuse!" he shouted, managing to throw himself over into the saddle and jerk back hard on the reins. "I'll say when we rest and when we run." He nailed his spurs to the horse's sides. The animal let out a painful whinny and shot forward.

"That's more like it!" Booker shouted, leaning forward low on the horse's neck as the courageous animal gained speed. He slapped the ends of his reins back and forth wildly. *"Yiiihiiii!"* But before the worn-out animal had gone a hundred yards, it veered sidelong off the trail, careened sharply down a steep hillside of sand and rock and jerked to a sudden halt.

With a loud scream, Booker shot forward over the horse's head in a high spray of sand. He turned a half flip and slammed upside down, backward into a thick, stiff saguaro cactus. He slid down onto his head and fell flat forward onto his face with a loud grunt, knocked cold, his back pierced with large cactus needles. The tired horse walked the rest of the way down the hillside to the cactus. It sniffed dryly at Booker's back, then walked away toward the faint smell of water in the night air.

A full twenty minutes passed before Booker moaned in a broken voice, "Good God almighty . . ." He pushed himself to his feet, his neck throbbing in pain. He staggered in place for a moment, until he righted the world beneath his feet. With cactus needles stabbing him at every move, he struggled forward two steps. Then he stopped with the tip of a rifle barrel poked into his stomach.

"What are you doing out here, you stupid son of a

bitch?" Jake Goshen asked, standing behind the rifle. Goshen gave the barrel an extra poke. "I told you and those other jackasses to stay south of the border, keep the money showing up down there."

"That is what we did, Jake," said Booker, pain racking him from every direction. "But we got singled out by some damn lawmen. They killed the others, far as I know. I got away by the skin of my neck."

"How many lawmen?" Jake asked in an angry voice.

"Two," said Booker, plucking a long, thick cactus needle from the back of his arm.

"Two . . . ," Goshen said flatly. He lowered the rifle at his side, then let out a breath, drew a long Colt, held it out at arm's length toward Booker's head and cocked it.

"Jake, please!" Booker pleaded. "They'll hear the shot!"

Before pulling the trigger, Goshen looked back along the dark trail Booker had ridden and stopped himself. He let the hammer down and lowered the Colt. "Those two lawmen just saved your worthless life," he said.

"Jake," Booker said, trying to regain some favorable standing with the enraged outlaw leader, "I rode all this way just to warn you about them. I knew you'd be in the hideout up in the hills."

"You rode all this way to get them off of your back and onto mine, Booker," Goshen growled. "Now, find your horse and get on it. We're headed for Hewes' place across the river."

Booker looked at the wagon bed filled with wooden

crates, covered with a tied-down black tarpaulin. "Is that what I think it is?" he asked meekly.

"Get your horse, Booker, before I change my mind and cut your throat," said Goshen. "If those lawmen cause us any trouble with this gold, you're going to be the first to die."

Chapter 20

———

Shaw filled the other two lawmen in on everything that had happened while Jane went to the saloon to find Ed Baggs. Instead of asking Baggs about any freight load he might have lined up for them, she warned him of the trouble coming to Banton. "I don't have to be told twice," Baggs said, tossing back his whiskey in one gulp. "I'm out of here. What about you?"

"I'm going for coffee," Jane said, giving him a look as she turned and walked back out of the nearly empty saloon. When she returned to the barn she carried a pot of hot coffee she'd picked up at a restaurant, along with four clean coffee mugs.

"Come and get it, fellows," Jane said. "There's nothing like a good mug of coffee before having to shoot a sumbitch or two."

Shaw stood inspecting his shooting gear when she came through the door. Ignoring her remark, he slipped his Colt back into its holster and took one of the mugs. "Obliged, Jane," he said as she poured the mug full.

"I figure it's the least I can do, to make up for introducing you to Lori Edelman," Jane replied. "I swear, I think Ed is right about me. I screw up everything I touch." She looked back and forth at the men checking their guns. "I had my shotgun stole from me, but if one of yas will lend me a gun, I'll be glad to pitch in and fight these outlaws with you."

Shaw didn't answer. He sipped his coffee, then set the mug down atop a feed bin and continued checking his rifle and his Colt.

"Well, don't everybody offer at once," Jane said with a sour expression.

"It's law work now, Jane," said Shaw. "You've been a big help. But it's best you sit the rest of it out."

"Sit it out? Why? Because I'm a woman?" Jane asked, offended by Shaw's remark. "You might be the fastest gun alive, but this place is my home." She thumbed herself on her flat chest. "I got a right to help defend it."

"Have you ever killed a man, Miss Jane?" Dawson asked, picking up a Colt from atop the feed bin where weapons and ammunition lay.

"No," Jane replied, her face taking on a grave, earnest expression, "but I've always known I could if circumstances ever called upon me to do so."

Dawson decided not to pursue the matter any further. He handed Jane the Colt and watched her check it and shove it down into her waist. "Here's how it's going to go," he said. "We've got nothing on Hewes. We'll have to wait until him and his men make the first move. Do you understand what I'm saying?"

"Oh," Jane said in a mocking voice, "you mean

we're not going to just start shooting as soon as we hear their horses riding in?"

"I just want to make sure you understand everything," Dawson said with no appreciation for her remark.

"I understand *everything*," Jane said solemnly. "I'll make no move until a move is made against us."

"That's right," said Dawson. "Before the smoke clears here, we're going to be on our way to get settled up with Jake Goshen and his men. Once this whole thing starts there'll be no backing out of it."

"Watch your language," Jane said. "I never crawfished away from trouble in my life. I ain't likely to start doing it now." She jaunted her chin proudly.

Outside, on the trail leading north away from Banton toward a distant line of hills, Anson, Wallick and Mean Myra finally slowed their horses to a walk and looked back toward town in the grainy starlit darkness. "Well, then, *smart boy*," Myra said to Anson, who sat nearest her. "What else do you have in mind for us?"

"Well . . ." Anson stalled for a moment. "I figure we'll ride on down to Texas. Wilbur and I can always stir us up something to do in Texas, to make us a few dollars." He tried a devil-may-care grin, but it didn't work well.

"Oh, a few dollars?" Myra looked unimpressed. "Tell me something," Myra said, "do you boys leave town that fast every time a lawman shows up?"

Anson said, "We both just got out of a Mexican prison. Excuse us if lawmen make us a little edgy. Like all desperadoes and long riders, we have to stay ready to make a getaway."

"Long riders . . ." She shook her head. "It's a miracle you two ain't starved to death."

"We are long riders." Anson stared at her. "You're welcome to come along with us and see for yourself. We'll even make you a partner."

"No, thank you," said Myra. "I make good money with my ass and ankles. I would've made seven or eight dollars already tonight if I hadn't wanted to see a man get shot down—which I didn't even get to see, as it turns out." She gave him a stiff, accusing glare.

"Stick with us, and you'll see me shoot a man sooner or later," said Anson, "I can promise you that."

Myra stared off as if in contemplation for a moment. Then she said, "I've been whoring two years and I've not yet seen a man shot. Most I saw was one get stabbed in his lungs." She shrugged. "It wasn't much." She put the stolen horse forward at a walk.

"Stay with us, Myra," Anson said. "Hell, I'll even see to it you get to shoot somebody yourself, if that's what it'll take to make you happy."

"Don't go making promises if you don't mean to keep them," Myra tossed over her shoulder to him.

"I mean it, Myra," said Anson, keeping his horse right alongside her. "I swear I do. If not the man back in Banton, then some other man, and it'll be damned soon."

"We'll see," Myra said, riding on a walk.

A mile farther along the trail, they stopped again, this time atop a sand crest, when they saw and heard the dark line of riders winding toward them. "Whoa, who's this?" said Anson, easing his horse off the trail, Myra and Wallick right behind him.

Behind the shelter of rocks alongside the trail, the three stepped down and watched the riders draw closer and file past them toward town. Recognizing Bowden Hewes as he passed less than fifteen feet away, Mean Myra stood up and dusted the seat of her coat. "I've got a feeling there's something coming to a head between Hewes and the lawmen." She looked at Anson and said, "Take me back to town. Maybe I will get to see a sumbitch shot tonight after all." Her eyes lit with excitement at the prospect. "I might see more than one!"

"But what about those lawmen?" Anson asked.

"To hell with them," said Myra. "Unless I miss my guess, they're the men I'm talking about." She grinned in her excitement and jerked her horse around in order to follow Hewes and his men. "Either way, I'll get to see somebody shot!"

Wallick looked at Anson warily as the two turned their horses to follow her. "What if it's us she sees killed?" he asked under his breath.

"Shut up, Wilbur," Anson said acidly. "Sometimes you just have to think positive and hope for the best."

The three followed Hewes and his men at a safe distance, the way scavenging wolves follow hunters on a game trail. . . .

Two miles before reaching the outskirts of Banton, Bowden Hewes brought his men to a halt and motioned them in close around him. He knew when the three dead gunmen came back to him tied down over their saddles that this drifter was not someone to be taken lightly. He didn't know what had happened out there in the sand hills, but the dead outlaws had been the drifter's way of calling him out to finish things between them.

But Hewes was no fool, he thought. He wasn't riding in blindly. "Everybody, listen up," he said. He paused for a moment, then asked, "I need three men to ride in ahead of us and check things out before all of us go riding in."

The men sat in silence for a moment. Finally Terrence Web asked bluntly, "Check out what things? He's either there or he ain't."

Hewes gave him a hard, silencing stare. "Are you giving me guff, Terry?" he said menacingly.

Web shrank back. "No, sir," he said meekly. "I didn't mean to at all."

"If we come across him while we're scouting," Collie Mitchum asked, "do you want us to kill him before we ride back?"

"Are you saying you're one of the three, Collie?" Hewes asked.

Mitchum shrugged. "Yeah, I'll go. I've never seen a bummer yet that caused me a loose stool."

"That's the spirit," said Hewes with a proud smile. To the others he said, "I always said Collie makes a big pair of dents in his saddle." He raised a finger and said, "A hundred dollars each for the three *scouts* if they bring this drifter's head back on a stick. It'll keep the rest of us from having to bother killing him."

Web, feeling he needed to do something to make up for questioning Hewes, said, "Count me in. I've been wanting to kill something for the past month." He looked around with a grin. "A hundred dollars just sweetens the pot for me."

"Keep your hundred dollars," Jesse Burkett said in a distorted voice through his still-swollen lips and his cracked, jagged teeth. "I'll kill that drifter son of a bitch on the cuff."

"All right," said Hewes. "Looks like these three all make big dents in their saddles." He stepped his horse to the side and said, "Well make a camp over there behind the rise. Be back by daylight. If he's not swinging from your saddle horn, then we'll all ride in and shake that town until it spits him up to us."

Terrence Web asked, "What if we run into Bert Willis, Maddox and Cooder? Do we have to share our hundred dollars with them if we kill him?"

"No," Hewes said flatly. "But you can give them this message from me. Tell them all three I want their sorry asses out here *pronto*. They were supposed to be back yesterday. Tell them they'd better have a damned good explanation."

"We'll give them your message," said Mitchum. Turning his horse and riding away, he said under his breath to Web and Burkett right beside him, "But they ain't helping me spend any of *my* hundred dollars."

From his hotel room overlooking the dirt street, Shaw watched the three riders appear out of the darkness into the flickering light of oil pots lined along the empty dirt street. They kept their horses at a slow, cautious pace, looking back and forth, seeing no one, hearing no sound save for that of a twangy piano playing halfheartedly at the saloon at the far edge of town.

"Here they come," Shaw said over his shoulder to the other three. "He only sent three men."

"*Only* three gunmen?" Jane asked in an exaggerated tone. She shook her head. "Three armed gunmen ain't nothing to sneeze at. Especially if they're Hewes' gunmen." She looked up from where she sat in a wooden chair, her right boot off, her bare foot crossed onto her knee. She held a pocketknife she'd been using to trim her toenails.

"Get your boots on, Janie," said Shaw, stepping back from the window. "It's time for you to go to the wagon."

She closed the pocketknife, put it away and pulled on a dingy, toeless sock. While she pulled on her boot, Dawson and Caldwell walked to the door. "We'll have you covered," Dawson said over his shoulder to Shaw.

Shaw watched the buckskin-clad woman stomp her boot into place and snatch her battered hat from a wooden table beside her chair. Shoving it down onto her head, she gave Shaw a wink and a grin and said, "I'll have you covered too—just don't shoot at me by mistake."

On the empty street, Terrence Web was the first to see the three wooden coffins leaning against the front of the barbershop, their lids standing beside them. Upon recognizing the bodies of Bert Willis, Parker Maddox and Fred Cooder inside the coffins, he jerked back hard on his reins and caused his horse to rear slightly in protest.

"Whoa!" Web called out, settling his horse as it made a full circle turn.

"Jesus . . . ," said Burkett as he and Mitchum also spotted their dead comrades. The men turned their horses to face the barbershop. "I guess they won't be needing a *good explanation* after all," he added.

The three corpses had been washed, dressed and properly attended to by Wheatis Buckley. Their cheeks had been circled with rouge, their lips reddened with lipstick, their skin coated thickly with paraffin. A single stitch of black thread held their eyes shut, another in the center of their lips kept their mouths from gaping. Their shirt cuffs had been sewn to the front of their shirts, keeping their hands crossed at their wrists.

"Get down from these saddles," said Jesse Burkett in his distorted voice. He slid his rifle from its boot on his way to the ground, eyeing the dark shadows of doorways and alleys in the flicker of oil light.

"What'd you see?" Web asked, keeping his voice low. He slid down from his saddle with his Colt coming up from its holster and cocking instinctively. He scanned the empty street.

"What I see is, we're sitting ducks here," Burkett said, the sight of the three dead gunmen having made a sudden sobering impression on him. "Spread out. This drifter is watching us right now. He got us in his gun sights."

From the dark shadow of an alleyway, Shaw said in mild, even tone, "You're right, I've got you covered. I have ever since you rode up onto the street."

"What the hell is your game anyway, Mister?" Web asked, stepping forward. His Colt was half raised, ready to fire. "Are you looking to be cut in on something? You've heard maybe there's some loose gold lying around?"

"Shut up, Terry," Burkett warned.

"Yep, I'm after the gold," Shaw said, stepping closer, getting too close for the gunman's comfort.

"That's close enough, drifter," said Burkett, recalling how quickly and unexpectedly this man had busted him in the mouth with a rifle butt.

But Shaw kept advancing. To Shaw's right, Collie Mitchum stepped sidelong, taking up a good position for himself. "I mean it," Burkett warned. His right hand slapped closed around the butt of his revolver, his other hand gripping his rifle.

But Shaw kept walking.

"That's *our* gold, in case you don't know it," said Web, still talking to Shaw as he came ever closer. "You've got no claim to it."

"I'm a lawman," Shaw said. "I saw the setup in Hewes' barn. I'm taking over the gold."

"You'll play hell," Web said.

"What kind of lawman goes around butt-whipping a man, and killing them like they're dogs?" Web asked.

"The kind who's been sent to clean up along the border," Shaw said quietly, still coming.

"If you're a lawman, where the hell's your badge?" Web asked.

"I'm not that kind of lawman," Shaw replied to Web as he stopped in front of Burkett.

"That's too close," said Burkett, nervously taking a half step backward, his left arm up, holding his rifle in front of him as if it were a shield.

"Who killed these men?" Web demanded, sounding outraged.

"Who do you think?" Shaw said to Web without taking his eyes off Burkett.

"What'd they do?" Web demanded. "A lawman can't go around killing men for no reason. What lawman would do something like that?"

"You're looking at him," said Shaw, his eyes still on Burkett. From the far end of the street Jane rode forward in a freight wagon from the livery barn.

"You best have some answers," said Web. "There's going to be—"

"Shut the hell up, Web," said Burkett through his swollen lips and busted teeth. He kept his eyes locked on to Shaw's. "Can't you see what this man is fixin' to do here?"

Web got it. "Not to me he ain't!" he shouted, raising his Colt quickly, already cocked and ready.

Even with Web's gun already out of the holster, Shaw's Colt streaked up and fired. The bullet bored through the gunman's forehead and slammed him backward up onto the boardwalk and into the three coffins. The coffins fell sideways like dominoes, spilling the three bodies out onto the boardwalk.

In front of Shaw, Burkett saw his chance to make a move. But before he could lift his Colt or swing his rifle, Shaw's big Colt snapped upward. The gun barrel struck Burkett under his chin, lifted him onto his tiptoes and sent him backward onto the ground.

Without stopping, Shaw's Colt finished its swing in a high arc, settled out at arm's length and sent a bullet slamming into Collie Mitchum's chest. Mitchum got off a wild shot as he fell on the ground backward, dead.

Jane had seen the fight begin, but it was all over in what seemed like a second. It had happened so quickly she'd had no time to stop the wagon and watch, or even duck down as the third outlaw's bullet sliced through the air over her head. "Dang!" she said, her mouth open in awe, the wagon still rolling along on the empty street.

Shaw stepped back and looked off along the street in the direction the gunmen had ridden into town. Smoke still curled from the tip of his Colt. His eyes searched the darkness beyond town. Then, seeing nothing, hearing no retaliation from anyone lurking in the shadows, he lowered the Colt and looked toward an alley where Dawson and Caldwell had stood waiting to back him up.

"That went smoothly enough," Caldwell said to Dawson.

"It always does when he's around," Dawson replied. The two remained out of sight as Jane Crowly eased the wagon to a halt beside Shaw and looked down at the dead lying all around.

Chapter 21

————

From the corner of an alleyway across the street, Myra Blount swooned headily at the sight of the bodies lying bloody and broken in the flickering firelight. "It's not what I thought it'd be like," she rasped, clinging to Anson. "It was so fast! They just flopped down like rag dolls. . . ."

"I saw it," said Anson, guiding her back into the sheltering darkness. "Now, let's get out of here before somebody sees us." Wallick stood farther back in the darkness, holding their winded horses. They had ridden hard, circling wide around Hewes and the rest of the men when they'd seen these three men ride on into Banton.

"Wait! Not yet," said Myra, halting, looking back toward the street, where Jane had stepped down from the wagon.

"You saw what you said you wanted to see," Anson whispered harshly. "It's over now."

"I saw what I wanted to see, but I heard some things I want to hear more about," she said, pulling herself loose from him with a hard shove. "Didn't you hear them talking about the gold?"

"It's just nerves talking, Myra," Anson said impatiently, wanting to leave before they were discovered lurking on the fringes. "It's the way men talk before they commence killing one another."

"Don't try telling me what men do or don't do," Myra shot back at him. "I've got more than my share of *knowing* about men. If that stolen gold is around here somewhere, I want to find it and take it off their hands." She gave a wicked grin. "If you boys are too short in the wick to help me, then cut out. I'm sticking."

Anson just stared at her, considering things for a moment. Wallick called out in a worried voice, "Are we going or staying, or what?"

"Shut up, Wilbur," Anson said over his shoulder. Then to Myra he said, "If I thought there was anything to that talk about gold I'd be all over it with you. But I don't believe there is."

"Your *time* is so important you can't stick around and find out?" she asked with a teasing expression.

"I'm not scared, if that's what you think," Anson said.

"Then stand still and keep quiet," said Myra.

On the street, Jane walked forward and watched Shaw stand up with Burkett's Colt in his hand. "Lord! I never seen nothing like that in my life, Lawrence. Had I batted an eye I would have missed it."

"It always goes fast," Shaw said flatly. He dropped the bullets from Burkett's Colt into his hand and slipped the empty gun back in Burkett's holster. The gunman lay groping in the dirt, trying to find his way back to consciousness.

"Yeah, but not *that* fast," Jane added. They both watched Burkett try to push himself to his feet.

Shaw reached out and gave the bleary-eyed gunman a hand. "Shake it off, Burkett," he said, pulling him to his feet. "You've got work to do."

"Huh?" Burkett staggered in place like a drunkard. His chin had already swollen around a gash made by Shaw's gun barrel. As his memory awakened, he felt around on his chest for any bullet wounds. "Who . . . ? What . . . ?" He stared all around at the bodies on the ground. A look of distress came to his face.

"That's right," said Shaw, "you're the last one standing. I had to kill these two." He gestured toward the bodies of Web and Mitchum. The other three bodies lay in the dirt, prepared for burial, their wrists still crossed, stitched to the front of their shirts.

Shaw's words had an awakening effect on Burkett, even through the pain throbbing in his chin and his previously busted mouth. A fire came into his eyes. "You should have killed me, Mister!" he shouted in his thick, distorted voice. His hand snatched the Colt from his holster and leveled it at Shaw. He clenched his broken teeth in spite of the pain. He wore the look of a man who had just felt the power of taking control.

But Shaw shook his head and said, "Burkett, don't make me smack you again. You're running out of face."

"Mister, get set to die!" Burkett growled.

"Your gun's not loaded," Shaw said calmly. "Drop it back in your holster."

Burkett cocked the Colt. "You're bluffing," he said.

Shaw angled his head in curiosity. "Why would I be bluffing about that? It's either loaded or it's not."

"Yeah, you idiot," Jane cut in. "Put the gun away. If he kills you, I'll be the one having to drive the gut wagon back to Hewes."

But Burkett would have none of it. He pulled the trigger. Nothing. He cocked and pulled it again. Still nothing. Again, nothing. Looking at Shaw, he let out a breath, lowered the Colt into the holster in defeat and said to Jane and Shaw, "What gut wagon?"

"This gut wagon," said Jane, gesturing a hand, "with *these* bodies in it." She gestured around at the ground.

Shaw stared at him intently. "Take them to Hewes. Tell him these are for Raul."

"All this over one dead vaquero?" Burkett said, shaking his head slowly. "Hewes won't buy it. You said it was about the gold a while ago. Which is it, Raul or the gold?"

"Tell Hewes to take his pick," said Shaw. "I rode out to his place. I saw what he's getting ready to do with the gold. I'm taking it over. Tell him he can ride in and try stopping me right here, or else I'll be coming across Fire River to kill him."

"That's bold talk for one gunman with nothing but a loudmouthed she-man on his side," said Burkett, giving Jane a scornful look.

"You son of a bitch—" Jane took a step toward him, but she was stopped by nothing more than a strong look from Shaw.

"Those odds have served us well so far," Shaw said calmly. "I think we'll keep playing them." Burkett hadn't seen Dawson and Caldwell, Shaw's aces in the hole. Jane gave a thin, proud grin, liking the idea of being included with Lawrence Shaw, Marshal Dawson and Caldwell the Undertaker.

"Then you're a fool, Mister. Bowden Hewes has enough men with him out there to ride through and level this town with one pass," said Burkett.

"Tell him to choose," said Shaw. "He can die right here tonight, or in his own front yard." He took a step backward and gestured a hand toward the ground. "Load up and haul them away."

In the alley, listening, Myra turned to Booth Anson and said, "There, did you hear that about the gold, or is this too much for you to take in all at once?"

"I heard it," Anson replied. "But there's only three of us. What can we do against Hewes and his bunch?"

"If this lawman or drifter or whatever the hell he is keeps killing them, pretty soon there's going to be none of Hewes' men left to worry about," said Myra, turning and walking quickly toward Wallick and the horses.

"Wait up," Anson whispered. "Where are we going?"

"You heard him," said Myra. "The gold is at Hewes' place. "We're going after it while these fools all kill one another."

Hewes and his men had mounted and rode forward at the sound of the gunfire coming from Banton. By the time they'd ridden a mile closer, they saw the black outline of the wagon rolling toward them. "Watch out for a trick of some kind," Hewes said. He and the rest of the men reined their horses to a halt, spreading out as they did so, their revolvers and rifles in hand.

"Bo, don't shoot! It's me, Jesse!" Burkett called out, seeing the dark figures strew out abreast before him.

Hearing the pained, stiff voice, Hewes said with a dark chuckle, "Everybody stand down. I'd recognize this beat-up sonsabitch's voice anywhere." He called out, not knowing Burkett was the only one left of the three-man scouting party, "All of yas get in here and tell me what's going on in there."

"This is *all* of us," said Burkett. The wagon rolled closer until he pulled back on the long brake handle and brought the rig to stop a few yards in front of Hewes.

"We heard shooting and was on our way," Hewes replied, stepping his horse forward to meet him. "What do you mean that's all of yas?" He craned his neck for a better look in the pale moonlight. "Where's Web and Mitchum?"

"They're lying back here dead," said Burkett, giving a toss of his battered head toward the wagon bed behind him.

Hewes and the men gathered around the wagon, looked in and saw not only Web and Mitchum, but the other three dead gunmen as well. "For God's sake," Hewes exploded. "Who is this drifter?"

"He's no drifter," said Burkett. "The son of a bitch is a straight-up lawman."

"What makes you say that?" Hewes asked, already turning away from the dead and looking at Burkett, seeing the bloody, swollen chin.

"He told me so," said Burkett. "I figure he's got no reason to lie about it." He winced at the pain throbbing in his face.

"Why are you still alive?" Hewes asked in a demanding tone.

Burkett sounded humiliated, saying, "He said he needed somebody to drive the wagon."

"That does it. We're riding in and finishing him off once and for all," said Hewes.

"Wait," said Burkett, "hear me out. This man wants all of us dead. He knows about the gold and he wants it for himself."

"What?" said Hewes. "How does he know? Did you tell him?"

"Hell no, Bo, you know me better than that," said Burkett. "But he knows; take my word on it. He said he was out at your place and saw everything being set up in the big barn."

"Jesus . . ." Hewes fell silent in grim contemplation, realizing someone had slipped past his men and spied on his operation. This wasn't going to sit well with Jake Goshen. Hewes had taken the responsibility for keeping the gold smelter a secret. He cut a glance toward Dean "Quick Draw" Vincent, who had sat staring in silence.

But now Vincent nudged his horse forward. He stopped beside Hewes and looked down at the bodies. "This drifter has seen our whole setup?"

"All that means is that we have to kill him before he starts any more trouble for us," said Hewes.

Burkett continued. "He says he aims to have that gold, and he aims to kill you firsthand. Says we can ride in and face him, and he'll kill you there. Or he'll ride out and kill you in your own front yard. It makes no difference to him."

"This is only one man we're talking about?" Hewes inquired.

"That's all I saw," said Burkett, sounding like a man beaten down and resolved to defeat. "That crazy she-male Jane Crowly is with him. She's prouder than a game rooster over all this. Other than Crowly, I believe he's all alone there—not that it seems to bother him any." He touched his fingertips gently to his throbbing chin. "I have to admit he's the fastest man I've ever seen when it comes to gun handling."

"You're easily impressed, Burkett," Hewes said in an angry voice, jerking his horse around toward the rest of the men. "All right, everybody heard it. This drifter thinks he's bigger than all of us together. He thinks he can take our gold from us, like we're a bunch of newcomers or something!" His voice rose as he spoke. "Can he do it? Are we going to *let* him do it?"

"Hell no," said a voice among the men.

"*Hell no*, is right," said Hewes. He settled down and said to Max Cafferty, "Take half the men and ride in and kill this son of a bitch. I'm riding back with Vincent and the other half to make sure this lawman didn't draw across the river while some other lawdogs snuck in on us."

"Hold it," said Quick Draw Vincent. "If this man is as fast as we're hearing he is, I want to meet him face-to-face." He looked at Max the Ax and said, "Any objections?"

Cafferty only shrugged.

"But what about Goshen?" said Hewes. "He'll want to know why you're not with me."

Vincent gave him a smug grin. "Tell him I had to take a few minutes, ride into Banton and do what the rest of yas can't seem to get done."

Chapter 22

———

Shaw stood at the bar in a dim glow of light from an overhead lantern. He stared into an unopened bottle of rye, his hands spread along the edge of the bar. "Tell them I'm a lawman. Tell them it's been a long night and it ain't over yet," he said over his shoulder to Wheatis Buckley, who stood, hat in hands, beside Jane Crowly a few feet away.

"I'm—I'm afraid that simply won't do," said the nervous barber, kneading his hat brim. "These good people demand answers. Their street has been littered with dead outlaws. They have been cowering in their homes this entire night."

"Where the hell else would they have been?" Jane cut in, giving him a curious stare.

"You keep out of this, Janie," Buckley said to her, his demeanor turning prickly. "This is just the sort of thing a wom—a *person* like you thrives on. But the rest of us aren't here to see how low we can sink or how hard and deviated we can live."

"*Deviated?*" Jane said, turning prickly herself. "Just

what do you mean, *a person* like me?" she demanded.
"What the hell *sort* of person am I?"

"I'm sure I wouldn't want to speculate," the barber
said, sorry he'd mentioned it and trying hard to bypass
the subject altogether. To Shaw he said, "And what
about those other two men lurking in the alleyways.
Who are they?"

"They're lawmen too," Shaw said flatly, offering
nothing more on the matter.

"Lawmen indeed," said Buckley. "If you truly are a
lawman, like I myself am, then where is your badge?"
As he spoke he thumbed the tin badge he had pinned
on the lapel of his coat.

"I'm not that kind of lawman," Shaw said, repeating
what he'd earlier told the outlaws in the street. He kept
his eyes on the full bottle of rye. "But since you are
wearing a badge, and do seem bent on seeing the law
upheld, go grab your shotgun and whatever rifle or
six-shooter you can find. We'll deal you in this hand."

Buckley's face tightened in fear. "I will not partici-
pate in some government endeavor to stir up trouble
along our western border. This town makes its liveli-
hood from both sides of the border. We know terrible
things go on along this border, but why must we dwell
on all this negativism?"

"Go home and get some sleep, *barber*," Shaw said,
not wanting to talk about it, knowing better than to
think he might change Buckley's mind. "Leave the
killing to the *kind of lawman* I am. Tomorrow you can
get up and run your business." He gave a thin smile.
"Even get up and wear your badge all around if it suits
you."

Seized by frustration, the barber cursed under his breath. His hands trembled so bad that he dropped his hat onto the dusty floor. Jane reached down and snatched it up before he could. She brushed it and handed it to him with a sharp grin. "Here's your hat. Now get the hell out of here before we lose our tempers."

Buckley clenched his teeth. But he snatched his hat from her hand and shoved it down onto his head. Turning stiffly on his heel, he walked out the door and into the flicker of oil pots. In the east the first rays of sunlight glowed silver beneath the distant horizon. "Why's he complaining?" said Jane, stepping over beside Shaw at the bar. "He got paid for attending the dead outlaws. Hell, he'll probably get paid for attending some more before this is over."

"He's like lots of folks," said Shaw. "He doesn't want to see a problem until somebody comes to fix it. . . . Then he blames them instead of the ones causing it."

Jane studied his face from the side, seeing how intently he stared at the dark, rich whiskey. "You ain't going to start drinking on us, are you?"

"If I am, are you going to talk me out of it?" Shaw replied.

"Well, I reckon I would try," Jane said.

Taking a breath, Shaw reached out and pulled the cork from the bottle. Jane watched him intently. He picked up a clean shot glass from a row of clean glasses stacked upside down along the inside edge of the bar. At the far end of the bar a bartender sat dozing on a tall ladder-back stool.

"Save your breath," Shaw said quietly. He filled the shot glass, corked the bottle, then slid the drink over in front of Jane. "Once I'm sober, I don't go around craving it. Whiskey doesn't tell me who I am," he said as if he'd long and carefully considered it and knew the answer. "I drink it when I don't want to know."

"Well . . . I'm glad to hear that, I reckon," Jane said quietly. She wrapped her gloved fingers around the shot glass and stared at him. *Fast Larry Shaw, the fastest gun alive . . .* She didn't want to become the voice of influence one way or another on a matter as deep and complex as this man's inner demons. After a moment she picked up the glass, turned it up and tossed it back in one shot. She let out a whiskey hiss.

Shaw stepped back from the bar. "Sometimes I wish I did have a craving for it," he said, his right hand resting on the big Colt on his hip. "I could say I felt something for *something.*"

Jane wiped the back of her gloved hand across her lips. She had to say something. Hell, it was not her nature to keep silent, not when someone was lost in the dark and a word from her might guide them, she told herself. "What about the widow?" she said. "Didn't you feel something with her, even if it was only for a little while? 'Cause sometimes a *little while* is all we can hope for." She shrugged a buckskin-fringed shoulder. "Hell, we're lucky to get it at all."

"I don't feel it now," Shaw said. His voice took on a slight bitterness as he added, "If I don't feel it now, I expect I never did."

"Whoa now, this ain't the time to go getting dark and morose on me," she said.

Shaw stopped before turning to walk out the door. "Are you going to be around?"

"What do you mean?" Jane asked. "I said I'd stick with you fellows. I meant it."

"I mean after?" Shaw asked.

"Yeah, I thought I might, if I'm not dead," she said. Her face reddened. "Are you wanting me to?"

Shaw didn't answer; he turned and walked away.

"You've heard what they all call me, what they all say about me, haven't you?" she called out.

Shaw stepped out the door and disappeared into the flicker of the oil pots.

"I'm not saying it's true," she called out, raising her voice to the outside. "But I'm not saying it ain't either."

When Shaw was out of sight, she pulled the cork and poured herself another drink. "Barkeep!" she said toward the dozing man. "Get over here!"

"What now, Jane?" the bartender said in a sleepy voice. He stood up and walked to where she stood leering at him from across the bar, above the shot glass of rye whiskey. A drop of whiskey dripped from the glass; he reached out with a damp bar towel and wiped it up.

"There's a fight coming, that's what, you pig-nosed turd," she said.

Used to her insults, the bartender ignored her pet name for him. "It's none of my business," he said. "I'll sell drinks to the winners."

Jane gave him a look of pure scorn. "Give me the shotgun you keep down there." She nodded at the bar top.

"What for?" the bartender asked. "You've already got a gun." He gestured a nod himself, at the Colt shoved down in her waistband.

"Did you not hear me, or are you just being belligerent?" she asked in an angry voice. She drew the Colt and pointed it at him.

He reached down, pulled out a shotgun by its barrel and handed it to her butt first, shaking his head. "There, don't lose it."

"Well, I'll do my best," she said, checking the short-barreled gun and shoving it up under her arm.

In the grainy darkness the gunmen had spread out silently around the small town. Dean Vincent and Max Cafferty waited while the rest of the men hitched their horses to trees and posts and crept along alleys and darkened side streets.

Cafferty turned and looked at Vincent as the arrogant gunslinger struck a match and lit a thin black cigar. "They saw that sure as hell," Cafferty said.

"So?" Vincent blew a stream of smoke and said sidelong to him, "Don't you suppose they know we're coming by now?"

"No need in shouting it out to them," Cafferty countered. "Our men are in there, trying to take up a position without being seen."

"To hell with the men," said Vincent, blowing another stream of smoke. "This is not something you and these gunmen are going to fix. It's all going to come down to him and me, man to man, one on one." He let go another thin stream of smoke and murmured studiously, repeating himself in Spanish, "*Hombre tripular, uno en uno. . . .*"

Cafferty eyed him dubiously. "You take that name Quick Draw awfully serious, don't you?"

"Yes, I do." Vincent gave a thin smile, staring straight ahead. "So should you."

"Maybe it's time somebody—" Cafferty's words stopped half-finished as he saw the Colt appear in Vincent's hand, cocked and pointed at his belly.

"Time somebody, *what*?" Vincent asked pointedly.

Cafferty stared at him, measuring his words, not giving an inch. "I came here to kill a sumbitch who's out to cause us trouble and cost us our gold, Vincent. Do you aim to stop me from doing that?"

"No, go help yourself," said Vincent, giving a wag of his gun barrel toward the town, the flickering oil pot–lit street in front of them. "I'll be along when it comes time to kill this bummer."

"*Lawman*, is what he told Burkett," Cafferty corrected him.

"*Bummer*, says I." Vincent gave a short, confident grin and gave another wag of his gun barrel.

Cafferty nudged his horse forward onto the dirt street. His and Vincent's job was to call the man down onto the street, into the open, where the rest of the men could strike from the cover of darkness. But now he would have to go it alone, not knowing if Vincent was really looking for a one-on-one fight, or if he was just finding himself a way to back out altogether.

All of this over one damn man, Cafferty told himself. Riding forward at a slow walk, he saw the dark figure step out into the middle of the dirt street facing him. *All right, let him have it,* he said to himself; and he nailed his spurs to his horse's sides and sped forward, rifle in hand, cocked and ready.

Shaw saw the lone rider coming, heard him let out a loud yell. But he knew the rider was only here to draw him out for the kill. No problem, Shaw thought, here he was. He only sidestepped slightly as gunfire exploded from the darkened doorways, alleys and side streets. From a rooftop above him he heard Dawson's Winchester go to work, shot after shot, the bullets probing the darkness like some night creatures thirsting for blood.

Max Cafferty saw shots streak orange-blue in the grainy darkness. "Kill this sonsabitch!" he screamed, firing as he raced forward, knowing that the lone figure should have already been shot down, or at least driven to cover by the hail of bullets. But that wasn't the case, and it was too late for him to change things, he thought. In the course of a split second he saw Shaw's gunshot blossom in a fiery circle before him. The bullet sliced through the air between his horse's lowered ears and hit him squarely in the center of his chest.

Seeing the horse and rider tumble forward, Shaw turned to his next target, a gunman crouched down in a doorway straight across the street from him. He fired as a bullet from another direction zipped past his head. His shot picked the rifleman up in the doorway and flung him through the large window beside him.

In the street, Cafferty's horse rolled back up onto its

hooves and raced away wildly. But Cafferty's body had flown forward and knocked out a wooden support post beneath a long boardwalk overhang. The overhang crashed to the ground in a billowing cloud of dust. The barber's battle-weary cat shot across the street with a long loud screech from beneath the boardwalk where it had been hiding.

From his perch atop the roofline, Dawson shot a rifleman as the man stepped into the open and took aim at Shaw. The bullet pounded the gunman backward to the ground. From his position in an alley across the street from Shaw, Caldwell shot at a gunman and missed when the man dove behind a stack of shipping crates out front of a mercantile store.

"Look out, Jed!" Shaw shouted, seeing two riflemen step forward and fire. Having stepped forward himself into the light of an oil pot in order to make his shot, Caldwell ducked back. But he wasn't quick enough. The two riflemen fired at once before Shaw's Colt silenced one and Dawson's rifle nailed the other.

As the two fell dead on the ground, Caldwell jerked sidelong when one bullet hit him high in his shoulder and the other sliced through his upper thigh. Seeing the lawman fall to the boardwalk as more bullets sought him out, Jane ran forward shouting a string of profanities at the hidden gunmen.

"I've got you covered, Undertaker! I've got you covered!" she shouted and cried, grabbing Caldwell and nestling him to her flat buckskinned bosom as if protecting a child. She waved the shotgun back and forth. "Stay back, you sonsabitches!" she screamed.

But a gunman named Lem Wright rushed in from out of nowhere and shouted, "Turn him loose, Jane. I'm killing him!"

"No!" she screamed. She swung the shotgun around one-handed, ready to fire. But a rifle shot from Dawson bored through the middle of Wright's back and sent him falling over atop Jane and Caldwell. "I would have shot him!" Jane bellowed through her tearful blood-splattered eyes. "I was going to shoot! He didn't think I'd shoot him! But I would!" She rocked back and forth, Caldwell pressed against her breast.

Shaw turned in time to see Bennie Ford running toward him from twenty feet away, a Colt in his hand. One shot spun Ford around and dropped him dead in the dirt, a bloody mist streaked in the air. From the roofline, Dawson levered a fresh round into his rifle chamber and searched the grainy darkness for a target. He found none. But listening, he heard the sounds of hoofprints racing away from behind the building along the dirt street.

"They're pulling back," Shaw called out, also hearing the horses' hooves.

"We're going after them," Dawson called down in reply. He turned and hurried across the tin roof, to a ladder he'd leaned up against the back of the building.

Shaw dropped the spent cartridges from his Colt into the dirt street and pulled six bullets from his gun belt in order to reload. Before he'd managed to get the first bullet into the gun, he froze when he heard the voice call out from thirty feet away, "We're not all gone, Fast Larry Shaw. I'm still here."

Shaw looked at Dean Vincent and said quietly,

"Quick Draw, what are you doing riding with this bunch of buzzard bait?"

"They weren't buzzard bait until they come upon you, Fast Larry," he said, stepping forward, a slight grin on his chiseled, cold face.

"Nobody calls me Fast Larry anymore, Vincent." Shaw shrugged. "How'd you know it was me, anyway?"

"The body count," he said, with the same slim grin on his face.

Shaw let out a breath. Was this it? Had it come to him this way, at the end of the fight he'd just won, a time when he least expected it? Not that he minded, he told himself. But he had been sober long enough that the world didn't look as bad as usual. *Well, what the hell . . . ?* This was what he went around wishing for most of the time. He had no complaints.

"You've got me cold, Vincent," he said. "You caught me with an unloaded gun in my hand." He turned the empty Colt and the loose bullets in his hand so Vincent could see. He heard running footsteps behind him and he said without looking back, "Stay out of it, Dawson. This doesn't concern you."

Dawson stopped, so did Jane, who stood with Caldwell leaning against her, his arm looped over her shoulder. Blood dripped freely down Caldwell's thigh. Vincent looked back and forth at them. After a moment of contemplation, he took a draw on his black cigar and said to Shaw, "Load up, Fast Larry. This is a fair fight. You know me. I won't have it any other way."

Shaw gave him a nod of appreciation. "Anything you say, Quick Draw." He took his time, putting one bullet after another into the big Colt. "I always knew you were fast. The fastest I ever saw, to the best of my recollection."

"Oh yeah, I am at that," Vincent said, his natural arrogance coming upon him. "I always thought you ducked me two or three times back when you was building yourself a reputation, *the Fastest Gun Alive*."

"Did I?" Shaw asked, almost apologetically. "I didn't mean to."

"Well, it seemed to me like you did," said Vincent, taking a moment to air his past grievances before the killing began. "That time in El Paso . . . that day in Hurrah Town . . . Eagle Pass." He took another step and stopped and spread his feet shoulder width apart. "But not this time, eh, Fast Larry?"

"Nope, not this time," said Shaw. He raised his Colt and fired, so quickly that Vincent didn't know what hit him until he sank to his knees and saw the smoking revolver in Shaw's hand.

"Ohhh . . ." The gunman dropped his Colt and gripped his chest with both hands, knowing he had only seconds left to live. "I . . . meant . . . holster your gun," he gasped.

"Oh, did you?" Shaw stared down at him. "You should have been more specific." He cocked the smoking Colt and added, "How dare you interrupt a gun battle just to prove how fast you are."

"I . . . always thought . . . I was faster than you," he said, gasping his few last breaths.

"Really? I didn't," Shaw said. He raised the smoking Colt and shot him through the forehead. Vincent flipped backward, dead in the dirt. Jane caught herself looking away from the spray of blood and brain matter.

"Let's get Caldwell patched up and ready to ride," said Dawson, stepping over to Jane and helping her seat Caldwell on the edge of a water trough. "We can't give them time to get ready for us."

Chapter 23

Mean Myra Blount rode hard across the rolling sand hills, leading Anson and Wallick as the sound of distant gunfire resounded from the streets of Banton. By the time first light sparkled and crested on the eastern curve of the earth, they had ridden upward into the line of hills separating the desert floor from the Fire River valley.

"Myra, we've got to stop!" said Anson as they eased their pace a little on a rough, rocky trail. "We can't afford to kill these animals. Besides, I thought I heard hooves back there coming along the trail toward us."

"I heard them too," Myra said. "So what?"

"So we best get off the trail and take cover, see who it is, and let them ride on past us," said Anson.

"Have you always been so damned scared of every little thing?" Myra asked. She nudged her horse and speeded it up.

Anson slowed and cursed under his breath. Seeing Wallick hurrying to keep up with her, he called out, "Get back here, Wilbur! I'm in charge here, not her."

"What am I supposed to do?" Wallick asked with a troubled look, glancing back along the trail as he nudged his horse forward. "You're the one wanted to bring her along with us."

"Damn it!" said Anson, nudging his horse up alongside him. "We can't keep up this pace!" But he rode on.

A few minutes later, at first light, Anson's horse veered suddenly and slowed down on its own, taking on a limping, guarded gait. "Oh man, I gone and done it!" he said, stopping and dropping from his saddle. "This horse is done for." Ahead of him Wallick stopped and turned his horse to face him. From farther back on the trail the sound of hooves had grown closer.

Myra circled, rode back and looked down at him. "What now?" she asked tightly.

"He's gone on me," Anson said angrily. "I told you we couldn't keep it up."

"Oh? Wallick and I did," Myra said in a critical, accusing tone. "Do you ride much?"

"Jesus, woman," Anson said, trying to hold his temper. He noted the rifle in Myra's hands. He had learned enough about her to realize she would most likely use it. "Let's not discuss it right now." He gestured back toward the sound of hooves and reached a hand up to her. "Give me a lift."

"Why?" Myra said, making no attempt to reach down to him. Instead, she sidestepped the horse farther away from him.

"Whoever's coming back there, they'll be here any minute," Anson said, worried about the sound of hooves speeding up toward them. "We're going to have to double up for a while!"

"No, we're not," said Myra. She also gestured toward the hooves. "You have a gun. You can get one of their horses and catch up to us. Wilbur and I are riding on."

"Jesus! Wilbur! Give me a lift!" said Anson, appealing to the big, cumbersome gunman.

Wallick started to nudge his horse back toward him, but Myra put her horse between the two in the middle of the trail. "Uh-uh, don't you do it, Wilbur!" she warned, gripping the rifle stock as if she knew how to use it. "He knew better than to let his horse go lame."

"Jesus, I never let him," Anson protested. "We were traveling too fast!"

"Then you should've slowed down," Myra said in a firm voice. She gigged her horse toward Wallick. "Come on, big fellow. It's you and me now."

"I'm sorry, Booth," said Wallick, still glancing back at the sound of approaching horses. "You can catch up to us." He turned beside the woman and the two rode away, Myra's tied-back hair flipping up and down with the rhythm of her horse's tail.

"How the hell . . . ?" Anson spread his hands in helplessness as the two faded off into the silver morning gloom. But he had no time to stand still and ponder his predicament. Hearing the hooves getting steadily closer, he jerked the lame animal by its reins and pulled it off the trail, into a tangle of brush and bracken.

From his hiding spot, Anson watched as the four riders slowed to a halt and then stopped on the trail in the grainy half-light of dawn. The first rider stepped down from his saddle and stooped and examined the fresh hoofprints on the ground. Steam billowed from their horses' nostrils.

Anson drew his Colt and held it at his side out of habit. There was nothing he could do here, he told himself, four against one, him on foot, them mounted and prepared for anything. But he wasn't going to give up hope, not as long as there was a chance he could get one of their horses under him and make a run for it.

He watched the man stand up from the fresh tracks, follow them to the edge of the trail and stand facing his direction. Even as Anson considered what he would have to do, he froze as the man called out, "Booth Anson! It's me, Juan Facil Lupo. Walk out here with your hands over your head."

"What the hell . . . ?" Anson stood stunned for a moment. Then he shook his head to clear it and said, "All right, Easy John, don't shoot. I'm coming out."

Leading his lame horse up onto the trail, his hands above his head, he said, "Don't worry about me getting in the wind. This horse has gone lame on me." Without lowering his hands, he let the horse's reins fall from his fingertips.

From atop their horses, Maynard Lilly and the three bounty hunters, Iron Head, Merle Oates and Bobby Freedus stared down at him, stone-faced. Anson only glanced at them in passing and said to Lupo, "If you don't mind saying, how'd you know it was me?"

Lupo only stared at him. But Maynard Lilly spit and ran a hand across his lips and said, "Your horse's shoe brand, idiot."

Anson looked down at the prints in the dirt. "Is that it?" he asked with a puzzled look. "All this time you kept track of me by knowing my horse's shoes?"

Lupo didn't answer. He continued to stare. He

didn't mention that earlier he had spotted Anson, Wallick and the woman on the trail below them.

"I was coming back, you know," Anson said, testing his situation a little. "That's all Wallick and I talked about, was getting back with you boys and getting this whole thing cleared up about the stolen gold."

Lupo remained rigid and silent, his eyes burning into Anson's.

Anson looked up at the others, then back to Lupo. "The fact is, we managed to pick up some information about the gold, where it's at . . . who's got it, and whatnot."

Still the silent stare.

"We was on our way there. Thank God I ran into you fellows, I didn't know what Wilbur and I would have done without all of yas backing us." He tried a weak grin. "It's kind of like we traveled one big ole circle and came right back to yas."

"Are you a man who prays?" Lupo asked.

Anson didn't reply; instead he went on as if he hadn't heard him. "A fellow by the name of Hewes has the gold at his place, across Fire River, not too far from here. Hell, lucky for you I can lead you there."

"You can lead us there?" Lupo asked.

"I sure can. Like I said, that's where we were headed," said Anson.

Lupo raised a finger and said, "Stop and weigh your answer very carefully before you give it." His eyes burned with resolve. "Have you ever been there?"

Anson shrugged and said with no regard for Lupo's advice, "Well no. But hell, that won't keep me from leading—"

The rifle lying across Iron Head's lap bucked once, then fell back into its resting place, a curl of smoke rising in a coil from the tip of its barrel. Beside Iron Head, Lilly asked Lupo, "Do you believe any of it, Easy John?"

"Yes, I believe it," Lupo said. "It was the confession of a condemned man. I was his confessor." He stared at Anson's body lying sprawled atop a stiff pile of dry brush. "He told us the truth, or as much of it as he was capable of telling."

Turning to Anson's lame horse, Lupo drew his pistol and cocked its hammer. "I am sorry, *caballo pobre*," he said. "But tonight the wolves will eat you. It is better for you that they eat you *dead* instead of *alive*." He fired one shot between the horse's eyes, then holstered his revolver and stepped up into his saddle.

But before he could lead the men forward, a voice from behind them said quietly, "Hello the trail, Juan Facil."

Turning as one, the mounted men saw Cray Dawson and Lawrence Shaw standing in the middle of the trail, their rifles cocked and ready in their hands. Glancing past the two, Lupo saw a gun barrel lying over a rock pointed at him and his men. On the other side of the trail, another rifle barrel stared at him from behind a sparsely branched juniper.

"Hello yourself, Marshal Dawson," Lupo said. Seeing the two on foot, Lupo knew they had led their horses up quietly and came prepared for a fight with whomever they found waiting for them around the turn in the trail. "I bet you are wondering why we killed this man," he said, sweeping a hand toward Anson's body atop the pile of brush, bobbing slightly on a morning breeze.

"The question crossed our minds," said Dawson. Both he and Shaw took a step forward. The other four mounted men returned their stares. "But I defer to your judgment," Dawson said, "knowing we're all after the same thing." Again his eyes went to the mounted men, this time to the bounty hunters. He added, "Unless you've changed the nature of your business since last I saw you."

"No," said Lupo, "the bounty hunters are with us because we are all after the same thing." He motioned again toward Anson. "He and another man were scouting for us, but they ran away and left us without horses or guns. That is what brought him to his present condition. The other man and a young woman are headed the same direction as we are."

"I understand," said Dawson. He motioned for Jane and Caldwell to come forward, now that he and Shaw saw who was here. "And are you men headed where I think you're headed, Easy John?" Dawson asked.

"Only if you think we are headed for the place across Fire River," said Lupo, watching Dawson's face for a reaction. For all he knew, Dawson and his men could be out to find the gold and keep it for themselves. "I hear the stolen gold is there."

"We heard the same thing," Dawson admitted, now that he heard Lupo admit that he had the same information. Again he let his eyes go to the bounty hunters, giving them a wary look.

"Don't worry about us," said Oates. "We're out for bounty."

"Not that we wouldn't take a stab at disappearing with the gold if we got a chance," said Freedus, eyeing Shaw, the big low-slung Colt, the familiar face.

"But we don't want to keep looking over our shoulders for the Mexican army the rest of our lives," said Iron Head.

"Are you who I'm thinking you are?" Freedus asked Shaw. "Are you Fast Lar—"

"I'm Lawrence Shaw. I don't go by Fast Larry anymore," Shaw said, cutting him off.

"Does everybody else know one another?" Dawson asked as Jane and Caldwell came forward, Jane leading their horses. Caldwell limped forward with a trouser leg cut off and a bandage around his thigh. Another bandage covered his shoulder beneath his open shirt front.

Both sides exchanged nods. "You were the cause of the gunfire we heard coming from Banton in the night," Lupo said. He offered a short, wizened smile. "It is unusual for me to see you and the Undertaker on your own side of the border."

"We go where it takes us," Dawson said without apology, "same as you."

Lupo sighed. "It is true, I am spending more and more time here where I don't belong. But I'm afraid it will be so until the border is secured from those criminals who use it to their advantage."

"Do you expect that to be anytime soon?" Jane asked, looking up at Lupo with a hand on her thin hip. "Those of us trying to live here could use a little encouraging word on the matter."

"*Sí*, but you will get no encouragement from me,

Jane Crowly," Lupo said. "I see no end of the trouble in sight. The border will remain wild and wide open so long as there are powerful men on either side who profit from it being so."

"I'd love to discuss it with you, Easy John," Jane said, "but as you can see, I've taken to tending horses for the law." She jiggled the sets of reins in her hands.

Dawson said, "Do you suppose we could ride across Fire River together, trust one another enough to get this job done?" As he spoke he looked at the bounty hunters again, letting it be clearly known where his doubts lay.

"We'll behave if you will," Oates offered. "I told you, all we want is the bounty due on any of these rascals, if nobody objects to it."

"None here," said Dawson, stepping over and taking his reins from Jane. "They're getting ready for us about now. Some of them made a run for it last night, but we managed to trim their numbers."

"Good for you," said Lupo, turning his horse on the trail. "We will make our plans along the way."

"Suits us," said Dawson, as Jane and Shaw helped Caldwell up into saddle. He waited until all three had mounted and gathered behind him, then rode forward and joined Lupo in the lead.

Behind Dawson, Lupo and the others, Jane sidled in between Shaw and Caldwell. In a guarded voice, she asked them both, "Do we really trust these buzzards?"

"No, we don't," Shaw said, but gave her a thin smile and added, "But who do you trust along these borderlands?"

"Good point," she whispered, the shotgun from the

saloon gripped firmly in her gloved hand. She looked at Caldwell's pale face in the thin morning light and asked him, "Undertaker, how're you holding up?"

But Caldwell didn't answer. He cut her a sidelong glance and stared grimly at the trail ahead. ·

Chapter 24

A gunman named Eddie Sheves, who had run away from the fighting at Banton, arrived at the edge of Fire River at the same time as Myra and Wilbur Wallick. Caught by surprise, Myra cursed under her breath, "Damn it to hell, Wilbur, why didn't you see him coming?"

"I don't know." Wallick sat staring, not knowing what to do.

Myra composed herself quickly and smiled as the man came riding up on them in the silver morning haze, his rifle in hand. "You-hoo," she said, waving a hand back and forth. "I sure hope you're not some highwayman come to rob me or have your way with me!"

Sheves stared curiously until he got closer and recognized both her and Wallick. "Myra? Mean Myra Blount?" He gave a bemused half smile. "What the blazes are you doing out here?"

Seeing how lathered and steamy his horse was, Myra thought quickly and said, "The same as you, no doubt. I came here to get some peace and quiet—all that shooting and killing going on in town. Lord, what a mess!"

Sheves gave a nod to Wallick and eased his hand on his rifle stock. "A mess don't come close," he said. "But that doesn't explain you riding all the way out here. Hewes ain't fond of company, you know." He eyed Wallick.

"Well, I'll swear," said Myra, acting suddenly hurt and put out. "He told me anytime I wanted a place to stay, I was welcome here. I hope he meant it. I hate to think I rode all this way . . ."

"Pay me no mind, neither one of yas," said Sheves, taking off his tall Montana-crown hat and wiping his wet brow. "I've been running hard all night. If I don't miss my guess, there's going to be law swarming here before the day's over. You might want to ask yourselves if this is a place you want to be. Especially you, Wilbur. I know you've had your ups and downs with the law of late."

"Obliged for telling us," Wallick said, "but I promised Myra I'd escort her, so I'm going to do it."

"And I'm going to be grateful to him from now on for doing it," Myra pointed out.

"Yeah . . . ?" Sheves pondered the benefits of having the gratitude of a young woman like Mean Myra. "How can I help too?" he asked.

"Well, since you asked, Eddie," Myra said with a warm smile, "maybe you'll lead us across the river and show us the shortest way to the hacienda?"

Sheves considered, then looked back along the trail behind him. "Well, yeah, I can do that. But let's hurry it

up. This is not a place to be right now. There'll be gunmen running here all morning, half spooked. A person
could get shot by mistake—that's something that's
concerned me my whole life."

"We'll just have to be careful, then, won't we,
Eddie?" Myra said.

"Yes, we will," he replied, returning her smile. "We
get to any of the trail guards you let me do all the
talking."

"Of course," Myra said. She gestured a hand toward
the river running before them and asked, "Shall we?"

They crossed the river before any more fleeing gunmen arrived from Banton. On the opposite side, Sheves
led them past a campsite where two riflemen sat sip-
ping coffee in the first light of morning. "Who's that
with you, Eddie?" one of the men asked without even
standing up.

"Boys, it's Myra, from town," said Sheves. "Hewes
invited her. This is Wilbur Wallick riding with her."

"Myra, Wilbur," said the men, touching their hat
brims toward them as they continued riding past them
at a walk.

"Morning, boys," Myra called out. Wallick only
touched his hat brim in return.

To Sheves one of the men said, "We're told there's
going to be law coming from Banton. Three men already rode in a while ago, said it didn't go well for
Max and some of the others there."

"You heard right," said Sheves, riding on. "Keep an
eye peeled. I expect they'll be riding here before the
day is over."

Once past the guards, Sheves gave Myra a grin and a wink and said, "See how easy it is, when you know somebody. I hope you don't forget what I did for you."

"How could I, Eddie?" Myra said. She looked all around, noting they were passing through a stretch of sparse woods and brush. "If you wasn't in a hurry, I'd do something real nice for you right now."

Sheves stopped his horse with a sudden jolt and said in rushed voice, "I've got a few minutes far as that goes."

"Oh good!" she said with a playful laugh. "Help me down, and carry me over to those trees."

Sheves gave Wallick a look; Wallick only shrugged and sat with his wrists crossed on his saddle horn. He watched as the two disappeared around a cottonwood tree and a wide stand of juniper and dried brush. "Is here all right?" Sheves asked, already letting her stand down from his arms and loosening his gun belt.

"Yes, this is fine," said Myra. She stopped him from opening his fly and said, "Take your shirt off, Eddie."

"My shirt, why?" he asked.

"I like feeling you against me," Myra said with a pout. "Is that so bad?"

"Naw, that ain't bad," Sheves said, grinning. He tossed his tall hat to the ground, unbuttoned the bib of his shirt and lifted it over his head. Before the shirt cleared his face, he felt a deep, harsh burn run across his throat. "Oh God," he said, or tried to say, in a gargling voice, feeling the rush of hot blood spill out and cover his chest.

"Careful, Eddie, watch the trousers," Myra said,

standing beside him and bending him forward as the blood spewed. Sheves struggled to get the shirt the rest of the way off, over his head. . . .

Moments later, Wallick stared as he saw the tall-crowned hat bobbing out of the brush. "Where's Myra?" he asked, looking farther back toward the small clearing beneath the cottonwood.

"Right here," Myra said, pushing up the hat brim and grinning up at Wallick.

Wallick looked confused for a moment. "Where's Sheves?" he asked, searching the brush in the early light.

"Sheves is no longer with us," Myra said.

It dawned on him what she must've done. "Did you—I mean, is he—?"

"Yes, I *did*, and yes he *is*," said Myra, stepping up into Sheves' saddle. She took the reins to her horse and jerked the animal up alongside her, then looked at Wallick from beneath the wide hat brim. "Are you ready?"

"Aw hell, Sheves was not a bad fellow," Wallick said with a sorrowful look.

Myra sidled over to him. "Listen to me, Wilbur. You and I are going to leave here with enough gold to move to England and build ourselves a castle. Do you understand? Only, you've got to pay attention and do what I tell you. Will you do that?"

"I don't want no castle," Wallick said.

"But you do want gold, don't you?" said Myra. "You do want plenty of this?" She gestured a nod toward her lap.

"Yes, I do," Wallick said, turning a bit breathless at the thought.

"All right then, pay attention," said Myra. "We're past the guards. All we've got to do now is find the gold, figure out how to take it and watch for our chance."

"You think it's that easy?" Wallick asked.

"Yes, it's that easy," said Myra. "So let's not go making it any harder than it is." She turned the horse and nudged it forward, leading the other horse behind her. Wallick followed with a stunned look on his face.

The front yard of Hewes' hacienda had been hastily set up like a battle encampment. Two overturned wagons lay end to end, forming a barrier and firing position between the large house and anyone approaching from the direction of the river. When Myra and Wallick rode up and stopped and looked around, Hewes shouted at them from a front porch full of gunmen.

"What the hell are you waiting for, Sheves?" he said. "Get your horses around to the barn and see if Goshen needs you back there."

With the tall, crowned hat mantling her forehead, Myra gave a slight wave and nudged her horse toward the barn. As she and Wallick rode around the house, Hewes called out again, "Is that Wilbur Wallick riding with you?"

Wallick called back before Myra had to answer, "Yep, it's me, Bo. I ran into Sheves, thought you might need an extra gun out here."

Hewes called out, "Good man, Wilbur," and turned away toward three men he'd been talking to.

As they headed toward the barn, Myra nodded toward a stand of spindly pine thirty yards away.

"There's where we need to be," she said to Wallick under her breath. As they veered their horses away in the direction of the pine cover, she noted a large heavily loaded freight wagon sitting near the rear barn door.

Once inside the tree line, the two dropped from their saddles, hitched their horses to a dead, fallen pine and crept back to a pile of brush for a better look. "Do you think that's it?" Wallick asked in a whisper, staring at the freight wagon.

"I'm betting it is," Myra replied, studying the wagon. There were six horses hitched to it, and next to it, through the half-open rear barn door, she could see the workers moving about inside.

"Are we going to take off with it now?" Wallick asked, wearing a troubled expression on his face.

"Sure we are," Myra said. "That way we'd make it about ten feet before every gun on the place chopped us up like kindling."

"So we're going to wait?" Wallick asked.

Myra stared at him for a moment, realizing this was how it would always be with him around. Then she searched along a trail filled with hoof and wheel prints from the wagon riding in on it. "Come on, Wilbur," she said. "I've got a notion the wagon is going out the same way it came in. We'll get down along the trail and wait for it."

Inside the barn, Jake Goshen called a gunman named Grady Dotson to the side and said, "You and Weasel Joe get ready. We're slipping away from here in a few minutes when Hewes calls everybody together. We're going to leave without making any big deal of it."

Dotson looked at a row of three-pound gold ingots lying stacked on a wooden pallet on the dirt floor. "What about the stuff we already melted down?"

"Leave it," said Goshen. "Let it keep cooling. Leave the sacks of coins waiting over by the furnace too. It'll keep everybody busy in here while we cut out. The rest of the men are busy getting ready for the law coming."

"What about Hewes?" Dotson asked.

"Hewes and I planned it this way. He knows we've got to move this gold out of here," said Goshen. "We're just doing it without any fanfare. The less men knowing about it, the better. Now get Weasel Joe and be ready to slip out back. I'll meet you both at the wagon when the time comes."

Hidden in the trees, Myra and Wallick spent the next twenty minutes watching more harried gunmen arrive from the direction of the river. The gunmen straggled in, one, two and three at a time, looking back over their shoulders. Finally, they watched Hewes step out away from the porch and stand beside the overturned wagons. He raised a hand and called out, "I want all of yas right here where I can see you when I talk to you."

As the men gathered around Hewes, on cue Grady Dotson and Weasel Joe Karr walked out of the barn and stepped up into the big wagon. "Looks like Hewes might be drawing everybody's attention while these men slip away with the gold," Myra mused under her breath. "I reckon nobody trusts nobody here."

A moment later, Jake Goshen walked out of the barn, pitched a shotgun up to Weasel Joe and walked back to where his horses stood hitched to a fence rail.

"Yep, they're making a run with it," said Wallick. "I wonder how much gold is there."

Myra looked at him and said, "A lot, Wilbur—one hell of a lot, if it takes six horses and a freight to pull it down the trail."

"How are we going to get away with so damned much gold as that?" Wallick asked, now that he'd seen what was involved and the enormity of it began to sink in.

"We're taking as much as we can right now and hiding the rest for another time," said Myra. She looked off up into the low jagged hills. "We'll stash it somewhere up there. That's the best I can think of right at this minute."

"Think we might buy a place somewhere and raise some sheep?" Wallick asked.

"Sheep?" Myra gave him a look. "Don't start spending it just yet, Wilbur," she said. "We've got some serious business to take care of first." She watched the wagon and Goshen on horseback move away along the back trail. "Come on," she said, turning toward their horses, "we've got to get ahead of them, then get them to stop for us."

"How are we going to get them to stop for us?" Wallick asked, following close behind her.

"Damn it, Wilbur," she said, getting more put out with his constant questions, "I'm going to show them these!" She stopped suddenly and spun around facing him, the bib of the shirt open and her large firm round breasts squeezed together between her hands.

"Lord God!" said Wilbur, too stunned to move.

"There, you see how well these work? It stopped you, didn't it?"

Wilbur couldn't speak. He shook his head and followed her on to the horses. When they had mounted, they rode wide of the trail and circled through stretches of brush and trees until they had gotten over a mile ahead of the heavy slow-moving wagon. "This will do it," Myra said, looking all around at where they sat atop their horses at a blind turn in the trail. "We'll wait right here for them."

From the direction of Fire River, past Bowden Hewes' hacienda, the sound of gunfire suddenly erupted. "I'd say that's the lawmen from town meeting up with some of the trail guards," Myra speculated. They listened for a moment, the gunfire not letting up, but rather growing more steady, more intense. "This makes everything a little easier for us," she said. "With the lawmen on their backs they won't have time to run back here to see what the shooting's about."

"What do you want me to do?" Wallick asked.

"Get down off your horse. As soon as they round this turn, cut loose on them," she said with a grin. Reaching up, she buttoned the bib of her shirt. "I might not need you girls after all," she whispered down to her breasts.

On the trail, Jake Goshen turned in his saddle and looked back toward the sound of gunfire in the distance behind them. "Damn, Hewes," he growled, "this is all on his head." He turned forward and gigged his horse up alongside the wagon as Dotson maneuvered the heavy rig around the turn.

In the wooden seat beside Dotson, Weasel Joe sat with the shotgun lying loosely across his lap. "When this is over I ought to stick this shotgun in his ear and see what he's been using for brains—"

Before his words were complete, Wallick and Myra opened fire at a distance of ten feet. Wallick's first shot killed Weasel Joe where he sat. Myra's shot hit Goshen in the head, but it only grazed him and knocked him from his saddle. He hit the ground, knocked out cold. Dotson let the traces fall from his hands and grabbed for a Colt on his hip, but both Myra's and Wallick's next shots hit him dead center.

"Grab the horses!" Myra shouted. But she didn't wait to see if Wallick would make the move. Instead she flung herself from her saddle over onto the seat beside Weasel Joe's limp, bloody body. "Got them," she shouted, grabbing the traces and sitting back hard on them to keep the frightened horses from bolting out of control. "*Yiii-hiiii!* I was born for this kind of work!" she shouted with jubilation.

"I was getting them," Wallick said.

"You wasn't fast enough, Wilbur," she said in an excited voice. Looking down at the loaded wagon bed, she said, "Oh my God! We did it! We got the gold!" Then she dropped onto the seat, saying, "Grab my horse, Wilbur, the other horse too! Let's take all of *our* gold and get the hell out of here!" Half standing, she slapped the reins to the big horses' backs and put them up into a run across along the trail toward the hill line.

On the ground, Jake Goshen felt the ground rumble beneath him as consciousness returned to him slowly. "Damn it all!" he grumbled, lifting himself to his feet and standing, wobbling in place, watching the big wagon roll over a rise and out of sight. He jerked his Colt from his holster and started to fire just as the wagon appeared to be swallowed by the earth.

"Son of a bitch..." Goshen looked down at Dotson's body lying dead in the dirt; then he looked up at the rise of dust in the wagon's wake, feeling a striking pain inside his forehead like that of a hammer against an anvil. *Now what...?* He cupped his palm to the long, bleeding gash running above his right ear. Now he had to have a horse, he told himself, turning back toward the sound of gunfire beyond the hacienda.

Chapter 25

————

Before crossing Fire River, Dawson, Caldwell and Shaw, Jane Crowly, Juan Lupo and the bounty hunters had gathered at the edge of a trail where they could see fresh hoofprints headed down into the water. Looking from one face to the next, Dawson said to the others, "Shaw here is the only one of us who's seen the setup at Hewes' place. We need for him to make a straight run for the gold, get his eyes on it and not let it out of his sight. Any objections?" He looked at Juan Lupo.

"None," said Lupo. "But I doubt the gold will be there. They knew we were coming. They have had time to haul it away."

"Then I'll follow it," said Shaw. "It won't be hard to track, if the rest of you can keep Hewes' and Goshen's gunmen off my back."

"I say we all make a run for it, and grab it as quick as we can," said Bobby Freedus. Then, seeing Lupo's and the lawmen's eyes on him, he added, "I mean, get it and hold it until Easy John here arrives, so's he can take it all back to Mexico."

Lupo and Dawson exchanged a glance, as if neither had to warn the other about the bounty hunters. "Are we in agreement about keeping Shaw covered while he makes a run for Hewes' barn?"

"Yes, we are in agreement," Lupo said.

Turning to their horses and mounting, Shaw and Dawson watched Lupo swing up into his saddle. "I'd advise Easy John and the Scotsman to keep those three in front of them at all times," Dawson said just between the two of them as Jane helped Caldwell into his saddle.

"That's some good advice for you to follow too," Shaw said. "Once they get a whiff of that much gold, I've got a feeling it'll go to their heads. They won't even be able to trust each other." He swung up into his saddle, drew his rifle and checked it. Then he turned his horse and nudged it toward the river.

"We'll give you a few minutes' lead so you can get out of sight before the shooting starts," said Dawson. Shaw only raised a hand in acknowledgment and rode on.

Turning to Jane, Dawson said, "If you want to turn back or wait here, we'll all understand. It's your choice. This is not your fight."

"Well, thank you for telling me that," Jane said a little sarcastically. "What do you suppose I've been thinking about all the way here? What color dress I should wear to the next town dance?"

"I just thought I ought to say something," Dawson replied, realizing he'd made a mistake.

Jane made sure Caldwell had his reins in his good hand; then she swung up atop her horse and gave

Dawson a hard stare. "Are you through, then?" she asked.

Dawson only nodded.

Jane said to Caldwell, "Come on, Undertaker, you stick with me. You might need somebody to reload for you once we get across this river and all hell breaks loose."

The group waited until Shaw had crossed the river and ridden out of sight. Then Dawson and Lupo led the others across the cool, flowing water and bore right of where Shaw had disappeared into a narrow valley filled with scrub piñon and juniper bush.

They had ridden only a few hundred yards when they ran into a hail of gunfire coming from a higher trail alongside them. From the other side of the valley, Shaw heard the gunfire in the distance behind him, but he stuck to his task and rode on. Keeping deep in the cover of brush, deadfall and bracken, he didn't stop until he saw the woman's dress lying beneath a cottonwood tree.

When he nudged his horse forward he saw the body of Eddie Sheves lying facedown in the dirt, wearing only a pair of ragged long-john underwear. "Well, well," he said to himself, recalling Lupo had mentioned the man and a young woman riding ahead of them. "It looks like somebody found themselves a way in." He looked down at the fresh tracks on the ground for a moment, then nudged his horse along, following them.

At the trail where Dawson and the others had met the first round of gunfire, six riflemen had taken position behind the cover of rock on the hillsides. But after being pinned down for over a half hour, Dawson and Lupo refused to stay and fight them any longer. Instead, the two led Caldwell, Jane and the group of bounty bunters away at a hard run, feigning a retreat.

"We've got them running scared! Ride them down and kill them," a rifleman shouted, reaching his horse and throwing himself into the saddle.

But only a mile farther down the trail, Dawson, Lupo and the others slid to a halt, dropped from their saddles and sent Jane and Caldwell leading the horses to cover among the rocks.

Emboldened by the retreat, the riflemen gave chase, wanting to kill the intruders before they managed to reach the hacienda. They didn't realize they were riding into a trap until it was too late.

Dawson and the others lay low until the thunder of hooves was almost atop them. Then Juan Lupo rose and shouted, "Fire!" and the battle began anew.

Less than an hour later, Shaw lay atop a rise and looked down onto the hacienda sitting three hundred yards away. He had gained ground while the lawmen and bounty hunters fought it out across the hillsides. Behind him he had heard the renewed gun battle rage off and on as he'd ridden closer to Hewes' hacienda. Now, on the land below him, he saw two mounted gunmen racing away from the hillsides and he knew Dawson and the men had fought their way through Hewes' men.

They would be coming soon, he told himself, scooting back from the edge and standing up. From the hillsides he heard rifle fire start again and decided it was Dawson and the others chasing the gunmen back to their lair. He'd seen no sign of Hewes. In the front yard he'd seen the overturned wagons and riflemen scattered and positioned everywhere. *But no Hewes,* he said to himself, thinking it odd.

His job for now was not to confront the situation below, but rather get past the gunmen and find out if the gold was still at the barn.

Back to work, he told himself. He stepped up into the saddle and rode on, circling wide around the hillside before riding toward the hacienda from behind.

Jake Goshen had walked most of the way back to the hacienda when he spotted the lone rider moving stealthily down a game trail on the steep pine-covered hillside. "It's about damn time something came my way," he growled to himself, crouching down and taking cover behind a sun-bleached log alongside the trail. Pain pounded in his bullet-creased head.

As the speckled barb stepped off the hillside onto the rocky ground, Shaw caught a glimpse of the man crouched down out of sight. He stopped the barb but made no effort toward drawing his Colt. His Winchester lay across his lap. Yet, instead of picking the rifle up, he crossed his wrists on his saddle horn and remained that way as Goshen sprang up facing him, his Colt aimed and cocked.

"Got ya!" Goshen said. "Don't make a move." He took a step sideways from behind the log and said, "Throw the rifle down."

Without moving his hands from the saddle horn, Shaw gave a nudge of his thigh and caused the rifle to slide off his lap and land at his horse's hooves. "Who are you, anyway?" Goshen asked, noting Shaw's calm manner in the face of a cocked gun aimed at his chest.

"You first," Shaw said in a mild tone.

Goshen gave him a bemused look, surprised at the attitude. With the drop on the man, Goshen had nothing to fear. Nothing he said would ever leave this spot. He could pull the trigger anytime. "I'm Jake Goshen. Your turn."

"I'm Shaw," he said, almost grudgingly, on the outside chance that Goshen might have heard the name *Lawrence* mentioned in connection with everything that had gone on. As he spoke, gunshots began to erupt in the distance, out in front of the hacienda. Shaw gave a nod of his head toward the sounds. "Shouldn't you be back there, watching over the gold?"

"You're a cool hand, Shaw," Goshen said. "How come I've never seen you among Hewes' men?"

"Was you really looking for me?" Shaw shrugged, going along with whatever the man said, hoping to find out what he could about the gold.

Goshen gave a short, dark chuckle. "No, come to think of it." He touched a hand to his throbbing head. "The fact is I'm chasing after the gold right now." He gestured down at the wagon wheel tracks and hoofprints. "I'm going to need your horse to catch up to it." He wagged his gun barrel toward the ground. "Now jump down."

"Catch up to it?" Shaw made no effort to get down from the barb's saddle. "You mean you've managed to lose all that gold?"

"Son of a bitch!" Goshen's mood darkened fast. "I'd hoped I wouldn't have to kill you," he said. "But now I see that's not going to be the case." He raised his gun out at arm's length, almost leisurely, and had started to pull the trigger.

Shaw's Colt came out in a streak and fired. The shot hit Goshen high in his right shoulder and spun him backward to the ground. His gun flew from his hand. Shaw holstered his Colt, stepped down from his saddle and picked his Winchester up from the dirt. Taking his time, he looked the rifle over. Then he walked over to where Goshen had managed to right himself and sit up in the dirt. The wounded gunman was leaning back on his left hand. His right arm hung limp and bloody at his side.

"Shaw . . . ," Goshen said as if having given the name some thought. "I . . . get it," he said, his voice sounding strained and weak. "You're . . . Lawrence Shaw, aren't you? You're the drifter . . . who found Doc's body."

"Yep," Shaw nodded. "You're probably wondering why I didn't kill you just now."

"You want to know . . . about the gold . . . I figure," Goshen said, leaning forward off his left hand and grasping his bleeding shoulder with it. "I was taking it . . . to the widow's house. This trail leads right past there . . . back across the river."

"What about Hewes?" Shaw asked, getting an idea why he hadn't seen Hewes back at the hacienda.

"He cut out . . . on horseback, right after I . . . left with the wagon," said Goshen. "He'll be there . . . waiting for me."

"What happened to the wagon?" Shaw asked.

"The fact is, some whore from Banton . . . and Wilbur Wallick bushwhacked us . . . took it away from us." He shook his bowed head. "Can you . . . believe that?"

"Tough break," Shaw said.

"I . . . I don't suppose I can talk . . . you out of killing me, huh?" Goshen said, looking up at him with sad eyes.

"I don't think so," Shaw said. "Like as not you're going to bleed to death in a few minutes anyway." He gave Goshen a searching stare. "Besides, do you really want to go back and face everybody, tell them what happened out here?"

"Naw, hell no," said Goshen. "Go on, get it over with."

"That's what I thought," Shaw said, stepping back, cocking his rifle hammer. . . .

Six miles ahead, at the top of the trail where the river had gone underground fifty yards up beneath a flat plateau of stone, Myra and Wallick had heard the distant sound of a single rifle shot. "What do you suppose that was?" Wallick asked.

More questions . . . Myra smiled and remained patient with him. She looked to their left, where the river roared back into sight from beneath the plateau and winded quickly away down the hillside. "They'll all be killing one another the rest of the day, I expect," she said. "We're lucky. All we've got to do is find us a good hiding place for this wagon and figure out how much gold to tote and how much to hide for later."

"Have you thought any about that sheep ranch I was talking about?" Wallick asked, driving the wagon slowly while Myra rode alongside on the horse.

She gazed ahead for a moment, seeing where this

thin winding back trail turned onto the larger easier trail leading toward the Edelman place and the deep valleys and endless hills beyond. "Stop the wagon!" she said suddenly, her eyes fixed on the turn ahead.

"What's wrong?" Wallick asked, halting the horses, searching the turn for any sign of what had caught her attention.

"Set the brake!" Myra said, still staring straight ahead intently. "Get down out of the wagon!"

"Lord, woman, what is it?" Wallick jerked back on the brake handle, spun the traces around it and jumped down from the seat atop the large flat rock surface beneath them. As he turned quickly to face Myra, the last thing he saw was the blast of smoke and fire from the tip of her rifle barrel.

"Sheep ranch your ass, idiot," she said. Stepping down from her saddle she levered a fresh round into the rifle and uncocked it before shoving it down into the saddle boot. She walked over to where Wallick was staring straight up, his mouth agape, a bullet hole in the center of his forehead. "You just can't know how much you were getting on my nerves," she said.

Myra was not concerned about leaving the body lying where it fell, but she did wonder how it would look bobbing and floating along the swift winding river. Bending, she dragged and rolled Wallick's warm corpse until a final shove sent it flopping off the rock edge into the rushing water.

"This is not so much," she said to herself, watching, letting out a disappointed breath. She put a hand on her hip and watched anyway as Wallick tumbled and rolled and bobbed and bounced along until he floated out of sight around a bend. "I don't even know why I thought it would be." She shrugged and walked back to the waiting horse and wagon.

When she had hitched the horse to the rear of the wagon, she walked to the side by the driver's seat and climbed up. Still standing, she reached out and unwrapped the traces from the brake handle. Then a rifle shot hit her center chest, picked her up and slung her backward onto the hard lumpy load that lay covered by a canvas tarpaulin.

Her eyes opened a moment later when she heard footsteps climb up onto the wagon and step over the driver's seat and stand over her. "I thought it was Eddie Sheves," said Hewes. "She's wearing his clothes." The tall Montana-crown hat lay on its overturned side, splattered by blood.

"Who . . . ? What . . . ?" Myra's voice had turned into a weak gasp.

"Never mind who I am," said Lori Edelman, staring down at her. Hewes' rifle was in her hands, the barrel still curling smoke. "Who do you think you are, bleeding all over my gold?"

Myra had no answer, but it didn't matter. Lori and Hewes both reached down, pulled her up enough to lift her over the wagon's side and drop her face-first onto the stone plateau. "Shall I shoot her again, Bo?" Lori asked, adjusting the rifle in her hands.

"No, let's get going," Hewes said, warily searching the trail back toward his hacienda. "I wonder how the hell this happened. We come out here to ambush Goshen, damned if we don't catch Mean Myra with the gold."

"Mean Myra, is it?" Lori said coolly. "I take it you two are acquainted?"

"Hell"—Hewes chuckled innocently—"everybody around Banton knows Mean Myra Blount. Killing her, you probably saved half the territory's cowhands from catching some terrible social malady." He stepped over into the driver's seat.

"Oh really?" Lori managed to return his smile as she stepped over and sat on the seat beside him. "Well, good health is always high on my concerns." Hewes slapped the traces to the horses' backs and drove the wagon on across the stone plateau.

Chapter 26

When Shaw rode up onto the spot where Myra lay dead and bloody on the broad flat stone, he stepped down only long enough to look around at the wagon wheel marks and hoof scrapings leading away from Myra's body. He followed the smear of blood where Myra had dragged Wallick across the plateau and rolled him into the water. Wallick's body was long gone downstream, but Shaw got the picture. He stared down into the roaring water for a moment, then turned, stepped back into his saddle and rode on.

He followed the wagon tracks to where they cut over onto the wider, better trail. Once upon the trail it dawned on him where the wagon was headed. He quickened the barb's pace. In the distance behind him, the sound of fighting had diminished from hard, steady rifle fire to a few random shots now and then. That was good, he told himself. Now for the gold.

He rode on . . .

At the Edelman hacienda, the Widow Edelman carried the last of her travel bags out onto the front porch. She stepped away from the travel bags and looked at the big house while Bowden Hewes hurriedly wrestled with a larger steamer trunk until he managed to drag it out across the yard and heave it up onto the wagon.

"I could say I'm going to miss this place, but I would be lying," Lori said. "This house, my life with Jonathan . . . our medical practice. What a worthless waste of time it has all been."

"We don't have time for reminiscing. We need to get a move on," Hewes called out to her from the wagon, adjusting the large trunk into place. "The fighting is all over by now. Either the law, or whatever's left of my men, will be showing here before long."

"I'm coming," Lori replied. "I just thought of one more thing." She stepped inside the door, took out a two-inch-long derringer and made sure it was loaded. Then she stood for a moment, calming and collecting herself in preparation for what she knew she had to do. *All right . . .*

Out front, Hewes stepped down from the wagon. He stopped and stood in reflection, gazing first at his stepbrother's grave, then at the house, then back at the heavily loaded wagon. He grinned and wiped a handkerchief across his forehead. "I've got to hand it to Mean Myra." He chuckled aloud. "I don't know what she did with Jake, but she had to have killed him to get the gold away from him. . . ."

Inside the door, Lori tucked the derringer up inside her blouse sleeve, smoothed the sleeve over it and walked out onto the porch. "Perhaps you should give me our travel itinerary, for safekeeping," she said, smiling as she closed the door behind her and stood pulling on a pair of white lace gloves.

But suddenly she froze; her smile withered as she watched Shaw step out from behind the weathered cottonwood tree and walk closer to Bowden Hewes. "They say talking to yourself is sign of going crazy, Hewes," Shaw said, stopping fifteen feet away.

"What the . . . ?" Hewes looked all around, making sure there was only one man to contend with. His right hand had already snapped tight around the butt of a big Remington in his waistband. "Jesus, drifter! What *is* it going to take to get shed of you?"

Shaw nodded at the big freight wagon. "A wagonload of gold," he said calmly.

"Gold?" Hewes almost sighed in relief. "Hell, why didn't you say so in the first place?" He made a sweeping gesture with his left hand toward the wagon. "Be my guest. Take all you can carry. Only hurry it up. Goshen could be topping the trail any minute now."

"Goshen's dead," said Shaw. "I killed him, after he told me where to find you."

"Damn, Jake spilled the beans, eh?" said Hewes in disappointment. "You can't trust anybody these days . . . not when it comes to gold anyway." His hand still lay wrapped around the butt of the big Remington. "Well, anyway, hurry up, I expect the law, or somebody, is going to show up."

"The law just did," Shaw said.

"What, you? You're trying to say you're the law?" Hewes stifled a laugh. "How much peyote have you been eating?"

"Watch him, Bo, he's fast," Lori warned him.

Shaw didn't look toward her. He kept his eyes on Hewes.

"If you really were the law, so what, drifter?" Hewes asked. "Would you arrest me, right here, right now? Wouldn't you still be willing to take enough gold to settle any grievances between us—let Lori and me get on our way? Let us all wind up happy?"

"No," Shaw said. "Forget the gold. You've got to settle up for Raul."

"For a dead Mexican? You'd turn all this down for one dead vaquero who was going to die sooner or later anyway? That's what this is about?"

"No, forget Raul. Forget the law too," Shaw said, a strange dark gleam coming into his eyes. "I just want to kill you. How's that?"

"By God, that's honest," said Hewes. His right hand jerked upward on the Remington. Shaw had seen it coming. He'd seen Hewes' knuckles whiten around the gun butt. He'd seen the sharp, intense look come to the man's eyes, the look that said he'd just bet his whole roll, heart and soul, on the flick of a wrist, the drop of a hammer. Shaw let him go the distance—no hurry, he thought.

He watched as if standing detached, somewhere above it all, seeing Hewes' Remington swing up at him. Shaw thought about those sparrows dancing above the old witch's fingertips that night in the fire glow. Had that been real or had it all been a drunken dream? Just one of many, he reminded himself. Then he felt the big Colt lift and fire and fall back into its holster as if it had never really left it.

Hewes slammed back against the freight wagon, a

bullet hole appearing in the center of his chest. He stared down at the blood, his Remington falling limply from his hand. He turned his shocked eyes back up to Shaw, the eyes of a man who had just seen everything lying at his fingertips, then watched it all vanish. "Damn . . . ," he said, and he slid down to the ground and fell forward on his face.

Seeing Hewes fall, Lori Edelman let out a short scream and came running down from the porch to the wagon. Shaw took a step back and let her run past him to Hewes, but not before kicking the Remington out of reach.

"Bo? Bo?" She shook him by his shoulders; then she checked the pulse in his wrist until she satisfied herself that he was dead.

Shaw watched. After a moment, the widow stood up and touched a hand to the side of her forehead. "I—I suppose I should hate saying this, but I'm glad he's dead. Now I am free . . . at last."

Shaw stood watching her in silence.

"You see, he was making me go with him," she said. "What choice did I have? I didn't know what had happened to you. For all I knew, he may have killed you, or had you killed like poor Raul." She stepped over beside Shaw; he let her. "Anyway, I'm not sorry he's dead. Now perhaps you and I—"

"I was here the other night when you and Hewes were in your bedroom," he said, cutting her off. "I listened through the window." He stared at her until she felt forced to look away.

"Then you must know what I had to go through just to keep myself from—"

"Stop it," Shaw said, cutting her off again.

She paused for a moment in reflection of what she and Hewes had said that night. Finally, she said warily, "I heard you say you are a lawman?"

Shaw just stared at her.

"Because, if you are, I want you to know, I believe Bowden killed my poor husband. Did you happen to hear me mention that to him?" she said, fishing for what Shaw may or may not have overheard.

Shaw didn't answer. If Dawson wanted to know about it, wanted to bring charges, investigate it, whatever, that was up to him, Shaw thought. Instead of answering he stepped forward and bent down over Hewes in order to drag his body clear of the wagon wheel, which had started to rock back and forth, the horses having turned skittish from hearing the gunshot.

"Tell me something," Shaw said as he began dragging Hewes a few inches. "Have you ever been to a place in Old Mex called Valle Del Maíz?"

"Valley of the Corn? Yes, I have been there. Why?" Lori asked.

"Do you recall ever seeing an old *bruja* there, who keeps a flock of trained sparrows?"

"A witch with trained sparrows?" she said. "No, I don't believe so. Anyway, I don't think sparrows can be trained."

"I wondered that myself," Shaw said. He stopped and stood up from dragging Hewes' body. Maybe it had all been a dream after all, he told himself. Then he turned around to face her and saw the open bore of the derringer less than three inches from his right eye, cocked, ready.

"Good-bye, Lawrence," she said with cold resolve.

All right, this was it, he told himself. Right here, in the front yard of the man whose body he had found, whose wife he had slept with both before and after burying him. Right here beside the corpse of Bowden Hewes, a man he'd just killed whose body was yet warm from the living. *Fair enough . . .*

"Good-bye, Lori," he said peacefully.

The gunshot was loud, but he didn't flinch. He heard it, but he knew right away that she hadn't killed him. Had she killed him he wouldn't still be standing hearing the rifle shot echo across the rolling hills.

Rifle shot? He felt Lori Edelman's warm blood on his face as he turned his eyes toward his horse. Beside the speckled barb he saw Jane Crowly. She stood with her mouth agape, her smoking rifle in hand. "Oh my Lord . . . Oh my Lord . . . What have I done . . . ? What have I done . . . ?" he heard her say over and over as if reciting a chant.

An hour had passed by the time Jane Crowly had settled down enough to take the hot cup of coffee Shaw held out to her. "Look at me, all shook up," she said, red-faced, sniffling, "crying like some young girl. You'd think I'd never pulled a trigger before in my life." She brushed a strand of hair back from her face and sipped the coffee. "Obliged, Lawrence," she said in a softer voice.

"Killing ought to shake up anybody in their right mind, Jane," Shaw offered.

"Well, you never seem too broken up over it," she replied. "I've noted that these past few days."

"I don't claim to be in my right mind either," said Shaw.

"True, you don't." Jane nodded, accepting his premise. She sipped her coffee and glanced over to where Shaw had laid Hewes and Lori beside her husband's grave and spread blankets over them. "I—I thought she was the most precious woman in the world." Her gaze hardened. "Turns out she was just as low-down evil, no-account as the rest of us."

Shaw didn't respond.

"Did you kill Mean Myra?" she asked quietly, knowing that if he did he would have only done so for good reason.

"No, one of them did it," said Shaw. "We'll never know which, any more than we'll ever know which one killed the doctor—his own wife or his own brother." Shaw squinted in grim contemplation. "Hell of a world sometimes." Then he gave Jane a gentler look. "Did I say *obliged* for saving my life?"

"Yeah, you said it, but I ain't greatly convinced you meant it. You didn't look none to happy about it."

"I was," Shaw said, still not looking or sounding as if he thought she'd done him any great favor. "Do you still want to ride with me some?"

She sat silent for a moment, then said, "Yeah, if it's all right. I've got to tell you though, I'm no good. I never have been. So don't go setting any high expectations on me." She gave him a bitter but honest look. "I just want to warn you beforehand. There's been terrible stuff said about me. Lots of it true."

"Me too," said Shaw. "I don't care." They sat watching as Dawson, Caldwell and Juan Lupo stepped their horses into sight and nudged them toward the yard. Lupo led the Scotsman and three of the bounty hunters' horses behind him. Each horse carried its rider's body lying facedown over its back. "Looks like Iron Head got away," Shaw said, noting the half-breed's absence from among the dead.

"I would not want to haul gold across this desert with Iron Head loose and knowing about it," Jane said.

"If I know Dawson he'll volunteer to escort him," Shaw said.

"Where do you and Marshal Dawson know each other from?" Jane asked, eyeing the riders as they drew closer.

"We grew up together," said Shaw. "We once loved the same woman." He surprised himself saying it. He had never said anything like that to anyone before.

Jane didn't reply. But after a moment, she said quietly, "Where will we go . . . you and me riding together?"

"I don't know," said Shaw, "back down into Old Mex, I suppose."

"Yeah, I like it there," Jane said. They saw the blood-stained bandage wrapped around Dawson's upper arm. Juan Lupo appeared to be unscathed.

On an outside chance, Shaw asked Jane, "Have you ever been to Valle Del Maíz?"

"Oh, hell yes, many times," said Jane. "I got drunk once and fell off the second floor of the hotel there, splattered mud and horse piss all over some local dignitaries and got asked to leave." She laughed under her breath. "You're the only person I've heard mention that place in the longest time."

Shaw watched the three riders look down at the two blanketed bodies on their way past them. "Did you ever see an old *bruja* there?" Shaw asked her. "She keeps a covey of trained sparrows? Gets them to dance above her fingertips?"

"You mean old Princess Anne," Jane said confidently. "Hell yes, I remember her. *Witch Anne*, I always called her. I never seen anybody get along with sparrows the way she did. Damn, this brings back some memories. . . ."

Shaw gave a half smile, listening, but not really hearing the rest of what she said. He gazed off across the brutal jagged land and saw the sun sitting low, wavering red and angry in the western sky. "I knew I saw her," he whispered to himself, feeling his eyes water a bit from the harsh sun's glare.

After the gun smoke clears
and the dust settles, what happens to
Fast Larry Shaw and the wagon full of stolen gold?
Don't miss a single page of action!
Read on for a special sneak preview
of the next novel by Ralph Cotton,
America's most exciting Western author . . .

ESCAPE FROM FIRE RIVER

Coming from Signet in November 2009

Trabajo Duro, the Mexican badlands

At the end of a clay-tiled bar, Lawrence Shaw lifted a water gourd to his lips and sipped from it. Outside, the shadows of evening had overtaken the harsh glare of sunlight and left the sweltering Mexican hill line standing purple and orange in the setting sun. In a corner of the Pierna Cruda Cantina Burdel, a guitarist strummed low and easy.

Yet even as the music seemed to soothe any tension in the warm air, the player doing the strumming kept a wary eye on the three trail-hardened *americanos* who had arrived only a moment earlier, slapping dust from their clothes. "Like the sign reads, 'Welcome to the Raw Leg Cantina and Brothel,' gentlemen," the owner, "Cactus" John Barker had said, translating the name into English for them as the three stood side by side at the bar. "What is your pleasure at the end of this hot, hellish day?"

"Rye whiskey if you got it. Mescal if you don't,"

said a man in a no-nonsense voice. A red dust-filled beard covered his face. He wore a weathered duster, and a long riding quirt dangled from his wrist.

Cactus John quickly set three shot glasses in front of them and filled each from a dusty bottle of rye.

"The Raw Leg, huh?" said another of the gunmen, casting a sour look all around the cantina.

"Yes, the Pierna Cruda," the owner said, beaming proudly. "It's your first time here, so I'll tell you: I serve the strongest drink this side of the border. I make it all myself, and I taste it myself, so I know it's the best." He gave a toss of his hand as if saluting his distilling abilities.

"South of the border takes in a heap of land," the red-bearded gunman replied flatly.

The three appraisingly eyed a couple of half-naked women up and down and threw back their shots of rye. The man with the red beard motioned for the owner to refill the glasses. "Pour them to the brim," he said gruffly. "I never liked drinking short."

"Yes, sir. I see you fellows have arrived with a powerful thirst," Cactus John said nervously. He'd immediately taken note of these men. They had walked in from the hitch rail like men who were there for a reason other than to quench their thirsts for strong drink or to sate their visceral needs for female companionship.

Like the owner and the old guitar player, Shaw had sensed trouble the second the three had pushed aside the ragged striped blanket covering the doorway and stepped inside. He had deftly pulled one corner of his poncho up over his shoulder. Also, like the musician, he had continued on with what he was doing as if they weren't there. Yet, unlike the guitar player and Cactus John, he had little doubt who these men were, why they were here or what was about to happen.

"*Gracias*," Shaw said to the young woman who had handed him the water gourd. She stood behind the bar, awaiting its return when he'd finished drinking. The three men had ridden with the late Jake Goshen's gang. They had found the hoofprints of Shaw's and his pal Jane Crowly's horses and began following them across the border the day before.

Their reason for trailing him was not because they wanted to reap vengeance on him for having killed Jake Goshen and leaving him lying in the dirt. They were following Shaw looking for stolen gold—a freight wagonload of it. There had been wagon tracks leading from Bowden Hewes' spread along Fire River where they had found Goshen's body. But then the tracks had vanished in the hill country, and only the hoof prints of Shaw's and Jane's horses remained.

The gold had been stolen from the Mexican National Bank in Mexico City more than a year earlier. A week ago Shaw, along with U.S. Marshal Crayton Dawson and his deputy Jedson Caldwell, aka the Undertaker, and a Mexican government agent named Juan Lupo had taken the gold back from Goshen and his gang. They had retrieved the loot just in time, before Goshen had a chance to melt it all down from German sovereign coins into untraceable ingots. But hanging on to the gold had proven to be no easy job. The borderlands were crawling with gangs of gunmen, outlaws intent on having the gold for themselves.

And here is where they find me, Shaw mused to himself.

"Puedo hacer más por usted, señor?" The young woman asked Shaw if there was more she could do for him, with a suggestive smile. She wore a string-tied peasant blouse that she kept pulled low and open in front, revealing her wares to the buying public.

"Gracias, no hoy," Shaw said courteously, turning her down but thanking her and leaving her offer open for another day. He laid a coin on the bar for the water and wiped his hand across his lips.

At the end of the bar one of the three gunmen said to the other two in a voice loud enough to make certain he'd be overheard by Shaw, "I hate a place that don't speak American."

The man with the red beard replied, "It is rude and unfriendly in Old Mex, and that's a fact." He dropped a gold coin onto the tile bar top. "Once across the border it appears all civil manners go to hell."

Facing the three from across the tile bar, Cactus John picked up the money quickly and said, "I myself am a born Texan, but I welcome all kinds of talk here." He gave a shrug of acceptance.

"Nobody asked you a damn thing, barkeep!" said the red-bearded gunman. "So keep your tongue reined down, 'less you want to lose it."

Cactus John stared back at him coldly, thinking about the sawed-off shotgun lying under the bar.

The girl standing across from Shaw gasped. She hurried from behind the bar, water gourd still in hand, knowing that at any second bullets would be flying.

Shaw almost sighed. He knew the gunmen would

get around to him shortly. First they wanted to make a strong impression, he decided as he felt their eyes all turn toward him.

"While we're here, there will be nothing spoke at us or around us but American," said the red-bearded gunman. "Everybody got that?"

Shaw only returned their cold stare.

"You there," one of the men said to Shaw. "Is that your speckled bard at the rail?"

Shaw's reply was no more than a single nod of his head.

"Where you coming from?" he asked.

Shaw didn't answer.

"Mister, I asked you a question," the red-bearded gunman demanded.

"No *hablo*," Shaw said quietly.

The three gunmen looked at one another. *"No hablo?"* one of the men said with a dark chuckle. "He must think we're joshing."

"Aw, to hell with this," said the youngest of the three. "Let's stop pussyfooting around here." He stepped back from the bar and faced Shaw with his hand poised near his gun butt. "You're one of the law-men, ain't you? One of them who raided Hewes' place over at Fire River. You helped Juan Lupo take back the gold."

Shaw made no move, no corrections in his posture, no drop of his gun hand to shorten the distance be-tween it and the big Colt standing holstered at his hip. It had all been done earlier, in unhurried preparation. "Yep," he said in a calm, flat tone.

The other two stepped back from the bar and

flanked the younger gunman. The one with the red beard said in a tight, angry voice, "You fellows thought you'd escape Fire River with a wagonload of gold? You were dead wrong. Now, where is it?"

Seeing that this trouble didn't involve him, Cactus John dropped low and ran in a crouch from behind the bar out the rear door. The guitar player and the half-naked women seemed to disappear into the walls like apparitions. "I spent it," Shaw said in the same flat tone.

"You spent—!" the third man started to say.

But the younger gunman cut him off. "You're real funny, Mister!" he said to Shaw, his hand grabbing his black-handled Smith & Wesson and raising it.

"Yeah, for a dead man!" said the tall red-bearded gunman, reaching for his Dance Brothers revolver at the same time. The third man took a step back and made his move a split second behind the other two.

Outside, Jane Crowly had seen the three sweaty horses that had shown up at the hitch rail while she'd gone to a small general store for a bag of rock candy. She'd returned with a bulging jawful of horehound candy and heard the language turn heated and loud on her last few steps toward the blanket-covered doorway. *Oh hell!*

She jerked to a sudden halt when she heard the roaring gunshots resound so heavily that dust rose from the window frames and the plank walkway. Then, recovering quickly, hearing the commotion of falling men and running boots, she raised her shotgun butt and slammed it hard into the striped blanket just as a gunman came fleeing through the doorway.

Inside, Shaw stood with his Colt in hand. Gray smoke curled from the gun barrel and upward, as if caressing the back of his hand for a job well done. He stared in surprise as the third man flew back into the cantina, striped blanket and all, and landed flat on his back on the dirt floor.

"Is it safe to come in there, Lawrence?" Jane asked, her voice distorted by the lump of candy in her jaw.

Shaw stared at the third gunman lying knocked-out cold, his head half wrapped in the dusty blanket. "It's safe, Jane."

Jane poked her head in first and looked back and forth, first at the two bodies lying dead in the dirt, then at the man she had nailed with the shotgun butt. "Lordy!" she said. "This one won't be coming to before Christmas." She noted a bloody bullet hole in the man's right forearm and inquired of Shaw, "Are you feeling poorly today?"

"I only meant to wound him," Shaw said. "I'd like to know how far word has spread about that gold coming across the desert." As he spoke he lowered his voice and looked all around the empty cantina, making certain no one had overheard him.

"A writer in the tradition of Louis L'Amour
and Zane Grey!"
—*Huntsville Times*

National Bestselling Author
RALPH COMPTON

**Available wherever books are sold or at
penguin.com**

No other series packs this much heat!

THE TRAILSMAN

**Follow the trail of the gun-slinging heroes of
Penguin's Action Westerns at
penguin.com/actionwesterns**